SWEET ANGER

SANDRA BROWN

SWEET ANGER

WARNER VISION BOOKS

A Time Warner Company

WARNER BOOKS EDITION

Jacket design by Jackie Merri Meyer
Jacket photography by Ron Rinaldi
Jacket typography by Carl Dellacroce

This Warner Books Edition is published by arrangement with the author.

Warner Vision is a registered trademark of Warner Books, Inc.

Warner Books, Inc.
1271 Avenue of the Americas
New York, NY 10020

Visit our Web site at
http://warnerbooks.com

ISBN 0-7394-0093-2

⦿ A Time Warner Company

Printed in the United States of America

Dear Reader,

For years before I began writing general fiction, I wrote genre romances. *Sweet Anger* was originally published more than ten years ago.

The story reflects the trends and attitudes that were popular at that time, but its themes are eternal and universal. As in all romance fiction, the plot revolves around star-crossed lovers. There are moments of passion, anguish, and tenderness—all integral facets of falling in love.

I very much enjoyed writing romances. They're optimistic in orientation and have a charm unique to any other form of fiction. If this is your first taste of it, please enjoy.

Sandra Brown

Chapter One

〜⚘⚘〜

"WE'VE GOT A TWO-ALARM FIRE WORKING ON CLERMONT JUST SOUTH of Sixth Avenue. It should be at about 42H on your Mapsco. And get there pronto. I want some good video."

The inch-long ash on the end of Pinkie Lewis's cigarette fell unnoticed on his battered, cluttered, littered desk. The harried news director paused long enough to say "Hiya, sweetheart" to the young woman who had just moved aside a day-old Moon Pie, a roll of masking tape, and two cups of cold gray coffee in order to perch on the corner of the desk.

"When you're done with the fire," Pinkie went on, returning his attention to the two men lounging by his desk, "swing by that elementary school where the third-graders are writing letters to the Russians. If we have any time left on the six o'clock, it'll make good human interest. Anybody hear from Jack lately? It's taken him four hours to shoot that bit on the drug bust."

"Maybe he's hanging around, hoping they'll let him sample the goods." The videotape photographer grinned as he heaved the camera to his shoulder. The reporter, who was pulling on his sport coat, thought his cohort's suggestion was funny and laughed.

"I'll have his ass," Pinkie growled. "So what are you two bozos waiting for?" The grins collapsed. That particular tone in Pinkie's voice could bring about miraculous changes in a man. "The damn fire will be out before you get there. I want to see flames, smoke, tragedy in the making," he yelled, waving his arms descriptively. "Now get out of here!"

The reporter and cameraman left, stumbling in their haste. Pinkie glowered after them and ran a hand through his hair. Or he would have if he'd had any hair. Actually, he ran his hand over a rapidly growing bald spot that blended into his beefy forehead. It was his florid complexion and fair hair that had given him his nickname.

"One of these days you're going to have a heart attack," the young woman commented. Disgustedly she stubbed out three cigarette butts left in the ashtray. They hadn't been properly ground out and were curling acrid smoke into the already polluted atmosphere of the television newsroom.

"Naw. I drink too much whiskey. It scares sickness off." Pinkie picked up a Styrofoam cup and took a swig. He made a face at the stale coffee. "Buy you a cup," he said, taking the woman's arm and guiding her into the hall and toward an alcove where numerous vending machines were tucked outside of the flow of continuous foot traffic.

As usual, Pinkie's pockets produced no change when he began slapping them in search. "Let me buy this time," Kari Stewart said, smiling. The coffee was too black and bitter, but it was hot. Crossing her ankles, she leaned against the wall and sipped cautiously.

Pinkie smiled at her with paternal affection. "God-amighty, you're a sight for sore eyes. Helluva day. One of the video cameras is on the blink. It'll cost a fortune to repair and then I'll catch hell for going over budget. I've got two unexciting but dependable reporters out with flu." He belched. "I need a drink."

"You need a hot, balanced meal, far fewer cigarettes, far less whiskey—"

"Yes, Mother—"

"—and a good woman to take care of you."

"Oh, yeah?" Pinkie asked belligerently. This was a familiar topic of conversation. "You got someone in mind?"

"Bonnie."

"That dried-up old prune! She's too old for me."

Kari laughed. The switchboard operator who handled all the calls coming into the television station with amazing alacrity and patience had carried a torch for the crusty news director for years. "You'll never change, Pinkie. You're biased, stubborn, grouchy, and predictable. That's why I love you." She poked him in the spare tire that sagged over his belt.

"How'd the interview go?"

"He was as wretched as he's reputed to be." That morning Kari had interviewed an aging television sitcom actor who was now doing "legitimate theater" on the dinner theater circuit. "I can see why his varied series went down the tubes. He was rude, obnoxious, and condescending. But I'll have the last laugh. I went to last night's rehearsal. The production is a turkey. And I didn't think anyone could ruin a perfectly wonderful Neil Simon."

Pinkie crumpled his empty cup and tossed it in the general direction of the trash can. It didn't make it, but he didn't notice. "Goose the old geezer right in his pride. Don't soft-soap it. I want gutsy stuff on the newscast, even during your entertainment segment."

Kari saluted. "Right, Chief."

Pinkie's beet-red face split into a grin as he lit one of his unfiltered cigarettes. "And *that's* what I love about you. You don't give me any guff." He sauntered away in the direction of the newsroom. "And you've got great legs," he called over his shoulder.

Kari took the compliment for what it was, a teasing gesture between friends. Pinkie had been her friend and ally ever since she'd signed on with WBTV five years ago. Where others were cowed by the querulous news director, Kari, as a green intern with no more television journalism experience than her college diploma afforded her, had called his bluff one day and forever won his respect. She talked to him as no one else would dare and got away with it because of their mutual affection. She knew he wasn't nearly as fierce as he pretended.

Pinkie saw in her a dedicated, thorough reporter with initiative. He could count on her not to "screw up," as he put it. At the same time, he liked her warm personality, her femininity. He had had a hunch that the viewers would be as charmed as he, and he had been proven right.

When Kari had married Thomas Wynne two years earlier, Pinkie had feared he would lose her. But she had assured him that she wanted to continue working. "Thomas agrees. Until we decide to start a family, he wants me to do anything I want. And I want to keep working for you."

"There might be a conflict of interests here, Kari," Pinkie had said. "How can you impartially cover the city hall beat when your husband is one of the city councilmen?"

"I've already thought of that. Much as I hate giving up that beat, I think it's the proper thing to do."

"So where does that leave us?"

"I've got an idea for an entertainment segment on the news programs."

His white eyebrows had jumped up then lowered into a thoughtful frown. "Let's hash it over."

Pinkie had trusted her judgment and her ability to implement her idea successfully. Kari Stewart's critiques were a highlight of every newscast. She was witty and incisive without being scathing or vicious. The viewers adored her.

Now Kari went into the editing room and closed the door behind her. She dropped into the chair and fished a cartridge of videotape from her oversized bag, which served as both purse and carryall. Pushing back a mass of untamed blond hair from her cheek, she inserted the cartridge into the computerized editing console and began watching the interview she had conducted barely an hour before.

She picked up the telephone and dialed an extension. "Sam, hi. Kari. Can you bring that tape you shot last night of the rehearsal to editing room three, please? Thanks."

A few moments later the door opened behind her and she said, "Just set it down, Sam. Thanks. I'm using that for B-roll. I'll be ready for it in a minute."

She was capably punching buttons while scanning the two monitors, one with the unedited tape playing, the other with the edited version she was electronically compiling. She was so engrossed that she didn't notice that the door didn't close.

"Kari."

Pinkie's voice and the unfamiliar tone of it brought her head around. She had seen him in moods ranging from elation when they had scooped all their competitors on a story, to drunken melancholia over a bad ratings report. She had never seen him as he was now: deflated, sagging, abject, and most uncharacteristic of all, pale.

She half rose out of her chair. "Pinkie? What is it?" He laid a hand on her shoulder and eased her gently back into the chair.

"An accident report came in over the police radio a few minutes ago."

"And?" A cold fist of dread began squeezing her heart. "What kind of accident?"

He ran his hand over his head, then dragged it down his face, distorting the features. "Auto/pedestrian. Just a few blocks from here, right downtown. I sent a cameraman over there. He just called in."

She did stand now, fighting off his hands as he tried to restrain her.

"Thomas? Something's happened to Thomas?" There was no one else in her life. Pinkie wouldn't be acting like this if it weren't Thomas.

She made a mad dash for the door, but Pinkie caught her. "It is Thomas, Kari."

"He's hurt? What happened? What?"

"A truck hit him."

"Oh, my God."

Pinkie dropped his eyes to the middle of her chest, which was just about eye level for him. "It was . . . fatal. He died at the scene. I'm sorry, sweetheart."

Several ponderous seconds ticked by. She remained motionless, speechless. Disbelief paralyzed her. Then quietly she said, "You're telling me Thomas is dead?" Her hands gripped Pinkie's shirtfront like claws and she shook him. "A truck hit him?! Killed him?!" she screamed. Several of the station's employees were now crowded into the doorway of the editing room. The women were weeping. The men looked distinctly uncomfortable.

"Kari, Kari," Pinkie crooned. He patted her back.

"There's a mistake. It couldn't be—"

"I made the reporter confirm it a dozen times before I came to tell you." Her eyes were wild in her pallid face. Her lips worked, but no sound came out. "Come on," Pinkie said gently. "They've taken him to Denver General. I'll drive you."

It was the cold that struck her first. She had never been in a room this cold. The dual swinging doors closed silently behind her and Pinkie as they entered. She shrank against him, hating this stark, clinical place instantly.

The fluorescent lights hurt her eyes. The brightness offended her. Shouldn't this room be dark and serene, lending death some dignity and reverence? But here death was considered only a physical phenomenon. This place was so very sterile. And so very cold.

She felt like turning to run, but Pinkie urged her forward. A man in a white lab coat looked up from his desk. He stood up immediately. "Mrs. Wynne?"

"Yes."

He led them to a large table draped with a white sheet. Beneath the sheet lay the still form of a man. Kari began to whimper involuntarily and mashed her lips flat with her fingers.

How could she bear to see Thomas's body mangled and bloodied? Would she disgrace him and herself by her actions? Would she scream? Faint? Dissolve into hysterics?

The pathologist pulled back the sheet.

At first she thought it must all be a tasteless joke someone was playing on her. Or some outlandish mistake. Her eyes flew up to the man holding the sheet. He read the unspoken question in them; saw her incredulity.

"He was killed by the impact," he said softly. "The truck struck him from behind. The trauma traveled up his spine into his brain. There is a bruise on his back. Otherwise . . ."

He left the rest unfinished.

Kari stared down at Thomas's body. He looked as though he were asleep. Nothing more. His face was relaxed. The silver hair that she had found so attractive the first time she met him was neatly combed. The hand lying by his side looked merely at rest, ready to lift up a tennis racket or caress her hair.

His tall body seemed as strong as it had that morning when she had kissed him good-bye. He exercised religiously at a gymnasium to maintain that hard muscle tone and to avoid middle-age spread.

"Thomas, Thomas, darling." Her whisper sounded loud in the silent room. She almost expected him to open his eyes and look up at her, to say her name, to smile. She would see again the sparkle in his blue eyes and hear the rich sound of his laugh.

She had thought it would be unbearable to see his body broken. It was almost worse to see it looking so normal. His untouched state made the whole thing seem that much more absurd and unreal. It simply hadn't happened!

But it had. He was horrifyingly still.

"Where would you like us to send him?"

"Send him?" she repeated vacantly.

"I'll telephone you later," Pinkie said to the man. "Mrs. Wynne hasn't had time to make her arrangements."

"I understand." The pathologist began to lower the sheet.

"Wait!" she cried. The word echoed eerily off the tile walls. She couldn't leave him. Not in this terrible place. Not in this cold, cold room. If she left him lying here, his face covered by the sheet, it would be official. She couldn't cope with that yet. She couldn't admit that Thomas, her husband, was dead.

"Kari, you have to go." Pinkie laid gentle hands on her shoulders.

"Thomas." Her eyes filled with tears that rolled heavily down her cheeks. Tentatively she stretched her fingers toward him. She touched his hair, his forehead.

Then, sobbing uncontrollably, she collapsed into Pinkie's arms. He led her out.

* * *

It was unexpected, unheard of, bizarre. The day of the accident had been clear. For some undetermined reason, the driver of the delivery truck had lost control as he turned the corner. The truck had swerved, jumped the curb, and robbed Denver of one of its leading citizens and Kari Stewart Wynne of her husband. He had been walking back to the courthouse after a luncheon appointment. Innocently. Feeling the false sense of security human beings are wont to feel about their mortality. He had died instantly of the impact.

Kari stared at the flower-blanketed casket and wondered how it was possible that Thomas, her vibrant, dynamic husband, was sealed life-lessly inside.

She gripped Pinkie's hand. He had been a bulwark for the last two days, seeing to the myriad details while she moved in a daze. She was grateful for this mental netherland she moved in. It protected her from reality. Without it, she wouldn't have been able to cope.

She had no parents to lean on for support. Her mother had died when Kari was a child. Her father, whom she had adored and ad-mired, had died just before she graduated from college with her de-gree in communications.

And now Thomas had been taken from her, too.

She went through the rites of burial feeling nothing but a deep hollowness inside her. It was only when she was returning home, rid-ing in Pinkie's car with him and Bonnie, that she began to weep. Bonnie silently passed her a box of tissues.

"Do you remember when we got married?" Kari asked them rhe-torically. "People were shocked." Her voice, she noted, was husky. Maybe she had cried more than she remembered.

"People are always shocked when a couple doesn't fit the norm. There was over thirty years difference in your ages," Pinkie said.

"Thirty-two years to be exact. But I never felt there was any differ-ence."

"Thomas didn't look as old as he was. He certainly didn't live like most men in their sixties."

Kari smiled at Bonnie. "No, he didn't." She turned her gaze out the window. It surprised her to see so much activity. To most people this was an ordinary workday. Life was going on.

"I was distraught over my father's death," she said reflectively. "I remember coming to work at WBTV with the sole intention of making that my life's focus. My work was going to be all I lived for. Then I met Thomas. He gave purpose to my life again. I don't know what I would have done without him. We were so happy." She sighed. "Is fate jealous of one's happiness?"

"Sometimes I think it is," Bonnie said kindly. "You're beautiful and talented. Thomas Wynne was rich and successful. The two of you seemed to have it all."

"We did," Kari confirmed as Pinkie turned his car into the lane that led up to the house she had shared with Thomas. "Please come in."

"You sure?" Pinkie asked. "We don't want to impose, but I could sure as hell stand a shot of something."

"I have a stock of your brand," Kari said, taking her key from her purse and opening the front door. She had dismissed the servants for the day so they could attend the funeral. And she had known she would only want her closest friends around her afterward. "No one else would drink that rotgut you prefer."

Pinkie appreciated her attempt at humor. He knew she was cracking up on the inside. She had worshipped Thomas Wynne. Privately he hadn't thought their relationship was healthy, but he had never dared mention that to Kari. She couldn't abide even a breath of criticism of her husband.

The house was chilly and gloomy, though a weak sun filtered beams of light through the mullioned windows. Kari turned up the thermostat as she entered the living room. She took off her coat and hat, then seemed uncertain what to do with them. They were finally dropped into a chair.

"I'll get the drinks," Pinkie said, crossing to the antique liquor cabinet. "What'll you have, Bonnie?"

"Whiskey straight."

"That's my girl. Kari?"

"Oh . . . whatever." Dispiritedly she sank into the sofa.

Bonnie Strand leaned forward from her place in an easy chair and took Kari's hand. Pinkie had unflatteringly referred to her as a prune. She wasn't. Not by a long shot. The strands of silver in her brown hair seemed to soften her features. Her face had character lines, but they added to rather than detracted from her expressive face.

She was a well-maintained woman in her mid-forties whose husband had left her after giving her three sons in rapid succession. From the time she was twenty-two, it had been an uphill climb to support herself and the three boys. But they were now grown, through college, and successfully on their own. Bonnie was tough yet kindhearted. In Kari's opinion, Bonnie Strand was one of the most "together" people she knew.

"I'll have to move from this house," Kari said, breaking the silence.

"Why?" Bonnie asked, incredulous.

"Sweetheart," Pinkie said as he came toward them with two drinks in his hands, "you're in no shape to be making that kind of decision."

"If I don't concentrate, if I don't think, I'm afraid my brain will atrophy and I'll slip into a coma." She had to force herself to go on living, couldn't they see that? No, she didn't feel like doing anything, certainly not planning the future, though she knew she must. "I'll move out as soon as I'm packed."

"You sure you want to do that?" Pinkie asked, shoving one of the glasses into her hand.

It was brandy. She sipped it and savored the burning elixir as it slid down her throat into her stomach. "Yes. This was Thomas's first family's house. You met his son and daughter today. They could have been hostile when we married. But they weren't. Their mother made this house a home. They grew up here. I never wanted them to feel like I was taking over something that didn't belong to me." She sipped again at her drink. "After we married and Thomas altered his will, I insisted that the house be left to his children."

"That was no small concession," Pinkie said. "This place is worth a million at least."

The estate, located in Cherry Hills, Denver's most exclusive area, sprawled over three acres. A blue-spruce-lined drive led up to the fifteen-room Tudor mansion that boasted a swimming pool in back, as well as a lighted tennis court and stables. The grounds were as spectacular as the house.

She spread her arms wide and painted on a bright smile as she asked, "What would a working girl like me do with all this?" She could tell by their dubious expressions that they weren't convinced. "I won't be entertaining in the fashion Thomas and I did. Most of our friends were actually his friends. I'll take my things and find a smaller place." She looked down into the brandy snifter and watched as the afternoon sunlight made its rich color jewellike. "Besides, I don't want to live here anymore without . . ."

It became necessary to dam a fresh fountain of tears. When she was more composed, she said to Pinkie, "I still have a job, don't I?"

"Don't worry about your job," he grumbled and ambled toward the bar to refill his empty glass.

"With Sally Jenkins just itching to get a spot on the air? No, sir. I'll be back to work in a week."

"For crying out loud, Kari," Pinkie shouted, whirling around. "Take your time. Let it heal. Forget Little Miss Hot Pants. She's filling in for you now, but when you come back, your spot on the news is waiting for you. You know that. And that Jenkins broad can *itch* all she wants to."

"What does that mean?" Bonnie asked suddenly, sitting up straighter.

"What does what mean?"

"The way you said 'itch.' "

"It means that there's a much more descriptive word for what she's willing to do to land a spot on the air."

"Like sleeping with someone who could put her there?" Bonnie's teeth were clamped tight.

"Yeah."

"She offered?"

Pinkie's meaty fists found his waist and dug in as he faced her. "Yeah. What about it?"

"What did you do?" Bonnie asked coolly.

"Nothing. I don't use the sack as a bartering table."

Bonnie smiled benignly and settled back into her chair. "What *do* you use it for?"

Growling like an angry dog, Pinkie faced Kari again. "You know your job is secure."

She had been fascinated by the exchange between her two friends. "Thank you, Pinkie. But I don't want to take extended time off. As soon as I've moved from here, I'll need to go back to work. Thomas would want me to," she finished quietly and bowed her head. Her finger trailed in endless circles around the rim of the snifter.

Bonnie gave Pinkie a speaking glance and stood up. "We'll leave you now, Kari, if you're sure there's nothing we can do before we go."

Kari stood with them. "No. Thank you both. I'll be fine. I need to be alone for a while."

At the front door, Pinkie took her hand. "Come back to work when you want to, when you feel like it; but don't be too hard on yourself."

"I'm not, really."

"That's what I like about you. You've got guts."

She smiled at him fondly. Even in his dark suit and tie, he looked rumpled and unkempt. "Don't forget my great legs," she teased softly.

He kissed her cheek and then awkwardly turned away. Bonnie was waiting on the opposite side of the car for him to open her door. "Well, what are you standing there for?" he said to her. "Get in."

He squeezed behind the wheel and Bonnie had no choice but to open her own door. She slammed it solidly and they drove away.

A smile curved Kari's lips, but it quickly faded as she turned away from the door and faced the emptiness of the large house, the emptiness of her life.

The beer was cold and biting. He didn't even taste it. He set the can aside.

He was slouched in his favorite chair. It conformed to his spine as if designed to do so. Over the tent formed by his fingers, he stared at the television screen. The sound was turned down. He already knew the audio portion of the news story by heart. But the video continued to intrigue him.

He must have been the only one in the city who hadn't attended that funeral. The First Presbyterian Church had been packed to capacity. The overflowing crowd had been forced to stand in the churchyard. Most everyone in attendance had joined the motorcade to the cemetery. This funeral had warranted news coverage on all of Denver's television stations.

Thomas Wynne, real estate entrepreneur and community servant, had been highly respected. He had had a bright and beautiful local television star for a wife. Together they had represented the American dream. But the dream had come to an end.

And he, Hunter McKee, must turn it into a nightmare for Wynne's widow.

His telephone rang. He shoved his tortoiseshell eyeglasses to the top of his head and leaned forward to stop the videotape machine attached to his television. "McKee," he said crisply into the receiver.

"Hunter, Silas Barnes."

"Hello, Silas. How has the first week of retirement been?"

"Restless."

Hunter laughed. "I'm sure that after being Denver County's D.A. for more than twenty years, so much peace and quiet will take some getting used to."

"I guess you've heard the news." The former D.A. cut through all the social chitchat and got right to the point of his call.

Hunter could appreciate that kind of verbal economy. "Yes," he answered soberly. "Helluva mess you've bequeathed me, Silas."

"I'm sorry. It was already a helluva mess. But now . . ."

"Yeah, now." Hunter's heavy sigh matched the exasperation of his gesture as he dragged his hand through his dark mahogany-colored hair. "Mr. Wynne's sins will be visited on his widow."

"She seems like a nice young woman."

"A rather tepid description, Silas."

The older man laughed. "I'm only trying to make you feel better. Do you think she'll cooperate with you?"

"I dread asking."

"You might not have the luxury of asking. You might have to force her to."

"I dread that even more."

"Well, if there's anything I can do to help . . ."

"You could have put off retirement for a few months until this was cleared up."

"My illness wouldn't let me. I hate having to dump this in your lap. I'm afraid you'll be up to your neck in boiling water soon, Hunter."

"Ah, well, that goes with the territory, doesn't it?"

"I'm afraid so. And if I hadn't thought you could handle that hot water, I wouldn't have suggested you for the temporary appointment. In all likelihood, you'll be officially voted in when they call the special election."

"I appreciate the vote of confidence. Thanks for calling."

"Good-bye."

Hunter hung up the phone and took another sip of beer. As the videotape in his machine was rewinding, he replaced his glasses on the bridge of his nose. He started the tape again, though he must have watched it a dozen times since it had first run on the six o'clock news earlier.

There she was stepping out of the limousine. Dressed in a black sheath, she looked so damn fragile, like a breakable doll. Her posture and carriage were sure and straight, even if her head was averted from the crowd and the cameras.

It must be tough, being a celebrity in the midst of tragedy. Because she was who she was, all eyes were on her, witnessing her grief. She was granted no privacy. Yet she looked the epitome of dignity and poise.

There. The camera focused on a close-up of her face. That face! Even though it was screened by a sheer black veil draping from her hat, it was a lovely face. Surely not the face of the enemy. The angles and planes were clearly defined, which was part of what made her so photogenic, he supposed. She wasn't wearing much makeup, which made her no less lovely, only softer, younger, and more vulnerable looking.

He cursed softly. Why didn't she look tough as a boot and hard as nails? Why didn't she look sly and worldly, jaded and cunning, shrewd and deceitful? It would make his job easier if she didn't look so damned tragically heroic, like the put-upon princess in a Grimm brothers' tale.

Her jaw was delicate but firm. Her nose was slender. Her mouth was soft and . . . hell! . . . suffice it to say, feminine. There was no direct shot of her eyes, which was just as well. He was probably better off not knowing about her eyes. Their shape, their color. Her blond hair was sleeked into a tight knot on the nape of her neck.

Now came the part that never failed to touch him. No matter how many times he masochistically watched the tape, the moment she took up that white rose, his heart began to beat unnecessarily fast and a suspicious clot formed in his throat. Through the veil, her lips kissed the perfect white bud. Then she laid it lovingly on the casket. Her fingers, as small and dainty as a child's, seemed reluctant to leave it.

Hunter, impatient with himself, reached for the proper button and snapped off the machine. Enough. He wasn't going to watch it anymore. He tossed his eyeglasses onto the end table and stalked into the kitchen for another beer.

He was borrowing trouble. It might never be necessary to interrogate Mrs. Thomas Wynne. But if it was, he'd do it and he'd go into the meeting with both barrels loaded. He had a job to do and nothing, *nothing*, would keep him from doing it to the best of his ability.

He was the acting district attorney for the city and county of Denver until the special election could be called to replace Silas Barnes. And if he wanted the post permanently, he had to shine, because the taxpayers would be watching him closely. Besides his own ambitions, justice must always be served. Right? Right.

Then why did he feel like hell? Why didn't he have his usual legal crusader's zeal to get to the truth? Where was his eagerness to rip the lives of the Wynnes wide open? Why instead did he feel a fierce instinct to protect Kari Stewart Wynne from everyone? Even from himself?

He went to the window of his condo and pulled up the blind. He gazed in the far distance at Denver's nighttime skyline. What was she doing on this night? Was she still wearing the black dress? Was her hair still confined in that tight bun? Was someone with her tonight? Comforting her, holding her?

He swallowed an emotion as bitter as the beer. It was jealousy.

The hardest day back would be the first one. She knew that, so she might just as well grit her teeth, walk through the doors, and get it over with. If only they wouldn't look at her with pity. If only they wouldn't look at her at all. She could stand the video and studio cameras. They were impersonal eyes. It was the human ones she couldn't stand peering at her.

Bonnie waved at her from her booth and made a thumbs-up sign. Kari walked down the hallways toward the back of the building, letting their familiarity seep into her comfortingly.

Nothing in the newsroom ever changed, except the personnel. The row of monitors mounted close to the ceiling for easy viewing from any point in the room offered a variety of television programming. The three major national networks were tuned in. Currently one showed an emoting couple in a clench on a soap opera, one an emoting winner on a game show, and one an emoting housewife lamenting the stains in her wash. Two private local stations were airing thirty-year-old situation comedies. The stock market report was charted on another monitor, and still another was tuned in to their own studio, empty and dark now.

A pall of cigarette smoke hovered over the rows of desks. There was a paper-ball-tossing contest going on in one corner. The contenders were idle videotape editors who were waiting for the reporters to return from the field with tapes and scripts. The producer of the six o'clock news was foully cursing his ex-wife to a sympathetic listener. Telephones were ringing incessantly. News service wires were clicking off stories from around the world.

Pinkie's desk was vacant. Kari wended her way to her own cubicle, which was separated from the others by seven-foot-tall portable walls. Her desk was covered with mail. She sorted through it, pulling what she knew was business correspondence and setting aside what she recognized as sympathy cards. An hour later, her right hand was cramped from writing acknowledgments to expressions of sympathy.

She had just finished when Pinkie's instantly recognizable vocabulary of obscenities punctuated the air. Kari stood and sighted him just as he rounded the corner at his desk, shouting deprecations at Sally Jenkins and the studio director, who were trailing in his wake. His cigarette had burned down to a nub, but he didn't notice as he rolled it from one side of his lips to the other. His hair was standing on end, fairly bristling.

Then he spotted Kari. His tirade ceased and he shoved the others away in his effort to reach her. "Thank God you're back. I'm losing my mind." He hugged her, then turned to the others. "Well, doesn't anybody have anything to do?" he roared. "Get to work."

Sally Jenkins laid a consoling hand on Kari's arm as she undulated past. "Back so soon?"

The red-haired girl was wide-eyed with innocence, which Kari knew to be feigned. A cinematographer had told her more lurid details than she had wanted to hear about his date with Sally. Her bosom had the comical dimensions of a Barbie doll. It had been given her, not by God, but by one of the city's plastic surgeons. And she had gotten her money's worth out of that bosom. Kari disliked her because she used her physical assets to get ahead in an industry that demanded hard work.

"You're so brave," Sally cooed before she glided out of the newsroom.

"Bubble Brain," Pinkie muttered as he lit a fresh cigarette. "She screwed up her intro cue last night, and the director went to the tape too early. She couldn't cover and—"

"I saw it," Kari interrupted.

"Then you saw what a disaster it was. God, I'm glad you're back. One more day with her and . . . She's got a great set of boobs, I'll credit her that. But I think that's where she stores her brains, because she sure doesn't have any in her head."

Kari laughed and it felt good. Pinkie eyed her closely. "You don't look so hot, but I've seen worse."

"Thanks, I think."

"Did you move?"

She nodded. "Into a condominium out by the reservoir. It's small, but spanking new with all the amenities. Pool and tennis court privileges. Security twenty-four hours a day."

"Sounds like you plan to hibernate."

"How could I hibernate when I'm seen by thousands of people every night?"

Pinkie wasn't satisfied. He poked a stubby index finger close to her nose. "I won't let you, so don't even think about it. Thomas is dead, but you're not, and I'm not going to stand by and let you pretend that you are. So," he said, jamming the cigarette between his lips and clapping his hands together, "end of sermon. You get your act together and cook up a good segment for tonight's broadcast or I'll put Booby Brain in your slot permanently."

Kari returned to her desk. Yes, she'd been right to plunge back in. This was what she needed, Pinkie's ribaldry, the constant deadlines to meet, the hustle and bustle.

If she could only take it home with her and not have to spend the nights alone.

Chapter Two

⤙ ❧ ❦ ⤚

SHE STEPPED ONTO THE SIDEWALK AND LET THE SUNSHINE BATHE HER
with light and warmth. Tears dewed her eyelashes, but they were
cleansing tears, happy tears. The rushing noonday foot traffic eddied
around her. She paid it no heed. Like an idiot she laughed deliriously
and hugged herself.

She was pregnant.

For the past two months, since Thomas's death, she had pretended
to live. She had gone through all the right motions, but her heart
hadn't been in it. She had approached each day lethargically. When
the annoying physical discomforts had beset her, she attributed them
to the lassitude plaguing her spirit. But her pervading illness hadn't
gone unnoticed, and at Pinkie's insistence, she had consulted her doctor. Only a few minutes ago, he had informed her that her malady was
one to be celebrated.

"I estimate you're in about your tenth week." Her face was awash
with gladness, but the doctor's wore a frown. "You're run down, emotionally and physically. You're far too thin. Eat. Drink milk shakes.
Gain some weight before I see you next time. You're anemic, so I'm
putting you on an iron supplement. Get plenty of rest."

She had listened to the doctor's instructions like a supplicant at the
mouth of an oracle. He had looked at her kindly. "Under the circum-

stances, I hope the news that you're carrying a child doesn't distress you."

"Distress me? Far from that, doctor. I couldn't be happier."

Relieved, he had smiled back at her and gone on with his list of do's and don'ts.

Now as she stood outside the doctor's downtown office, the euphoria still ran through her like a crystal river. She was carrying Thomas's child! A living part of him was growing inside her body.

She skipped toward the parking lot where she had left her compact car and drove to the television station. Pinkie looked up from his intent perusal of the morning newspaper when she stepped in front of his desk. "Well?" he asked, scowling.

Kari hesitated. Should she tell him now? Or was the secret too precious to share just yet? Wouldn't she rather savor it for a while? Besides, Pinkie might not take the news too well. What was the station management's policy on pregnancy? Especially since she was an on-air personality.

"The doctor prescribed a tonic," she said, her eyes dancing.

"Gin and tonic. Good for you. I always thought so. I think it's the lime."

"Not gin and tonic, you idiot," she laughed. "Vitamins and iron and stuff. I'm going to be fine. Wonderful in fact. Are you free? Let's go to lunch."

"I sent out for a hamburger."

She grabbed his arm and hauled him from his chair. "From that greasy spoon across the street? You'll get ptomaine. I'm on a diet to eat right and you've got to help. Let's go someplace where they serve salads and vegetables. Things like that."

Pinkie made a grimace of distaste. But he wasn't about to refuse her invitation. For the first time since she had become a widow, Kari was acting more like herself and he didn't want to reverse that trend.

"I just got an interesting call." Three weeks had gone by since she had learned of her pregnancy. She had had her hair trimmed. Her complexion glowed, thanks to the facials she had resumed giving herself once a week. Her cheeks had filled out and no longer looked ashen. There was a sparkle in her eyes. Because it had a purpose, her life was good again.

Pinkie didn't know the reason for her rejuvenation, but he was grateful for it. The zombie role she had played right after Thomas's death had scared the hell out of him. She had withdrawn into a private world of misery, and he had been afraid she would never come out of it. Thank God she had.

"Who called? Or are we gonna play Twenty Questions?" he asked crossly, as he swung his feet down from his desk. He was no longer so careful in his manner toward her. They had returned to their old comfortable relationship and were continually engaged in conversational skirmishes.

His affected annoyance didn't put her off for a moment. "Hunter McKee, our acting D.A."

Pinkie had worked on a metropolitan newspaper's city desk before transferring to television journalism. He'd been in that environment for over fifteen years. Little shocked him. He boasted that in his career he had seen and heard it all, from heads of state being assassinated to quintuplets being born in taxicabs. Nothing surprised him. He came close to being surprised now. The talk he heard from downtown was that McKee was no pantywaist, but someone to reckon with. "Oh, yeah? What'd he want? To talk over your last movie critique?"

Her smooth brow wrinkled into a puzzled frown. "That's just it. He didn't say. He only asked if I would come to his office tomorrow."

"Curiouser and curiouser. Could be he thinks you've still got the city hall beat. Maybe he has a story for you."

She was shaking her head. "I don't think so. I didn't gather that from the way he sounded. He didn't live in Denver when I had that beat. I'm sure that if he knows me from television at all it's as the entertainment reporter."

"You've never met him? Seems likely that in the circles you and Thomas ran in, you would have."

She had no recollection of ever having met Hunter McKee. "No. Not that I remember. What do you know about him?"

"Only what I read and what I've heard. He's a hotshot. Smart as a whip. Ambitious. Shrewd. Capable. Old Silas Barnes spoke highly of him and he was no easy man to please. He's always been a prosecutor, never a defense lawyer. He wants to be the D.A. of Denver County and probably will win the election when it rolls around."

"What about a personal life?" Her reporter's instincts were twitching. "Is there a Mrs. McKee?"

"Not that I know of. I think he's the all-work-and-no-play type. Maybe that's why you've never run into him at a cocktail party." Pinkie ground out his cigarette. "What time are you meeting him?"

"Ten o'clock tomorrow morning."

"Fill me in afterward."

She smiled as she spun around and headed back toward her desk.

"Well, don't hold your breath in expectation. It couldn't be anything important."

Shirt-sleeves or coat? Shirt-sleeves might make her feel more relaxed and at ease. The first impression she would have of him would be that of a trusted friend. But such casualness might offend her, too.

Damn it! What difference did it make? She was going to be offended anyway. So he would wear the coat of his three-piece suit and look official.

After pulling on the coat, he sat down behind his desk and fingered the manila file folder lying on its polished surface. Glancing over a few of the documents it contained, he cursed again and muttered an obscene epitaph for Thomas Wynne. What had the bastard been thinking? He'd had it all, public admiration, money, position . . . her. Why had he risked it all? Or had that been the allure? The thrill of the risk. Certainly the money was pocket change to someone with his bankroll. Why would he——

The buzzer on his intercom interrupted his thoughts. "Ms. Stewart is here."

"Send her in."

His palms were damp. He wiped them down his pants legs as he stood up. He, Hunter McKee, who had been described as having nerves of steel, who was the scourge of criminals, felt like one hundred and eighty-eight pounds of Jell-O.

What was wrong with him? He had faced vicious murderers screaming threats of what they were going to do to him if they ever got out of the prison he had helped to send them to. He had remained unmoved. In a moment's time, he would be facing one dainty woman, who looked no more threatening than a fragile butterfly, and his insides were churning. What was he afraid of?

She walked through the tall door. The sunlight streaming through the windows fell on her hair, on her skin, on the soft blue dress that draped over and clung to her perfect figure.

His loins knotted painfully.

One mystery was solved. Her eyes were green. Pale green surrounded by a forest of dark lashes.

She wasn't wearing her hair as she had on the day of the funeral, but as she did on her television segments. It was a wreath of undisciplined curls left free about her shoulders. There must have been a thousand shades of blond in that riot, varying from the palest white to the richest hue of gold.

The taste-oriented words usually used to describe complexions crowded his mind. Peaches, cream, honey. None by itself was quite adequate. But a delicious combination of them came close. Add to it the tint of apricots that stained her cheeks and mouth, and it was no wonder he wanted to take a bite of her and hold it on his tongue for a long time.

One look at her in the flesh and he knew what he had been afraid of. He had feared it from the time he saw her on television attending her husband's funeral. His unflagging objectivity had just taken a suicidal leap out the window.

"Mr. McKee?"

The tall athletic-looking man seemed to come out of a trance and then moved toward her. "Thank you for coming. Do I call you Ms. Stewart or Mrs. Wynne?"

She extended her hand. "How about Kari?"

Her hand was swallowed by the warm pressure of his. He had a good handshake, firm and solid, but not crippling. It lasted a bit long while his eyes probed intently into hers. He finally withdrew his hand and, placing it beneath her elbow, guided her to the chair opposite his desk.

"Are you too warm?"

"No."

"Too cool?"

"No," she said, smiling. "I'm fine."

She was accustomed to such overblown solicitousness. Ever since Thomas's death, people had walked on eggshells around her. It had begun to grate on her nerves. The photographers who went out to shoot stories with her had taken to treating her like an elderly maiden aunt. One had cursed viciously just the week before, then turned to her abashedly and said, "I'm sorry, Kari."

"Oh, for God's sake," she had cried. "Will you stop being so nice to me? I didn't become mentally or physically impaired when Thomas died!" Apparently word had gotten around. Everyone had begun to relax around her and return to their old camaraderie.

Now Mr. McKee's overabundance of politeness amused her. He went to the blinds behind his desk and adjusted them so she wouldn't be looking into glaring sunlight.

"Would you like some coffee?"

"No, thank you."

"Ice water?"

"No. I'm comfortable, Mr. McKee. Only curious. Why did you want to see me?"

He disregarded her question and made an observation of his own.

"You're more . . ." he gestured awkwardly, "*slender* than you look on television."

This was a remark she heard frequently. "Television cameras add about fifteen pounds. You're very young." His brows shot up. "I mean for the office you hold," she added quickly. "I expected someone older."

"Someone more like Silas?"

"Yes."

"Disappointed?"

"Surprised." She tilted her head to one side. "Where did you come from?"

"My last post was in St. Louis."

"Why did you leave?"

"Is that important?"

She had the grace to smile self-deprecatingly. "I used to cover city hall as a reporter. I guess it's natural for me to fire questions at the district attorney."

He produced a hint of a smile. "Then I'd better answer honestly. In St. Louis I was too far down on the ladder. There was no room to move up."

She nodded her understanding. "I wonder why we never met before."

"Should we have?"

"I came to the courthouse frequently. My late husband was on the city council."

"Yes. I know."

"You knew him personally?"

"I met him a few times."

He moved behind the desk, sat in the deep leather chair, and pulled on a pair of eyeglasses. They didn't diminish his attractiveness. If he wanted to stay in public life, Kari predicted he would go far. His physical appearance certainly wouldn't be a handicap.

He was over six feet tall. Even under the cover of his immaculately tailored charcoal-gray suit, she could detect a trim body of lithe muscle and graceful coordination. His hair was well cut, but had about it a boyish disorder that most women would find endearing. It was dark brown, threaded with reddish highlights.

His forehead was broad and high and bespoke intelligence. His brows were thick and arched over eyes neither gray nor green, but the mossy, woodsy color in between. An aristocratic nose divided two high cheekbones. His lips were finely shaped, the lower one having a sensual fullness to it. His mouth was wide. She imagined that when he smiled, he would be heart-trippingly sexy.

He gazed at her across the desk for several moments before he said quietly, "I'm sorry about your husband."

"Thank you." Was that what he had called to say? she wondered. Why couldn't he have said that over the phone?

He spoke the words she had heard repeatedly over the past months, but there was something unique in the way he said them, an element of intensity. She thought it was more than Thomas's demise he was sorry about. And the piercing way he was looking at her made her distinctly uncomfortable, as though he were weighing her reaction to everything he said.

"I've seen you on television," he remarked with seeming nonchalance. Actually she thought it was a calculated comment. She doubted if Mr. McKee ever said anything off the top of his head.

"That's like saying 'I've seen your baby.' What's your opinion?"

He grinned. She had been right. He was handsome and sexy. She could think of a dozen young ladies who would love to remedy his single status.

"I used to turn off the TV after the hard news stories." He glanced away and unnecessarily opened his lap desk drawer, then closed it. "Lately I've been making it a point to watch your entertainment features. They're very good."

"Thank you," she said with a formal nod of her head and a wide smile.

"You have a clever way with words and you always look . . . beautiful." The last word was uttered softly after a slight, almost imperceptible pause.

Kari's heart did a fancy little dance it had never done before. An odd but thrilling feeling slipped past her tight control and feathered up through her stomach and chest. She caught her breath at the strange sensation, and barely quelled the impulse to place her hand over her stomach. Could it have been her baby moving? No. It was too early. Then what? Certainly she wasn't reacting in schoolgirl fashion to Mr. McKee's compliment.

"You could have saved yourself this visit and written me a fan letter." She smiled, but it was shaky.

"I am a fan and I wanted to tell you so." His brows drew together into a frown. "But I'm afraid there's more to this appointment than that."

"I thought there was. If it's a news story, you should call our assignments editor. He'll send over the—"

"No, it's not a story. At least, not yet. It will be by this afternoon."

She recrossed her legs and shifted in her chair impatiently. When was he going to get to the point? "Why don't you tell me what this is about, Mr. McKee?"

"It concerns your late husband," he said bluntly.

That stilled her rising impatience. She blinked in surprise and watched as Hunter McKee opened the file lying on his desk. His movements were methodical, official. He no longer had the aspect of a gracious host, an admiring fan, but of a public servant about to carry out an unpleasant duty. "Thomas? What about him?"

He drew a deep breath. "For several months this office has been conducting an investigation into the disappearance of huge sums of money. The funds went into the city council's coffers. There was never anything tangible to show for this money, though the ledgers showed a place for every penny. But only on paper. The funds allocated for several projects were never forthcoming."

"I don't see what—"

"Please," he said calmly, holding up both palms. "The funds were being misappropriated. We have the evidence now to go before the grand jury. This afternoon two councilmen will be arrested on charges of fraud and embezzlement of city funds. I wanted to speak with you before the issue became public knowledge."

She wet her lips with the tip of her tongue. "Why?"

His eyes speared into hers. "Because Thomas Wynne was allegedly in on the scam."

For a long moment she sat perfectly still. So did Hunter. It was silent. Sounds of typewriter keys and ringing telephones filtered down the hallways and through the insulated walls, but overall the room was silent.

In one abrupt motion, Kari bolted from the chair and made a bee-line for the door. Nimbly Hunter rounded his desk and caught up with her just as she reached it. His strong lean fingers circled her upper arm.

"I'm sorry, Kari—"

"Mrs. Wynne," she hissed, "and please let go of my arm."

"I want to explain."

"There's nothing to explain." Her eyes were hot with anger. "Thomas served this city for more years than you've been out of law school. He was a scrupulous, conscientious businessman and public official. He would never . . ." She halted to draw a deep breath when her air ran out. "Your allegations are wrong and will be proven so. Let me go."

She wrenched her arm free, but his hand flattened wide on the door. His arm was held ramrod straight and had the support of his hard body behind it. She couldn't open the door against such strength. Furious, she glared up at him.

"Sit down," he ordered softly. "I have some questions to ask you. You may have an attorney present if you wish."

Her chin went up. "Certainly not. I have nothing to hide and neither did Thomas."

"Then you won't mind answering a few questions," he said smoothly.

She had backed herself into a corner and the only way to save face was to brazen it out. Forcibly she relaxed her posture but not her hostility. "What do you want to know?"

"Will you sit down? Please." He was all kindness and good manners again. He placed his palm beneath her elbow, but she jerked it away. She returned to the chair under her own power and rigidly sat down on its edge.

He returned to his chair behind the desk and consulted his files. "Did Mr. Wynne ever travel to San Francisco?"

"I don't remember," she said flippantly.

His brows lowered. He peered at her from behind the lenses of his glasses and she knew the first taste of fear. He was serious about this. "Did he?" he repeated.

She swallowed. "Yes. Occasionally."

"How often?"

"That's hard to say."

Again she was subjected to a hard suspicious stare. "Why?"

"How often is often?" she cried. Judging from his impassive expression that he still wasn't satisfied, she said on a long-suffering sigh, "He traveled to San Francisco with some frequency."

"Can you name specific dates?"

"Of course not! Thomas had many business interests. I didn't keep track of them."

"He traveled extensively?"

She made a hopeless gesture with her hands. "I suppose you could say that. He went out of town twice or three times a month. Do you consider that extensive?"

He didn't answer her question, but fired another of his own. "To San Francisco, New Orleans, New York, Puerto Rico?"

"Yes, maybe, I guess so. As I said, I didn't keep track."

"You never knew where your husband was when he went out of town?"

Her lips narrowed angrily and her eyes flashed at him. "Yes, I knew. He called me every night when he was away."

She thought McKee muttered something vulgar under his breath, but she couldn't be sure. He was riffling through the papers in the file. "Do you have any idea what your husband's annual income was?"

"No."

His head came up. "*No* idea?"

"I know we didn't lack for anything. We lived well. But I had my own bank account."

"Money that he gave you?"

"Money that I earned," she snapped. "Are you done, Mr. McKee?"

"With you, yes. I only wanted to know if you were privy to your husband's dishonesty."

Hot color surged to her cheeks as she jumped out of her chair. "He was *not* dishonest."

Hunter, too, got to his feet and leaned across the desk to speak directly to her. "I have the documentation. I'll get a conviction on the other two with or without your help. I'd appreciate your help, though. If you could remember dates, names—"

"Go to hell," she said, whirling away from him and storming toward the door.

He went after her, this time managing to wedge himself between her and the door to block off her escape. She was quaking with fury. How dare he accuse a man like Thomas Wynne of something as despicable as misusing public funds!

"Let me call a court reporter to take your deposition," he said. "If it's as you say and you don't know anything, then that will be that."

"I don't want to be any part of your shoddy investigation, Mr. McKee."

"Like it or not, as Wynne's widow, you're already a part of it."

"A wife can't be forced to testify against her husband."

"Your husband isn't on trial. His co-conspirators are. Tell me what you know and I won't bother you again."

"I don't know anything."

"Then testify to that in a deposition. However, you might know more than you're aware of, some small fact that you consider insignificant. Let me ask you some pertinent questions."

"Forget it. I'm leaving." She fumbled near her hip for the doorknob.

He grabbed her wrist and yanked her hand hard against his chest. "Then I'll have to subpoena you. You'll have to testify in court."

"I'm sure you won't shirk your duty, Mr. McKee." Ineffectually she tugged on her imprisoned wrist.

"I don't want you to be hurt!"

They had been engaged in a shouting match. But at his last sentence, her head came up and she stared at him. He had spoken with an earnestness that she couldn't ignore, with a soft emphasis that was more puissant than his raised voice had been.

He was bending over her closely. He had tossed his eyeglasses on his desk and the eyes that looked down at her now were dark. His face was resolute and hard, but . . .

Compassionate? She shook her head. No. Not compassionate. That was impossible. How could he be compassionate toward her and intend to malign Thomas? That was one and the same as insulting her personally.

She gained control of her voice and said levelly, "I've already been hurt, Mr. McKee. It hurt to identify my husband's body as the victim of a needless, grotesque accident. He was a wonderful man and now you want to . . . Oh, God!" she groaned as she felt the prickle of tears behind her eyelids. "Just let me out of here."

She didn't want to cry. Not in front of anyone. Certainly not in front of him. But tears of rage and anguish filled her eyes. She ducked her head to hide them.

He couldn't bear it. He had known it wasn't going to be a picnic, but he couldn't stand being the villain of the piece. Why must he be the one to bring her more pain when she'd suffered so much? She looked so utterly helpless and forlorn.

Damn Wynne! Why had that crooked sonofabitch died and gotten off the hook, leaving her to suffer the consequences of his double dealings? Had Wynne still been alive, Hunter couldn't have held him in more contempt than he did now as he gazed down at the halo of blond hair on his widow's head.

He was alarmed to see that his fingers were strained white around her wrist. Immediately he relaxed them, but didn't let go. The hand she had squeezed into a tiny fist flexed at the lessening pressure. He studied that hand. More than anything he wanted to press the inside of her wrist to his lips and hold it there until the pulse slowed down. He wanted to open her hand and lay his mouth against the palm.

With his other hand he unthinkingly reached out and let one errant blond curl wind around his finger. It was as silky as it appeared. He wanted to crush each curl in his hand, bury his face in a mass of them, feel their caress against his lips.

Instead he lowered his hand without her ever knowing of his touch.

He was sure she would have flinched with loathing. For, whatever her husband had been, it was evident that she had idolized him.

He, Hunter McKee, was the man who was going to knock that idol off his pedestal. And where would that leave him in her opinion? It was common knowledge what happened to the bearer of ill tidings.

"I didn't want you to be hurt." He hadn't intended to repeat the words, especially with such heartfelt regret and in such an intimate whisper and with his thumb lightly grazing her inner wrist.

But she heard him and raised her head to glare up at him, condemning him more with the eloquence of her green eyes than she could have with shouted insults.

"Good-bye, Mr. McKee," she said coldly. This time when she pulled on her hand, he had no choice but to release it.

His mouth formed a grim line as he moved aside and held the door for her. Tossing back her hair and proudly straightening her shoulders, she marched past him.

He followed her into the corridor and watched her go.

If he had fashioned her himself, she couldn't have been more perfect. Just the right size. Slender, but feminine. Her derriere was gently rounded beneath her skirt; her breasts filled out the bodice of her dress. Oh, yes. He had noticed them, too, and cursed himself all the while for being a lecher while he was noticing. Forbidden thoughts about shape and color and texture and taste had also filtered through his mind.

Her legs were long and shapely in their high heels and silk stockings. He *knew* they were silk. If he imagined hard enough, he could feel their texture against his palms and the way the curve of her calf would fit his hand.

And her hair, and her face, and those animated expressions were so exactly what he had always wanted in a woman. And her scent and her eyes and her mouth. God! *Don't even think about her mouth.* He was already aching.

When she left the building by way of the front door, he closed the door to his office and returned to his desk. "Hellfire and damnation," he sighed, sinking into the chair and running a hand through his hair.

She was a widow of three months. And even if it had been three years, she would hate him forever for what he must do to her husband's memory.

Still, how did one turn off desire, desire stronger than any ever felt before? He hadn't arbitrarily turned it on. He hadn't picked her out of a crowd to be the recipient of his desire. Because of the situation, she would have been the last one he would have willingly selected. He hadn't asked to be attracted to her, it had just happened. Now what the hell could he do about it?

The whole thing was insanity, lunacy of the highest caliber, political and professional suicide, yet like a sap he had gone and done it anyway.

He had fallen in love with the enemy.

Chapter Three

WHEN KARI RETURNED TO WBTV, THE NEWSROOM WAS BUZZING. Some big story had just broken and she had a fair idea what it was. As she passed clusters of people conversations ceased. Covert, speculative glances were cast at her. Everyone already knew.

She went to her cubicle and carried on as though nothing were wrong. Let them talk, she thought. Hunter McKee, in his attempt to win public approval, would make a monumental fool of himself. Accusing Thomas Wynne of misappropriation of community funds was preposterous! Everyone would laugh at McKee, scorn his petty unfounded allegations, just as she had.

"Hi, baby."

She had a smile ready; albeit a stiff one. "Hi."

Pinkie glanced over his shoulder. Private conversations were hard to come by in the beehivelike room. "It's no longer a mystery why McKee wanted to see you."

Her chin tilted at a proud angle. "No."

"Word just came down. They arrested Parker at home, Haynes on the golf course. 'Course they'll be out on bond in a matter of minutes. Still, helluva mess for city hall." He placed a comforting hand on her shoulder. "Helluva mess for you."

"Why?" she asked defensively. "If there was a scam, Thomas certainly wasn't involved."

"Is that what McKee told you? That Thomas wasn't involved?"

Pinkie's eyes were as fair as the rest of him, a pale, almost transparent blue. They could be compelling. As they were now. She looked away from them. "No. He thinks Thomas was in on it. The man's a fool."

"Foolish maybe, but chivalrous. I never heard of a public official warning the kinfolks beforehand that someone in the family was about to be zapped."

"Nor did he. He wanted me to give him information." She stood and began to pace the small cubicle that was barely large enough to contain her desk and chair. "He actually thought I would help him get a conviction on the others. Can you believe that? The gall of the man? He wanted to have a court reporter take my statement so he wouldn't have to subpoena me."

Pinkie fanned out the match he had just used to light his cigarette and dropped it into the wastebasket. His eyes never left Kari's face. "So he *was* extending you a courtesy."

"Like hell he was," she said acerbically. "He probably thought that as an emotionally weakened widow, I'd break down, blubber out all Thomas's dark secrets. What he doesn't understand is that Thomas didn't have any secrets, dark or otherwise. He'll find that out soon enough and then he'll look like an idiot."

"You're sure of that?"

"That he'll be made to look a fool?"

"No. That Thomas didn't have any secrets," Pinkie said quietly.

Kari spun around to face him, ready to do battle. For several tense seconds she stared at him defiantly, daring him to expound on that theory. Finally Pinkie looked away. Kari dropped into her chair and gave him her back.

"I'm sorry, sweetheart. We've all been thrown out of whack. This is a sonofabitchin' thing to happen to you so soon after . . ." He laid his hands on her shoulders and administered a gentle massage. Her muscles were knotted with tension. She had just begun to get a handle on things. Now this. He didn't know whom he would rather strangle first, Wynne for doing whatever the hell he had done, or McKee for making his widow pay for it. "Why don't you go home? We'll fill your segment with a human interest piece tonight."

"Not on your life," she said tightly and stood up abruptly, throwing off his comforting hands. Her eyes were brilliant and fierce. "I don't want to give Mr. McKee the satisfaction of thinking he's frightened me. He'll be watching tonight and my smiling, shining face is going to be on that television screen. I'm not guilty of anything and neither was Thomas. And if Mr. McKee thinks I'll skulk around as though we were, he has another think coming!"

Kari had deluded herself into believing that if she bluffed her way through it, ignored it, it would go away. She hadn't counted on the scope of the scandal. It rocked the foundations and rattled the rafters of city hall. That evening's *Denver Post* carried the full story, disclosing the estimated amount of money involved based on figures provided by the D.A.'s office.

Apparently Pinkie had warned the station's reporters to lay off her, but other media reps weren't so restricted. As she left the building, she was swarmed by reporters from the newspapers and other television stations. She said nothing, only shoved her way to her car. Anger and fear were warring forces inside her. Her hands trembled as she drove home. Her heart was pounding.

Once at home and safely inside, she forced herself to calm down. This kind of anxiety couldn't be good for the baby. She mustn't panic. She must remain composed and give this thing time to die down, as it surely would within a few days.

Another delusion. She had underestimated McKee's diligence. The story continued to sprawl over the front pages of the daily newspapers. Every newscast on every television station seemed dedicated to fanning the fires of the scandal. McKee won an indictment for Parker and Haynes from the grand jury and a trial date was set.

McKee was highly visible. Kari watched or read every interview, hating him more by the day. Her eyes were blinded to him as an aggressive D.A. She saw him only as the adversary who would drag Thomas's name through the mud, who would destroy her, who would threaten the future of her child.

During the day, she drove herself like a Trojan, burying her distress in work. At night, she tossed and turned restlessly, trying to think of something she could do to clear Thomas's name.

She was convinced that if he were guilty at all, it was only by association. Did she have something in her possession that would exonerate him? A file, a letter, a memo? Was there something she should remember that would absolve him?

If such a thing did exist, or if she could recall something, she would have gladly swallowed her pride and taken it to McKee. Futilely she searched. But her efforts produced nothing. She felt helpless.

The pressure began to tell on her. She hoped she didn't look as bad as she felt. There was no worry that her pregnancy might begin to show and give her away before she was ready to announce it. She was rail thin.

Pinkie found her in the small makeup room adjoining the studio where she taped her segments for the newscasts. She was dabbing cover-up as thick as putty on the dark circles under her eyes. Over her shoulder, he peered at her image in the theatrical mirror.

"Why don't you let this be your final telecast for awhile? You've been put through hell these last three weeks since that story broke."

"I'm fine." She ran a brush through her hair and whisked more powdered blush across her gaunt cheeks.

"You're not fine, Kari." Pinkie's patience snapped. "The situation's far from fine. You look like death warmed over. I've seen pounded crap that looked better than you do. Take a few days off. Don't be so damned brave about this."

Unaffected by his tirade, she stood and picked up her script. "They're waiting for me on the set." Pinkie caught her arm as she went past him. Seeing his concern, she let down her guard and laid an affectionate hand on his cheek.

"Everyone's hassling me, Pinkie. The D.A., the press. I've been hounded for weeks. Please don't you hassle me, too." She kissed his balding head and made her way into the studio.

Pinkie let out a string of colorful oaths. He admired her courage, but he questioned her common sense.

The telephone was ringing as Kari inserted the key in the lock of her front door. She hurried into the apartment and yanked it up. "Hello," she said breathlessly.

"Ms. Stewart?"

She recognized his voice instantly. "Yes," she said coldly.

"This is Hunter McKee."

I know damned well who it is, she wanted to shout. Stubbornly she remained silent.

"How are you?"

She gritted her teeth. "Does it matter?"

"Believe it or not, it does."

"Well I don't believe it, Mr. McKee. If my well-being were your concern, you wouldn't be carrying out this campaign to discredit my late husband."

"It isn't a campaign. It's an execution of duty."

"It's an execution of reputation. Thomas's."

He ignored the interruption and went on. "The purpose behind the investigation was not to discredit anyone, especially your late husband."

"That's not the way I interpret the headlines."

"Then your interpretation is wrong."

She laughed shortly. "You're making your name a household word. Do you deny you're using this trial to gain the public's attention? What better way to win voters than to produce thieving civil servants, robbers of hard-earned tax dollars? You're making certain that the post of D.A. will be permanently yours, aren't you?"

"I'll admit I want to hold the position permanently, yes."

"And you'll condemn an innocent man in order to win it." She was breathing hard. One fist was clenched around the telephone, the other hand was balled at her side.

"If you're so certain of Wynne's innocence, why won't you help me? If you'll recall, I gave you the opportunity weeks ago."

"I can't help you. I told you that weeks ago, too."

"Can't you?" he asked softly

His tone made her wary. "What do you mean?"

"Do you have documents in your possession, records your husband kept that might shed light on the case; prove his innocence?"

She sank into the nearest chair, rubbing her forehead with her three middle fingers. Was that it? He thought she was withholding evidence. Didn't he think she would have turned it over if she had discovered anything? Then again, she didn't even want him to know she had searched. That would be tantamount to admitting the possibility of Thomas's guilt, wouldn't it? By an act of will she shook off the depression and fatigue that weighed her down, not wanting to reveal a trace of weakness.

"You want me to let you paw through Thomas's personal effects, is that it?"

An exasperated sigh preceded his clipped reply. "I wouldn't put it that way."

"But that's what you want?"

"Something like that, yes."

"I can't help you, Mr. McKee. When I moved from the house, I took only a few items that had special significance to me and left the rest for his children to handle as they saw fit."

"I've gone through those things, with Mr. Wynne's attorney present, I might add. I found nothing incriminating in them."

"Then that should be your answer!" she exclaimed.

"I found nothing to absolve him, either," he retorted. "You know as well as I do that a man who has as many irons in the fire as your husband did is bound to keep several sets of books. Do you have them, Ms. Stewart?"

"No!" The truth of it was, she didn't. Thomas had never written anything down, not telephone numbers, addresses, errands to run, things to pack, nothing. He carried information in his head. In desperation she asked, "Do you think I'm deliberately trying to keep something from you? What's that called?"

"Obstruction of justice."

"Do you think I'm guilty of that?"

"Are you?"

"No."

"You'll swear to that?"

"Yes."

After a lengthy silence, he sighed heavily. "That's just what you'll have to do then, Ms. Stewart. I've tried to spare you an appearance in court, but you've forced me to put.you on the witness stand."

"I have nothing to hide."

She prayed he would hang up. The tense silence between them was almost palpable. What more could either of them say? Yet he made her feel much had been left unsaid. At last he muttered a gruff "good night" and hung up.

She laid the telephone back in its cradle. The simple task seemed to require all her energy. Then she tried to stand. That was when she felt the first cramp.

Pinkie was nursing a bottle of Scotch and watching an old John Wayne movie on TV when his telephone rang.

"Yeah?"

"Pinkie?" Her voice was weak, but he knew who it was. He pulled his stockinged feet from the coffee table, knocking over a bowl of potato chips in the process.

"Kari? What's the matter?" He didn't have to ask if something was wrong. Something definitely was. He only wanted to know what.

"I'm bleeding." Her voice cracked. "I think I'm losing my baby."

"Your *baby*!?" he shouted. Blasphemous language poured through his lips. "I'll be right there."

He arrived at her condominium within twenty minutes. Bonnie, her hair wound in pink foam curlers, was with him. He had picked her up on his way over. Leaning weakly against the door, Kari let them in. Her eyes were red from weeping.

"Thank you for coming," she said needlessly. "I called the doctor. He thinks I should come to the hospital just . . . to . . . uh . . . be sure." Then she collapsed against Bonnie and began to sob rackingly. "I've lost my baby. Thomas's baby. It's gone. Oh, God. My baby, my baby."

"More soup?"

Kari smiled wanly. "No, thank you, but it was delicious. I don't remember anyone ever making me homemade chicken soup before."

Bonnie lifted the tray off Kari's lap and patted her hand. "Do you want anything else? A Coke? Juice? The doctor said you must build up your blood sugar."

"Nothing for now, thanks. You've both been terrific. I don't know what I would have done without you. First Thomas's . . . accident. Then the scandal. Now this." Her voice trailed off and she lowered her eyes to the satin border of the blanket she was pleating between her fingers.

She had been home less than an hour after spending the night in the hospital. Bonnie and Pinkie had driven her home. They were fussing over her like mother hens, making her a bed on the living room sofa, fetching and carrying, talking softly. She was reminded of the days just following Thomas's funeral. In a grim way, their attitude was appropriate. Her baby had died.

Pinkie was sitting across the room beside the open window. Bonnie had dictated that if he insisted on smoking, he had to sit by the window. With unaccustomed meekness, he had complied. Not out of deference to Bonnie, but to Kari. "How do you feel, sweetheart?"

"Empty," she said softly. Neither he nor Bonnie missed the fragile hand that smoothed down her concave abdomen.

"For God's sake, why didn't you tell us you were pregnant? Why didn't you—"

"Pink-ie," Bonnie ground out.

He glowered at her and took a deep drag on his cigarette. "I was only going to say that if we had known, we would have made damned sure she took better care of herself."

"Don't blame yourself, Pinkie," Kari said. "There's only one person to blame for this." *Hunter McKee, Hunter McKee, Hunter McKee*, her brain chanted. How she hated the name.

The doorbell startled them all. Pinkie jumped up to answer it. "Is Mrs. Kari Stewart Wynne here?" the uniformed official asked.

"No," Pinkie said curtly and was about to close the door.

"It's all right, Pinkie," Kari said from her resting place. "I've been expecting this. It's a subpoena, right?" she asked the official as he stepped around Pinkie into the room.

"That's right, ma'am." He laid the document in her outstretched hand and took his leave as briskly as he'd come. Pinkie called him a rude name and slammed the door behind him.

"I'm to appear in court on the seventeenth," she said, reading from the subpoena.

"The seventeenth?" Bonnie said. "That's only—"

"The day after tomorrow!" Pinkie finished for her. "Out of the question. I'll call McKee myself, tell him the circumstances, tell him—"

"You'll do no such thing," Kari said, springing erect. The sudden motion taxed her strength. She fell back onto the cushions. "I'll be there when I'm supposed to be."

"But you can't," Pinkie protested. "You can barely make it from bed to chair. My God, Kari, you've had your insides scraped out. . . ."

"Pinkie, shut up!" Bonnie yelled. "You've got about as much tact as a steamroller. Now be quiet." Properly subdued, he hunched down in his chair. Bonnie knelt beside Kari and took her hand. "Honey, are you sure you should put yourself through that right now? It would be a terrible ordeal at any time, but now . . . Let us call him and say that you've been ill. We won't mention the miscarriage if you don't want us to. We'll just say that you're not feeling well."

"No," Kari said firmly. "He'd think I was goldbricking to avoid facing him. I won't let that man think I'm a coward. He called it, but it's going to be *my* day in court."

She was wearing black.

He saw her the instant she entered the courtroom. It was a two-piece suit with a cream-colored blouse underneath. The skirt was narrow. The jacket fit her to perfection. All that showed of the blouse were the bow beneath her chin and an inch of cuff at her wrists. Her hair had been pulled into a short curly ponytail at her nape, secured with a sedate black velvet ribbon. There were small pearls in her ears. Her green eyes were the only vibrant color about her. They looked unusually large in her pale face.

They flickered toward him, stopped, and stared unblinkingly and emotionlessly, then gradually moved away. They didn't come back.

She looked like a victimized angel. He had never felt so villainous.

Guy Brady, one of his junior assistants, whistled softly under his breath. "Jeez, what a looker she is. Even better in person than on TV."

Hunter swiveled around and scowled at him so menacingly that the young attorney quickly absorbed himself in the legal briefs spread out before him.

As unobtrusively as possible, Hunter watched Kari. She took a seat in the second row. Accompanying her was a short, stocky yellow-haired man with a ruddy complexion. He hovered over her like a bodyguard.

The judge's entrance was announced; the court was called to order; Hunter proceeded with the case he had been building against the defendants for the last few days. He called two witnesses. Their testimonies were cut and dried and only repeated information the court had heard from previous witnesses. Cross-examination was equally as boring.

The next name on Hunter's list was Kari Stewart Wynne.

He pondered the name. This was it. *Do I or don't I?* If he didn't call on her to testify, he might have a chance at winning her confidence, and then her friendship, and eventually . . . Maybe, but it was an optimistic pipe dream.

If he did call her to the stand, he ruined his chances for anything.

But it was his sworn duty to uphold justice. It wasn't his fault her husband had been a crook. If he didn't do what he knew he should, wouldn't he be as guilty of dereliction of duty as the defendants?

"Your Honor, I call Mrs. Kari Stewart Wynne to the witness stand."

A murmur rose from the spectators. Everyone knew her from television and unless they had been living under a rock for the past month, they were well acquainted with her connection to this case.

"Do you think she'll cooperate?" Guy asked out of the side of his mouth.

"No," Hunter answered as he watched her making her way to the witness box.

"Then, why call her?"

"If she won't cooperate, the jury will wonder why, won't they? They'll automatically think 'guilty.' "

"She's not on trial."

"No, but whether she wants to think so or not, her late husband is."

Guy gave Hunter a respectful nod, but Hunter didn't see it. He was watching Kari being sworn in. The hand resting on the large black Bible looked as delicate as porcelain. He could see the faint blue veins, each fragile bone. He remembered holding her hand against his chest. It had weighed virtually nothing, yet it had left a lasting impression there that his imagination could conjure up at will.

She took her seat and calmly met his gaze. His heart went into double time. Why did she have to be so damned beautiful? And why did he have to rip her to shreds? With a gesture of frustration, he put on his eyeglasses. "State your full name, please."

"Kari Elizabeth Stewart Wynne."

"You were married to Thomas Wynne?"

"Yes."

"For how long?"

She showed the first flicker of emotion. She seemed surprised by the question but answered it calmly. "Two years."

Of course the question had no real bearing on the case. Hunter had a personal reason for wanting to know. "Are you acquainted with Mr. Parker and Mr. Haynes?"

"Yes."

"To what extent?"

"They served on the city council with my husband . . . before his death."

Clever, this woman. She had slipped that in to make him look like the tormentor of hapless widows. Which was exactly what he felt like. If they weren't already, the members of the jury would soon be eating out of her hand. He couldn't let her get away with such sly tricks or even he himself might succumb to her charm.

"While your husband served on the city council, did he often take trips?"

"Yes."

"Business trips, pleasure trips? What kind of trips, Mrs. Wynne?"

"My husband is dead. How can he be on trial?"

Score two for her. Hunter addressed the judge. "Your Honor, would you please direct the witness to answer the question."

"Her husband isn't on trial, Mr. McKee," the judge reminded him.

"No, Your Honor, he isn't. But were he still alive I have no doubt that he would be. However, that is irrelevant. I do believe that this witness's testimony could be relevant to the involvement of Mr. Parker and Mr. Haynes in the alleged misappropriation of funds."

"Very well. Proceed. Mrs. Wynne, you will please answer the question."

She wet her lips. "He often took business trips."

"Alone?"

"I think so."

"But you're not sure?"

"Yes, alone," she said with a conviction he knew was counterfeit. He was certain the jury knew it, too.

"You never went with him?"

"Not on business trips, no."

"Never?"

"Not on business trips," she repeated.

He turned away from her abruptly and went to the table where Guy was ready with a file. He opened it and began shuffling through a stack of receipts. "You went with him on vacations, I suppose."

"Of course."

"Pleasure trips."

"Yes. Vacation trips, pleasure trips, whatever you want to call them."

He could tell by the way she shifted in her chair that she was growing impatient with this questioning that seemed to be going nowhere. But every time she glanced at the file he was consulting, he could discern her unwilling interest in it.

"Would you consider the chartering of a private airplane to be the kind of luxury associated with a pleasure trip rather than one taken for business purposes?"

The question was planned to confuse her, and as he had anticipated, she was unprepared to answer it. Weighing her answer in her mind, she stammered, "I'm not sure I understand—"

He jumped in. "If a commercial airline is available to fly you from point A to point B, would you consider it a luxury to charter a private jet? A simple yes or no, Mrs. Wynne."

"I don't—"

"A simple yes or no."

"Yes!" she exclaimed.

He retreated somewhat. He didn't like the twin spots of color that had bloomed in her cheeks, making the rest of her face look even more pale. Her fingers, gripped tightly together in her lap, looked bloodless. Had she lost weight?

He forced his mind back to business. *You want this conviction, don't you? You don't want these crooks who have been bleeding taxpayers for years to go free, do you? Then, get with the program, McKee, and stop thinking about her as a woman. Stop thinking that you'd much rather be holding her protectively than attacking her with leading questions. And for God's sake, stop looking at her face like a lovesick calf.*

Impatiently he shoved his glasses higher on the bridge of his nose. He noticed that Guy was looking at him curiously. Was his uneasiness that obvious? "And would you say that rented boats and limousines, etc., were also luxuries associated with pleasure trips?"

"I suppose so, yes."

He turned on her belligerently, as though to prove to himself that he still could. "Then as long as you're supposing, why do you suppose

Mr. Wynne arranged for these luxurious means of transportation when he was ostensibly conducting business for the city of Denver?"

"He didn't!"

"Objection," the defense attorney said from his table. "Mr. McKee is calling for a conclusion from the witness."

"Sustained," the judge intoned.

If Hunter had allowed himself to smile, his expression would have been smug. The jury had already heard his accusation and Kari's vehement denial. "Is this your late husband's signature on this charge receipt?" He shoved a slip of paper in her face.

Her eyes scanned it rapidly. "It . . . it looks like it. I can't be—"

"And this." Another paper was thrust at her. "And this."

The defense attorney came to his feet. "Your Honor, Mr. McKee is badgering the witness. She can't swear to the validity of the signatures on those receipts. Only an expert could."

"Sustained. Mr. McKee, I think you've made your point."

"Yes, Your Honor." He looked back at Kari and was alarmed by the faint trace of perspiration beading her upper lip and the rapid rise and fall of her chest. He leaned forward and whispered. "Are you all right? Would you like a glass of water?" He had an almost irresistible impulse to take her hands between his and warm them. Instinctively he knew they were as cold as ice.

"No, thank you," she said stiffly, not meeting his eyes, but looking over his shoulder.

He didn't press, but stepped back. She despised him. And he hadn't even gotten to the bad part yet. To give her time to restore herself, he needlessly studied his notes. When he had wasted as much time as he could, he approached her again.

"Did your late husband entertain on these business trips of his, Mrs. Wynne?"

"I've already told you. I wasn't with him. I don't know."

"Take a guess."

The defense attorney came to his feet again. "Objection, Your Hon—"

"I retract the question," Hunter interrupted. He ambled toward the witness box and propped his forearm over the railing in a relaxed pose, as though he and Kari were doing nothing more than having a casual chat. "When your husband was alive, did you entertain in your home frequently?"

"Yes. Thomas had many friends. He liked to entertain."

His right eyebrow rose. "But you didn't?"

"I didn't mean to imply that," she snapped. "Yes, I did; very much."

"And you said that Mr. Wynne enjoyed entertaining."

"Yes."

"Then it's reasonable to assume that Mr. Wynne played host when he was away as well."

"Your Honor, counsel is—"

The judge held up his hand. "I think I know where Mr. McKee is going with this line of questioning, and I'd like to hear Mrs. Wynne's answer."

"But again it calls for conclusion on the part of the witness," the defense attorney persisted.

"I'll rephrase the question," Hunter said obligingly. "Do you know of any specific occasions when your husband entertained while he was away?"

Her gaze was unsteady. She didn't know how to respond and was groping for an evasive answer. "No," she said at last. Hunter sensed she was telling the truth.

"He never mentioned hosting a party or dinner or lunch?"

"He might have. I don't remember."

"You don't remember? Weren't you ever curious as to what he did while he was away from you?"

The question was way out of line. He knew it. And she was smart enough to know it, too, because she looked at him just as probingly as he was looking at her. "I trusted my husband."

He continued to stare directly into her eyes for several moments while jealousy for Thomas Wynne ate at him like gnawing teeth. Wynne had had the absolute love and trust of this woman. And he had betrayed both. So help him God, if Hunter could have choked the life out of Wynne at that moment, he would have.

He turned away from the sight of her to regain his composure. Over his shoulder he asked, "Based on your husband's personality, his liking to play host, his charisma, is it reasonable to assume that he entertained on his business trips?"

He glared at the defense attorney, daring him to object. When the other man remained still, Kari answered slowly. "Yes. I suppose that's a reasonable assumption."

"And since we've already established that all the trips he took alone were for business purposes, we have to assume that all his entertaining was for business purposes as well. Right?"

She directed a pleading glance at the defense attorney's table, but he was busy scribbling notes. "I guess so," she answered softly. "Although I don't know that for fact. And remember, Thomas had business interests other than those concerning the city."

Now it was going to get nasty. If there were any other way . . . But there wasn't. He had no choice but to drop a ton of bricks on her head, to publicly humiliate her. Drawing a deep breath, he consulted the file again before returning it to the table. Slowly, resolutely, he walked toward the witness box.

When he was so close that the tips of his shoes were touching it, he asked, "Did you ever hear your husband mention a business associate by the name of Gloria Patten?"

"No."

"A Gloria Patten of San Francisco?"

"No."

"What about a Serena Holly of New Orleans?"

She swallowed hard, but her eyes remained unflinchingly on his. "No."

"A Miss Divine of New York City or a Miss Ortega from San Juan, Puerto Rico? Do any of those names ring a bell?"

"No."

"Yet these are women your husband must have conducted business with. City of Denver business. Because at its expense he entertained them frequently."

She gasped and pressed a closed fist against her heart. "Stop," she whispered.

"What business do you think your husband had with these women, Mrs. Wynne?"

"I don't know," she rasped.

A low hum of response buzzed through the spectators. The judge began to tap his gavel. Hunter rounded the witness box and came to stand directly beside Kari. With her eyes wide and wary, she followed his movements. "You don't know what business your husband had with these women?"

"No."

"It must have been extensive. Think back—"

"Your Honor, this is outrageous. The witness—"

"Mr. McKee—"

"Please stop," Kari cried.

He placed one foot on the step of the witness box. "He entertained them frequently. Every time he was in their respective cities."

"No!"

"In his hotel suite."

"You're lying!"

"Your Honor—"

"Mr. McKee, please limit your questions—"

"In his bedroom. All night."

"No!" she screamed.

She shot to her feet. She reeled. Her eyes closed. She pitched forward.

Chapter Four

HUNTER'S ARMS WERE THERE TO CATCH HER. HE SWEPT HER UP against his chest, alarmed that she weighed no more than a child. Her head lolled against his arm. She was drastically pale. Her eyelids, shadowed by fatigue to a soft lavender, lay perfectly still. The chalky lips were slightly parted.

The courtroom had been pitched into bedlam, first by Hunter's unorthodox questioning, then by Kari's dramatic reaction to it. Reporters and photographers were scrambling for vantage points. Spectators were on their feet, clambering for the aisles. Bailiffs were valiantly trying to restrain them. The judge was banging his gavel and shouting for order. The defense attorney was apoplectically demanding attention.

With the reigning pandemonium providing a diversion, Hunter carried Kari toward a side exit. "Get out of my way," he snarled at the bailiff who ill-advisedly blocked his path. The bailiff swung open the door for him and stepped aside.

Down the corridor from the courtroom was a small unmarked office. It had been placed at Hunter's disposal because the main D.A.'s office was a separate building several blocks from the courthouse. It was a room where he could retreat during court recesses or use to privately receive key witnesses. He now headed toward that office with rushed footsteps. He didn't want anyone to follow him or know where he was taking her. No one would take better care of her than he would. He went into the office, kicked the door shut behind him, and deposited her on an aged leather sofa.

Jerking off his glasses and dropping them to the floor, he knelt beside her. "Kari? Kari?" His voice was laced with apprehension. God, what had he done to her?

"Please wake up," he whispered. He touched her cheek. It was cool. He laid his palm on it and stroked her cheekbone with his thumb. "I'm sorry. God, I'm so sorry for everything."

Her chest was barely lifting and falling with her light respiration. With fumbling fingers, he began unfastening the buttons of her jacket. When they were all undone, he levered her up. She sagged against his chest like a rag doll.

He peeled the jacket off and heedlessly tossed it aside. Then he held her against him, tight against him, possessively and protectively against him, rubbing her back, trying to massage her into consciousness.

Her hair had come down with his fingers entwined in it. He pressed his face into the blond mass and breathed the flowery scent he had always imagined would perfume it. His mouth came maddeningly close to her ear. Gradually he lowered her back to the cracked leather cushions.

His eyes were busy surveyors of her face, watching for signs that she was coming around. She lay as still as death. Her breathing was shallow.

Tugging on his lower lip with his teeth, he indecisively considered the bow beneath her chin. His hands began to perspire. He would catch hell from her if she woke up and her blouse—

But she had fainted and showed no signs of waking up. He caught the ends of the tie between his fingers and pulled until the bow fell away. Then he unlooped it from around her neck. The pulse in her throat was weak. He could see its meager fluttering in the small triangle at the base of her neck.

Of their own accord, his hands went to the first button. They were pearl buttons that slipped easily from the holes. Still it was no easy task. His hands were trembling. He only unfastened three buttons, then adjusted the blouse so her throat and upper chest were exposed to air. She didn't stir.

She hadn't planned on taking off the suit jacket. That he knew. Otherwise she would have worn a brassiere, and one less sheer than the camisole with the cobweb-fine lace. It was about as substantial a garment as smoke.

He tried not to let his brain register anything, but it was photographing and filing as rapidly as his eyes were scanning. He was human, wasn't he? And male. And what heterosexual human male wouldn't look, wouldn't gaze at the dusky shadows her nipples made beneath the two layers of soft, sheer fabric?

God, she was beautiful.

He closed his eyes for a moment to ward off the shaft of desire that speared through him. When he opened his eyes again, they fell on that dent at the base of her throat and this time he didn't see a pulse at all. Or didn't he want to? Was he looking for an excuse to lay his hand over her heart?

In any event, that was what he did, gently at first, just enough to make the silky fabrics of the two garments slide together and bring his palm fully over the small mound. Soft, full, warm. Woman flesh. Her flesh. Filling his hand.

She whimpered. The sound tore through him like a bolt of lightning. He lifted his face over hers. "Shhh. It's all right, Kari." He stroked her hair. "I never wanted you to be hurt. I swear I didn't. Forgive me."

He lifted her against him and again pressed his face into her neck. "It's all right. It's all right."

When she first began to come to, she felt better than she had in a long time. She was being held in strong arms and the protection they offered was sublime. Warm, tender lips were moving up her neck, around her ear, along her jaw to the corner of her mouth, where they laid a gentle kiss.

Oh, that felt good. She turned toward the masculine face; beard-rough, smelling of cologne and shaving soap and male skin. Her lips located his and pressed against them.

He reacted instantly by tensing and pulling away. Was he going to leave her again? No! her mind screamed. She wound her arms around his neck. She wanted to be held against this large, hard body. Its strength made her feel safe. *Go on touching me; kiss me,* she wanted to cry out. But somehow her brain wasn't able to communicate the command to her voice.

Finally the lips returned. They stayed and moved over hers with tender rubbing motions. They whispered loving words, soothing, comforting words. Moaning, she opened her mouth. The wet velvet thrust of his tongue parted her lips wider until it was nestled deep inside her mouth, where it prowled hungrily.

Strange. Thomas had never kissed her this way before. Never with this degree of wantonness. She felt this kiss all over her body. In her breasts, which tightened and tingled and strained against the powerful chest. And in her womanhood, where one hot curling sensation followed another until she thought she might explode with pleasure. Or pain. She ached to be pressed there, stroked, filled.

She found handholds in his thick hair and pulled him closer, deepening the kiss by closing her mouth around his tongue. She wanted more, more. Plaintively she called the name of the only lover she had ever had. "Thomas, love me. Thomas, Thomas."

Abruptly he left her. He shook free her shackling hands. The pleasure-giving lips were withdrawn, though their moisture lingered on hers. Reluctantly she opened her eyes.

Everything inside her went dangerously still. She wasn't looking into the face of her beloved husband, but into the hated face of Hunter McKee.

It was too hideous to be believed. She dared not move. If she moved, if she felt anything, then she would know this wasn't her imagination. It couldn't be anything but a nightmare. She couldn't countenance it as real. But it was.

He stood up, his eyes falling on her unbuttoned blouse. His guilt-ridden face was the giveaway. "I undid it while I was trying to revive you," he said hoarsely, apologetically.

A small squeaking sound involuntarily escaped her lips as she looked down at her front. Her eyes swung back up to his. Her breath, so light before, now came in great gulps. Running a hand through his hair and whispering a heartfelt curse, he turned away.

She swung her feet to the floor and sat up dizzily. "You . . . you . . ." She couldn't think of anything bad enough to call him. She grappled with the buttons on her blouse.

He faced her again. "Listen to me, Kari. I'm sorry. About everything. You fainted on the witness stand. I carried you in here. I . . . You . . ." He shrugged helplessly.

She tried to stand, but immediately her knees buckled beneath her. He lunged to catch her, but she jerked backward. "Don't touch me," she grated. "If you ever touch me again—"

"Kari, please. I know you thought I was someone else. I know I took advantage of the situation."

"You're damn right you did." Her chest was now heaving with rage. "Aren't you finished yet with humiliating me? You're—"

The door opened and Pinkie barreled in, looking like either an avenging angel or the duped stooge in a farce. His hair was standing on end, like an electric halo around his head. "Kari, thank God!" he cried. "I couldn't find you."

"Close the door," Hunter said with remarkable calm. "Does anyone else know where we are?"

"No. All hell broke loose. The defense declined to cross-examine Kari, making you look like a real sonofabitch, Mr. D.A.," he said with undisguised satisfaction. "The judge called a recess. How are you, baby?" Pinkie bent down to examine Kari's face. His hands wandered over her arms and shoulders as though searching for wounds.

"Just get me out of here. Please, Pinkie." She leaned against him weakly as he helped her to her feet.

"Is he a friend of yours?" Hunter demanded. She only glared at him as she retrieved her suit jacket. He addressed Pinkie. "Ms. Stewart isn't well."

Pinkie looked from one to the other. Something was wrong here. He could smell it. He hadn't liked the D.A.'s method of questioning. In fact he'd felt like killing him when he was firing those questions at Kari, questions that raised doubt as to Wynne's moral character.

But he'd also seen the way the man had risked everything, including his own reputation, by carrying her from the courtroom and out of harm's way. McKee couldn't be all bad.

"Name's Pinkie Lewis. I'm news director at WBTV. And Kari's friend. Though lately I've felt more like her keeper."

"I think she should see a doctor. She was unconscious for some time."

"Let's go, Pinkie," she murmured.

"Yeah. I'll see that her doctor's called," Pinkie said to Hunter. "I warned her against appearing in court so soon after—"

"Pinkie," Kari said sharply, showing a spark of life even though she seemed on the verge of collapse.

"So soon after what?" Hunter stalked them as they made their slow progress toward the door.

Pinkie opened the door, but turned to eye the D.A. speculatively. He had put Kari through hell. But he looked like a guy with a conscience. Maybe he should get back some of what he had been dishing out. "So soon after her miscarriage," Pinkie said over Kari's protests. "She lost Thomas Wynne's baby three days ago."

Stunned into speechlessness, Hunter watched them go. Pinkie shot him a knowing look as he closed the door after them. Hunter wheeled around, digging the heels of his hands into his eyesockets. He uttered a foul expletive; repeated it with more emphasis. Then, bellowing in rage against fate, he slammed his fist into the nearest wall.

* * *

Pinkie padded to the front door. He stood only in his socks, one of which had a hole in the big toe. His shirttail had long since been pulled from his waistband. A cigarette dangled from the corner of his lip. He held a glass of Scotch in his hand.

He swung open the door and for a long moment stared at the man on the other side of the threshold. At last he said, "I'll say this for you. You've got guts."

"May I come in?"

"This isn't my house."

"May I come in anyway?"

Pinkie fortified himself with another sip of Scotch, all the time assessing Hunter McKee. Maybe it was the bouquet of yellow roses he was holding. Or maybe it was the unmistakable signs of fatigue ringing his eyes, or the haggardness deepening the vertical laugh lines on either side of his mouth. But for whatever reason, Pinkie experienced a rare twinge of sentimentality. He felt sorry for the poor bastard. He stood aside and permitted Hunter to enter Kari's living room.

"How is she?" Hunter asked, turning around and cutting through the preliminaries.

"She's not so hot right now, but she'll be fine. The doctor instructed her to stay in bed for two weeks at home or it'll be a month in the hospital."

Hunter's hard swallow was visible. "Is she that ill?"

"Exhaustion, both mental and physical fatigue, anemia, hypoglycemia."

Without invitation Hunter dropped into a chair and remorsefully stared at the floor between his feet. It was a long while before he raised his head and said, "I had no way of knowing about the . . . illness. I swear I didn't mean to hurt her."

This morning Pinkie had wanted to murder the man. Tonight? The hell of it was, he believed McKee. He might be a demon in the courtroom, but he hadn't deliberately set out to hurt Kari. Still, Pinkie's first loyalty was to her, and he wasn't going to let the man off easy. "Drink?"

Hunter paused momentarily before giving Pinkie a lopsided grin. "Please." Gingerly he laid the bouquet of yellow roses on the coffee table and unbuttoned his sport coat.

Pinkie splashed a double shot of Scotch without ice, water, or soda into a glass and extended it to Hunter. He tossed it down in one swallow. Little did he know how that escalated him in Pinkie's opinion. The newsman never could abide a man who drank like a gentleman.

"Are you . . . uh . . . staying here with her?" Hunter twirled the empty glass in his hand.

Pinkie wasn't fooled by the seeming indifference behind the question. If he didn't know better, he'd think the man was jealous. Hell. The man *was* jealous.

This time he brought the bottle to Hunter, tipped it toward his glass, and poured him another drink. "No, I'm not staying here with her. Bonnie and I came by after work to check on her, bring her some supper."

"Is Bonnie your wife?" Hunter asked hopefully.

Pinkie sputtered and choked on his drink. "God forbid. She works down at WBTV; hangs out with us sometimes. Kari likes and trusts her. She's with her now, helping her get ready for the night."

"I see." He was distinctly uncomfortable. All afternoon he had weighed the decision whether he should come to see her or not. He'd finally talked himself into it, but he wasn't certain it was the proper thing to do. He had caused her collapse. But even if he were innocent of that, what had happened *after* she fainted was definitely his fault and she wasn't going to miraculously forget it.

And her friend or watchdog or whatever the hell this Pinkie Lewis was to her was scrutinizing him like a bug under a bell jar. He felt like a kid on his first date who was having to meet the girl's father alone in the formal parlor.

Feeling a need to justify himself, he said, "How could I have known about her baby?" The thought of her losing her child made him sick to his stomach. "Why didn't she call and tell me she couldn't come to court? I would have understood and excused her from testifying."

"Would you?"

"Look, Mr. Lewis, I know what you must think of me, but—"

"Call me Pinkie. I can't stand that Mr. Lewis crap."

Behind his eyeglasses, Hunter blinked. He liked this man's honest and abrupt approach. One never had to guess where one stood with him. "All right, Pinkie. You're obviously very close to Kari . . . to Ms. Stewart."

"Very."

"So, tell me, why wasn't I informed that she was ill? Why did she force me to put her on that witness stand?"

Pinkie sighed. "We tried. Bonnie and I offered to call you and explain the circumstances." He pointed toward the hallway that led to the bedroom. "That girl is as stubborn as a mule. She must think she's Superwoman. She wouldn't hear of having herself excused."

"That's ridiculous."

"Is it?"

"Yes. I wouldn't have insisted she appear in court. Why would she do that to herself?"

"She didn't want to lose face with you," Pinkie replied bluntly, watching for Hunter's reaction.

His blank expression showed his incredulity. "Why?"

"Because you attacked Wynne and she was crazy about the man."

Hunter looked like he had taken a blow on the chin. His head went back slightly and he sank down into the cushions of the chair. "I see," he murmured, his eyes no longer on Pinkie but staring vacantly at the roses. "Then, there was no getting around hurting her, was there?"

Pinkie felt that itch again. Right between his shoulder blades. He was in administration now, but a field reporter never got rid of that sixth sense, that radar that tells him something's out of sync, something's amiss, something's not all it appears to be.

And, worried as he'd been about Kari this morning when he found her in that office with this man, he had begun to itch the moment he entered the room.

Wild horses wouldn't be able to drag what had transpired in there out of Kari. And Hunter didn't seem the type to rap about his personal dealings with women.

Pinkie would probably go to his grave curious about what had happened in that office before he appeared on the scene. But as sure as God made little green apples, *something* had happened. If his guess was right, it had had nothing to do with what had gone on in the courtroom. And whatever it was, it had knocked the socks off both of them.

Otherwise why had Kari retreated into herself and barely spoken a word for hours afterward? And why would a D.A. come bearing flowers to a witness he had had to run through the gauntlet?

In his opinion, the man looked gut-sick in love.

Pinkie braced his elbows on his knees and leaned forward in his chair. "Why did you come here tonight, McKee?"

"I want to see her and apologize."

"That's out of the question, Mr. McKee."

At the ringing sound of his name, Hunter launched himself to his feet, barking his shin on the edge of the coffee table and sloshing his drink. If he had thought Pinkie Lewis was intimidating, he was totally unprepared for the sour look on Bonnie Strand's face when she saw him. She could have been smelling last week's garbage.

Pinkie made the introductions. Bonnie's concession to them was a cool nod. "You're the last person she wants to see, Mr. McKee," Bonnie said tartly.

Pinkie was beginning to think McKee deserved the benefit of the doubt. Besides, he resented Bonnie's interference. "How do you know what Kari wants?" Pinkie demanded of her.

"I know," Bonnie retorted.

"Well, maybe you ought to mind your own damn business," Pinkie shot back.

Tossing her head, Bonnie looked at Hunter. "Did you bring the roses?"

"Yes."

She sized him up with a critical eye. "She doesn't hold you in the highest esteem, and frankly neither do I. Not if the accounts of what happened this morning are true."

Hunter wondered if she could know what he'd done in the office and decided that she was referring strictly to the courtroom scene. Kari wouldn't have told anyone that they had kissed. "I'm afraid the accounts are true, though I didn't know Ms. Stewart's physical condition when I put her on the stand. I hope to prove to you and her both that I'm not a complete monster."

The faintest of smiles curved his lips, but it was enough of a smile to make Bonnie's heart flutter. After all, she was a woman, and the first word that came to her mind after this close-up look at the charming good-looking D.A. was "hunk." Humility was always appealing in a man so strong. But Bonnie was too jaded to be put off by a pair of broad shoulders and a set of white teeth and a self-effacing manner. "I don't want her upset again," she said by way of warning.

"I swear to you that if she shows the slightest hint of getting upset, I'll leave immediately."

Bonnie cast a glance at Pinkie, who shrugged in answer to her silent question. Making up her own mind about the man, she moved from the doorway leading into the hall and said, "Second door on your right."

"Thanks," Hunter said. He picked up the roses and made his way to the door. He glanced back at Bonnie. "Is it all right if I just . . . ?"

"Yes, go on in. She's in bed, but she's still awake."

Hunter garnered all his courage and opened the door. The room was shadowed. Only one small lamp burned on a glass-topped rattan table beside the bed. The headboard of her bed was also rattan. The walls of the room had been painted a dark cream color. There were splashes of navy and cinnamon in the print bedspread, in baskets of dried flowers, in the Oriental rug on the floor. Oversize pillows covered in a ropy unbleached cotton were piled in one corner in front of a natural wicker screen from which hung belts and scarves and one huge straw hat. A ceiling fan with caning blades was suspended from the ceiling. The room looked exactly like her, neat and tidy on the surface, but hinting at the possibility of an intriguing mystery beneath.

He closed the door softly behind him and advanced into the room. She turned her head at the sound of his footsteps and opened her eyes. Immediately she sprang to a sitting position. "What are you doing here? How did you get in? Get out of here."

She spoke in hoarse whispers and he thanked God for that. From her expression she could just as easily have been screaming bloody murder.

He patted the air in front of him in a calming gesture. "Please, Kari. Pinkie and Bonnie said I could come in. I want to apologize to you."

"I don't need your apology. I don't want it. You could apologize from now till doomsday and it wouldn't change my mind about you. Now please leave."

He shook his head, and she saw the futility of arguing with such determination. She fell silent as he came forward and stood at her side. "These are for you," he said, laying the roses on the bed and thinking what an ass he was to present her with flowers after all the antipathy between them.

"Thank you," she said, thinking what an ass she was for accepting flowers from a man she loathed.

His eyes sought hers and when they captured them, refused to let them go. "I'm sorry about your baby."

Those softly spoken words seemed to prick her like a needle deflating a balloon. She fell back against the pillows. "You can't know what sorrow is, Mr. McKee."

"I can't know yours, no. But I'm very sorry I didn't know about your miscarriage when I put you on the witness stand this morning."

She looked at him then and her eyes belied the paleness of her complexion. They were smoldering with an inner fire. "Would it have made a difference if you had known?"

"You wouldn't have been called to testify."

"But then your case might have suffered, Mr. McKee," she said with sarcastic sweetness.

He glanced down at the floor. "Perhaps. But not significantly."

"You still think you'll get a conviction?"

His eyes speared straight into hers through the dim light. "I'll get a conviction." It was a firm statement that left no room for doubt. Her chest began to heave with agitation. He recalled his promise to Bonnie Strand, but nothing could make him leave her now.

"If you were so sure of the outcome, why was it necessary to attack Thomas and me?"

"I wasn't attacking you. Never you. I told you from the beginning that I didn't want you to be hurt. I meant it."

She threw back her head and laughed bitterly. "You don't think your lying implications about Thomas hurt me?"

They weren't lies! he wanted to shout back. But he held his tongue. Wynne had died her hero and her hero he would remain. He couldn't hang Wynne without hanging himself, too. "I publicly humiliated you. I realize and admit that. I'm sorry I had to do it, but I did."

As the memory of the morning assailed her she clamped her top teeth over her lower lip. Hunter swiftly moved closer. "Are you in pain?" he asked.

"No, no," she said, shaking her head miserably. "Just leave me alone. I don't want you here."

Even twisted in anguish, her face was one of the prettiest he'd ever seen. He longed to lay his palms on her cheeks, to soothe away all her heartache. He wanted to touch his lips to hers once again. God, why had he kissed her? Not knowing what she tasted like had been hell, but now knowing and not being able to have it again was worse.

He straightened and moved away, cramming his hands into his pockets to keep from touching her. She smelled delicious, like dusting powder. In the soft lamplight, her skin glowed with a pearly luminescence. Her hair looked alive and healthy enough to crackle. The bedcovers were pulled up only waist-high. Beneath the blanket he could see the outline of her thighs and the merest suggestion of the delta between them. The nightgown she had on was chaste, but soft and clinging. It molded to her shape. He couldn't really see her breasts, but he could imagine them.

In fact, his vivid imagination was causing him a great deal of discomfort.

Damn, he cursed himself, ashamed of his arousal. She had belonged to another man. For all practical purposes, she still did. This was a hopeless infatuation. It was a dead end. She obviously couldn't stand the sight of him; indeed, hated him.

What the hell was he doing here, making her more antagonistic with each passing second, and torturing himself? But he couldn't leave without apologizing for one more thing.

So he could think more clearly, he put distance between them, going to stand in front of her dresser. He itemized the articles she used every day, the personal things she touched without thinking about them. A hairbrush. A gold wristwatch. A bottle of scent. He was tempted to lift the crystal bottle to his nose and breathe deeply of the perfume, but he didn't dare.

"I owe you another apology." His quiet voice vibrated across the room.

She reacted as though he had actually touched her. Her stomach was sucked in on a sharp breath. She knew what was coming, but talking to him about it was unthinkable. "I don't want to hear it," she whispered. "Just go."

"I'm sorry I kissed you."

She groaned and covered her mouth with her hand. "Go away. Leave me alone."

"Or, more honestly, I'm sorry for doing it when you had no choice in the matter. I'm not sorry I kissed you."

Her head came up and she sought his reflection in the mirror. "Wasn't it enough that you crucified my husband's reputation? Wasn't it enough that you exposed me to public ridicule and caused me to lose my baby?" Her small fists were balled at her sides and she thumped the mattress angrily. Tears slid down her cheeks. "But aside from all that, you had no right to touch me, much less . . . touch me the way you did."

His eyes closed briefly in a spasm of guilt. "I know."

"Then how could you have kissed me?" she demanded.

He spun around. He wasn't entirely to blame. She wasn't faultless and by God he wasn't going to be branded as the only culprit in the crime. "I'll tell you how I could." His new tone stopped her tears and snatched the breath out of her lungs. "I've wanted to kiss you from the first time I saw you. Now you can kick and scream, pitch a fit, summon your watchdogs out there to come in here to haul me out, but that's a fact. I *wanted* to kiss you. And you didn't seem to mind. In fact, when I tried to pull away, you wouldn't let me."

"Wouldn't let . . . You outweigh me seventy-five pounds!"

He looked properly chagrined. It was absurd to suggest that she could physically best him. But resolutely he came forward until he stood at the foot of the bed. "Your arms embraced me. Your hands caressed me. You pressed your mouth against mine. You—"

"Stop!"

"—opened your lips and—"

"No more, I said."

"—you kissed me back!"

She was breathing hard, laboring for every breath. "I was dreaming, practically unconscious. I wasn't kissing you. I thought you were my husband!"

Frustrated in his own right, Hunter whipped off his eyeglasses. He leaned forward and trapped her feet and lower legs between the straight arms that braced him up over her. He spoke softly, enunciating each word. "Well, I'll tell you something, Kari Stewart. If I were your husband, I wouldn't do something so stupid as to risk losing you."

His meaning was clear. Thomas Wynne had been that stupid.

"Get out." She pushed the words through her teeth.

"And you can deny it to me and to yourself till hell freezes over, but you participated in and enjoyed that kiss."

"I did not!"

Then, with his eyelids partially closed as he studied her mouth, he leaned closer and said in a soft, declarative whisper, "Liar."

"Get out!"

Her shout brought Pinkie and Bonnie on a run. They arrived in time to see Hunter calmly putting on his glasses. Apparently the bouquet of yellow roses that were hurled at his retreating back didn't faze him. He shouldered past them muttering "Excuse me," and seconds later the front door slammed.

Chapter Five

HER CONVALESCENCE WAS LIKE A SENTENCE, BUT SHE SERVED IT. When she passed the doctor's muster and was allowed to go back to work, she had to admit that the time of complete rest had been to her advantage.

She felt renewed. It had been almost five months since Thomas's death. It was time to get on with her life. Before her miscarriage, she had felt she was moving in limbo, but now she had a definite goal—to see that the acting D.A. got his comeuppance.

Hunter McKee had won his conviction of councilmen Parker and Haynes. Even though Thomas Wynne was dead and unable to defend himself, he had been sentenced in shame just as the other two had been. Kari Stewart Wynne was not going to forgive and forget that.

She had been back at work for three weeks when she heard a rumor that sent her flying out of an editing room and straight to Pinkie's desk in the newsroom.

"I just heard that Dick Johnson is leaving to go to KABC."

Pinkie blew a cloud of cigarette smoke ceilingward. "The grapevine around here is shorter than a hooker's timer," he said crossly. "I just heard it from the horse's mouth not fifteen minutes ago."

"I want his beat."

Pinkie frowned up at her. His eyes stayed hard on her face even as he shouted to a passing videotape photographer to get his camera and meet a reporter at the heliport. "It's a chemical explosion, so take plenty of equipment," he shouted. Then to Kari he said, "Let's talk."

Eagerly she followed him into his private office, which he rarely frequented. The glass-walled room sat adjacent to the newsroom and provided the news director a view of what was going on, who was available, who was busy, who wasn't. When Pinkie summoned someone into the inner chamber, it was usually for a serious discussion. After closing the door, he sat behind the desk and Kari took the chair across from it. "Why?" he asked without preamble.

She blinked. "Why what?"

"Why do you want the city hall beat?"

"I had it before I married Thomas. You know why I gave it up then, and you also know it's always been my first love."

"Uh-huh," Pinkie didn't sound convinced. He lit another cigarette and watched her through the rising smoke. "You've made a niche for yourself on that entertainment beat."

"But I'm bored with it, Pinkie. I miss the city hall. I still have well-placed sources over there."

"That's a helluva sales pitch, Kari, but this ain't no dumbo you're talking to." He propped his stocky arms on the edge of the desk and leaned forward. "You want that beat so you can cook Hunter McKee's goose."

Guiltily she looked down at her hands. "I'm a good reporter, Pinkie. I wouldn't let my personal feelings color my journalistic judgment." He glared at her suspiciously and she cried, "I wouldn't!"

He sat back in his chair and hitched one foot over the corner of the desk. "What's going to happen to your spot on the news? Hypothetically. I'm not saying you've got the other job yet."

"Give the entertainment segment to Sally Jenkins. She did an okay job while I was away."

"You know the business, Kari. It's cutthroat. Sometimes you come back from vacation to learn you have no job. If you give up that peachy spot to Miss T. and A. and screw up over there," he hitched his head in the direction of downtown, "there'll be no coming back. Are you prepared to take that chance?"

"I won't screw up. Don't you believe in my ability anymore?"

"Yes. But I also believe that you're a woman who thinks and feels things passionately. You're also stubborn. You've got this grudge against the D.A. and—"

"It's not a grudge."

"The hell it's not!" Pinkie snapped. "Don't play word games with me. *Grudge* is probably too mild a word for what you feel toward him." He aimed his index finger at the tip of her nose. "I don't want this newsroom to get in a battle with McKee."

"I would never let that happen."

"You'd better make damn sure you don't," he said, as his feet hit the floor.

Her eyes lit up. "Then I have it?"

"You have it."

"Thanks, Pinkie," she said, surging to her feet. "When?"

"Dick's leaving at the end of the week. Monday?"

"Monday." She spun on her heels to leave, then paused. "Can I reserve Mike Gonzales as my cameraman?"

"Are you going to ask for more money?"

"I hadn't planned on it."

"Then, you can have Mike." He smiled at her and she laughed, fairly dancing with excitement. Pinkie came to his feet and took a drag of his cigarette. He didn't look happy. "I love you like a daughter, Kari, so I'm going to warn you about something. Revenge is a two-sided blade. It usually comes right back and smacks you in the ass."

She winced. "I'll remember."

Pinkie doubted seriously that she would.

"Kari, I don't like this."

"Come on, you big coward. Where's your sense of adventure? Besides, what can they do to us if they catch us?"

Mike Gonzales moaned as he hauled the heavy camera and recorder up the stairs. A video camera on a hospital elevator attracted too much attention. That was what they were trying to avoid. "It's not the hospital staff I'm worried about, it's Pinkie."

She laughed softly. "If we deliver him a tear-jerking story for the six o'clock news, he won't care what we did to get it."

"But the D.A. is going to raise hell. He didn't keep this man's whereabouts a secret for nothing, you know."

"That's what bothers me. Why the big secret? Why haven't any of us seen this man since he was arrested for murdering his wife? What's McKee up to?"

"How did you know this guy had a heart attack in his jail cell?"

"I overheard it at one of the coffee machines in the courthouse." Mike chuckled. "My unwitting informers said he'd been taken to the hospital."

"Who did you weasel the room number out of?" he asked.

She smiled at him with mischief. "That's my secret."

They finally reached the floor they were looking for. Kari pulled the stairwell door open to peer into the hall. "I hope the illustrious Mr. McKee hasn't posted a guard."

There was none. Silent and unseen, they slipped down the hall and into the patient's room. The middle-aged man lay in his bed awake, twisting the sheet between his hands.

"Who are you?" He looked like a frightened rabbit as Kari and Mike moved into the room.

"I'm Kari Stewart, Mr. Hopkins. How are you feeling?" she asked kindly.

His fearful eyes darted from Kari to Mike and the camera, then back to Kari. Recognition dawned. "Are you the girl on TV?" he asked, no longer showing apprehension but interest.

Kari had learned a long time ago that when people see someone in their living rooms every night, they feel that they know him personally. In situations like this, that feeling of familiarity came in handy.

"Yes." She sat in the chair next to the bed and unobtrusively switched on the small tape recorder she carried. She nodded to Mike and instantly heard the soft hum of the video recorder as the camera clicked on. "You've watched me on television?"

"Sure Emma and me—" He broke off as his lip began to tremble and his eyes filled with tears. "She's gone now."

"I read that in the newspapers. Would you like to talk about it?"

"I didn't mean to kill her. I don't even remember doing it." He began to cry in earnest and the focus on Mike's camera rolled in for a close-up.

"You've got to admit, it's powerful stuff."

"Yep. So is something else when it hits the fan. And that's exactly what's going to happen if we air this piece."

Exasperated, Kari let loose a deep sigh and turned her back. She paced the small confines of the editing room as Pinkie watched her interview with the alleged murderer Hopkins one more time. "It's good, Pinkie."

"I didn't say it wasn't good." He stood up. "I just don't know if it's journalistically good."

"What do you mean?"

"You haven't presented both sides."

"The other side has already been presented. You read McKee's statement in the paper. He wants a conviction and a death sentence."

"He wants a conviction. He wasn't quoted as saying he wanted a death sentence."

"He'll get around to it." She placed her interlaced fingers beneath her chin as though she were pleading with him. "Think of all the times bad press has convicted someone before he ever came to trial."

"So, you're going to set that right by making it your business that Hopkins gets off?"

"No. I'm just giving him a forum."

"He has one. In court."

She forced down her rising temper. "Pinkie, I've had this beat for almost two months. Have I slandered Mr. McKee?"

"You've come as close to the wire as you can without actually doing it," he reminded her.

"And people are paying attention. Our ratings are up."

He had to admit that and, after all, that was where the bottom line was drawn. Whether he approved her methods or not, Kari had made her reports on city hall, and particularly those regarding Hunter McKee, as colorful and stimulating as her entertainment critiques had been.

"All right," he conceded. "Against my better judgment, it airs on tonight's news."

"Thanks, Pinkie." She kissed his cheek.

Querulously he rubbed it off. "I just wouldn't want to be around to see McKee's reaction."

As it turned out, no one was around except Kari when he came storming into the newsroom. She had arrived early, excited over the impact her interview with Hopkins had had and wondering what she would do today as a follow-up.

At this time of morning, a few reporters and photographers were straggling in, but they were congregated around the coffee machines. She was alone in her cubicle when she looked up and saw McKee looming over her angrily.

"Well, good morning, Mr. McKee. To what do I owe this unexpected visit?"

"Don't be cute with me, Kari. I saw your story on last night's news."

"Oh?"

"And I'm mad as hell about it."

"Isn't that bad for your public image?"

His lips compressed into a hard, thin line. "How did you get into Hopkins's hospital room?"

"I walked."

He took a threatening step toward her. His large frame seemed to fill the small space. To keep herself from feeling at a disadvantage, she rose to her feet. But when she raised her eyes to meet his, she realized just how minuscule the office was. He was standing far too close.

"I've let you get by with the sly innuendos you sneak into your reports. Oh, yes, I've heard them, but I let them pass without comment."

"How commendable."

"Because I thought a true professional would soon tire of the little game you're playing and would start reporting honestly and without bias, as other reporters do."

That stung. Her eyes flashed furiously. "I *am* a true professional. I report what I see."

"After you strain it through that spiteful brain of yours," he said with rising volume. "What did you hope to accomplish by airing that tearful interview with Hopkins?"

"Nothing. It was a good interview. I thought the public should see the broken, guilt-ridden man you're going to ask the state to kill for you."

He looked like he might very well take the state's business in his own hands and wring her neck on the spot. "You wanted to win public sympathy for him and make me look like Adolf Hitler's second cousin just for taking him to trial."

"He had a heart attack!"

"You should have been more thorough in checking out the medical reports, Ms. Stewart. He has angina. Has had for years. He suffered some chest pains in jail, and as a safeguard, I had him hospitalized. Can we speak off the record?" She set her jaw stubbornly, giving him the impression she wouldn't agree to it. "You're not trustworthy enough for me to speak off the record?"

"I certainly am."

"All right, then." He stuck out his hand. "Off the record."

She looked down at his extended hand and warned herself against touching it. A premonition so deep she couldn't find its source warned that if she touched him, it would lead to consequences. Nonetheless she took his hand and shook it twice before quickly releasing it. "Off the record," she said brusquely.

"Hopkins, no matter how pitiable he looks and acts, murdered his wife. It was two weeks before he disposed of the body— You *do* know how he disposed of the body, don't you?"

She swallowed the nausea that filled the back of her throat and nodded. "If the newspaper accounts are true."

"They are. I was there while they dug up the twenty-six holes in the backyard." She squirmed uncomfortably.

He took off his glasses and folded them into the breast pocket of his coat. He had remarkably unusual eyes, she noticed. And for an infinitesimal second, he seemed just as captivated by hers. Her heart flipped over in her chest, just as it had that day in his office when he had told her she always looked beautiful on television.

"Where was I?" he asked distractedly.

"It was two weeks . . ."

"Oh, yes. It was two weeks before anyone noticed that she hadn't been seen around their house. Now if he was so shook up over it, why didn't he come crying to us with a confession right after he axed her?"

Kari made a squeamish face. "I don't know, Mr. McKee. He was probably overwhelmed by what he'd done. Terrified. He was under tremendous pressure. He said that for thirty years she had nagged him."

Hunter laughed. "So, you think we should look the other way every time a man kills his wife because she nags him?"

"Don't laugh at me."

He sobered instantly. "I'm not laughing at you. I didn't see anything funny about what you did yesterday. And the issue here isn't whether Hopkins murdered his wife or not, whether he's crazy as a bedbug, or saner than us all. The issue is your yellow journalism. What's your motive, Kari? To swing public opinion against me?"

"Maybe it should be swung against you."

"Why? I'm doing my job. It's my job to prosecute criminals and help maintain law and order. Why do you persist in taking potshots at me for doing what the taxpayers expect me to do?"

"I don't like your methods." She turned away from him but was brought back immediately. His hand had firmly gripped her upper arm and spun her around.

"And I don't like yours. I don't like my orders being disobeyed, and my orders were that no one was to get to Hopkins. Who let you in that room?"

"No one! And let go of me. You're hurting my arm."

That wasn't quite the truth. He wasn't hurting any part of her. But they were standing chest to chest and she found that proximity to his body disquieting, not to mention the strange vulnerability she felt each time his warm scented breath struck her mouth and throat.

He glanced down at his fingers, which were curled around her arm. Slowly they were released. He seemed embarrassed by his show of temper. To cover her own discomfiture, she rubbed her arm where his fingers had been to let him think he'd bruised her.

She took up the conversation in a lofty voice, as though she were speaking to a brute who had been brought to heel. "There wasn't a policeman at the door. I merely walked in."

He'd hardly been brought to heel. "Someone gave you the room number. Who was it?"

"Is this off the record?"

"It sure as hell is not! I intend to go straight from here to the hospital and read the staff the riot act."

"Then, I'm sorry, Mr. McKee. I never, *never*, reveal my sources. You should know that that's the unwritten creed of any reporter who values his credibility."

He was quaking with rage, and Kari knew the exhilaration of triumph. She had him right where she wanted him. He was tasting humiliation and frustration and was powerless to defend himself against them. Wasn't that how she had suffered when he accused Thomas of wrongdoing?

But she was soon to learn that Hunter McKee wasn't a defeated foe. Not yet. He took a step toward her, until their clothes were brushing together. He was as close as he could come without actually touching her. Those intriguing eyes homed in on her mouth and stayed . . . and stayed. At last he said softly, "You're asking for trouble, Kari."

His eyes remained on her mouth. She refused to move away and give him the satisfaction of knowing that this intent inspection disturbed her greatly. Unable to bear it any longer, she wet her lips with the tip of her tongue. "I'm not afraid of you," she said huskily.

The corner of his mouth twitched with the need to grin. Then his eyes lazily strayed up to hers. When they collided, her stomach dropped.

"I think you are."

Without another word, he left.

"You've got a real tiger by the tail this time."

Hunter, sitting at his desk, his feet propped up on the corner of it, took off his glasses and rubbed his eyes. "Yeah, don't I know it. Jury selection was bad enough."

He and Guy Brady had been poring over briefs and legal tomes for hours. It was late and he was tired. He swung his feet down and stood. He stretched, arching his back as his fists dug into the small of it.

"Of course the judge's ruling is a break for us. We can try that kid as an adult," he said.

It had been a month since the Hopkins incident. Hopkins never came to trial. After extensive psychiatric tests, he was judged by several doctors as being mentally unfit to stand trial. He was committed to a state hospital on the condition that if he was ever released, he could be tried for the murder of his wife.

This case was just as touchy. Hunter had no choice, other than releasing a killer back into society, than to go all the way with it.

Guy frowned down at his scribbled notes. "Some social-conscience groups are gonna raise hell. Why does he have to be just sixteen?"

"In years he's sixteen," Hunter said, playing devil's advocate. "He's far older than that in experience. Have you read his arrest record? It's as long as my arm. Petty theft, burglary, robbery, assault, vandalism, possession of controlled substances, possession of a lethal weapon. This is not your ordinary sixteen-year-old high-school kid. Since he was nine, this kid's been in trouble. He's been a violent crime waiting to happen. It finally did."

"He's pleaded self-defense. That's a helluva hard thing to prove."

"And that's the defense's job. I think the coroner's report is a definite plus for our side. Is it conceivable that he stabbed his father forty-three times if he didn't intend to kill him?" From an assortment of vending machine junk food lying on the table, Hunter picked up a Twinkie, studied it dubiously as he unwrapped it, then bit into it. "As far as I'm concerned, it's open and shut. I've questioned the boy, studied the reports. He's amoral."

"But defense will come back with the low socioeconomic level of the family, the crowded home, the irresponsible mother, the abuse the boy suffered from his alcoholic father, the—"

"You ought to join the Kari Stewart camp," Hunter commented dryly. "I can just hear her now."

Guy chuckled. "She's really got it in for you."

"Yeah, and this trial is going to be right up her alley. It will give her all the ammunition she needs to make me come out the villain. I hope to God no one else thinks I will enjoy getting a conviction on that kid. It's necessary. That's what I'm paid to do."

Hands shoved into his pockets, he went to the window. A late evening rain had washed the downtown streets. They reflected traffic lights in blurred ribbons of red and white. It was still coming down, rain mixed with sleet now. Hunter's gaze crawled over the skyline to the WBTV broadcast tower.

Was she still at the station? Probably not. It was late. He hoped she wasn't. She had no business driving home this late alone.

What in hell was he thinking?

She despised him. She had made a campaign of making him look like a bungling buffoon at best and a political manipulator at worst.

But here he was, like an idiot, worrying about her driving home alone on ice-slick streets.

Face it, buddy, she's never off your mind.

That was the hell of it. Furiously he would watch her reports on TV, then go to bed and dream erotic dreams about her. It didn't make any sense to a man who was usually pragmatic and logical to a fault.

He had even gone so far as to reexamine his motives for the way he had handled the city council scam. Had he been out for Wynne's head just because he happened to desire the man's widow? Rarely did Hunter question a decision once he made it. Such self-analysis was a new experience for him.

But no matter how many times he turned the question over in his mind, he knew he had done the right thing. All his actions had been within the law, motivated by his duty to uphold it. That Kari Stewart could have ever made him doubt himself only showed how much influence she had over him.

"I'm going to shut her up this time," he said now.

Guy choked on the swallow of tepid Coke he'd just taken. "You're going to put a muzzle on Kari Stewart? How?"

"By getting the judge to bar cameras from the courtroom. Without a video camera to back her up, she's virtually ineffective. This is a hot trial. It's made national news already. We'll have a tough enough job without it turning into a circus."

"This judge likes his publicity, Hunter. Do you think he'll do it?"

Hunter returned to his desk and sank into the chair. He pulled on his glasses and picked up another file. "I'm going to do my best to see that he does."

His best wasn't good enough. The judge denied his request. "Let's give it a day or two and see how it goes. If it becomes as rowdy as you predict, I'll reconsider."

Hunter cursed all the way back to his office. His mood didn't improve the next day when the trial opened and the first reporter to question him as he entered the courtroom was Kari Stewart.

"Is it true that you tried to have cameras and sketch artists banned from the courtroom?"

Who the hell were her sources? If he had informants like that, there wouldn't be a criminal left on Denver streets. "Yes, I did." God, she was gorgeous. A red sweater with a high cowl neck made her complexion glow and her hair look like a golden flame.

"Why, Mr. McKee?"

"I have no further comment at this time. If you'll excuse me."

He went around the cluster of reporters. They followed him into the large corner courtroom and competed for the best seats. The trial commenced.

That evening according to Kari Stewart's report on WBTV news, the accused was portrayed as a victim of his environment. The audience was treated to shots of him crying on his mother's shoulder. He was quoted as having said that he was remorseful, that he'd been forced to murder his father. Hunter knew better. The report dwelt on the deprived environment the accused had grown up in.

The next morning when he entered the courtroom, Kari flashed him a bright guileless smile that caused his eyes to darken threateningly.

To Kari's surprise, he came directly toward her. "Ms. Stewart, will you meet me for coffee after we adjourn today?"

The invitation almost struck her speechless. Mike, sitting beside her, gazed on, equally dumbfounded. "No, thank you," she said politely. "I'll have to get back to the station to edit my story for tonight."

"I promise it won't take long."

His tone of voice was just challenging enough to make her reconsider. She wasn't about to back down. Ever. "All right. Where?"

"The Ship Tavern at the Brown Palace?"

Again, she was surprised but hoped she didn't show it. "I'll be there fifteen minutes after court is adjourned." He nodded curtly and withdrew.

"What's that all about?" Mike asked from the side of his mouth as the judge came in.

"I haven't the foggiest," Kari replied in a whisper. "But I wouldn't miss it for the world."

Chapter Six

$\smile$ ❧ ❧ $\smile$

THE LOBBY OF THE BROWN PALACE HOTEL, A DENVER LANDMARK, was one of Kari's favorite places. It settled around one like a comfortable, warm shawl. The stained-glass ceiling, several stories above, shed a soft glow and added to the feeling that the lobby was an overgrown Victorian parlor. The paneling shone with the patina of age. The brass appointments sparkled. The potted palms flourished. The furniture invited visitors to lounge. Everything was sedate and understated and tended to make one want to whisper to maintain the restful atmosphere.

Down the hall, the Ship Tavern, with its rich maritime motif, was no ordinary bar. It was as cozy and gracious and intimate as the lobby.

It wasn't crowded at that time of day. The lunch rush was over. Kari felt awkward going into a dimly lit downtown hotel bar in the middle of the afternoon. Only a few men, probably out-of-town businessmen, were loitering at the long polished bar. She had no trouble spotting Hunter at one of the scattered tables. She wended her way toward him, trying to ignore the knowing looks the other patrons gave one another.

Hunter stood and waited until she sat down across from him before he slid back into his chair. "Thank you for coming. Are you hungry?"

"No. Just something to drink, please."

"What would you like?"

A waiter wearing an austere black suit had materialized from nowhere. "Perrier and lime, please," Kari said to him, smiling.

"Good afternoon, Ms. Stewart," he said formally.

"You know me?"

"From television. It's a pleasure to serve you. May I say that you're even more attractive in person than you are on TV?"

"You may, and thank you."

He turned to Hunter, apparently expecting another celebrity. "I'm nobody," Hunter said with a wide grin. "But I would like a black coffee."

"Yes, sir."

Hunter was still smiling when he turned back to Kari. He wasn't wearing his glasses. She couldn't help but notice that the lines forming sunbursts around his eyes squinted together when he smiled. So, he was good-looking. So what? "Why did you choose this place for our meeting?"

"I like it," he said simply.

"I like it, too, but it isn't exactly conducive to . . . to . . . Never mind."

"Come on, what? Isn't conducive to what?"

"Isn't conducive to anything you and I might have to say to each other. Do you know what those men at the bar are thinking?"

He glanced over his shoulder, then turned back, leaning across the table in order to hear her. She was barely whispering. "Mind reading isn't one of my strong points. What are they thinking?"

She didn't like his mischievous, teasing manner. "They're thinking that I'm either a call girl transacting the business part of our arrangement, or your illicit lover."

Hunter's eyes locked with hers a moment before he looked back at the men. "Is that so? Shame on them."

"I'm leaving."

"Wait." His hand shot across the table to trap hers.

He was being charming and joking and affable. She didn't want him to be charming and joking and affable with her. She didn't want him to pretend to be anything but the calculating opportunist she knew him to be. "I've got work to do, Mr. McKee."

"What are you thinking? That I deliberately chose this place to make you feel uncomfortable?"

"It crossed my mind," she said tightly.

"Damn!" he said, lifting his hand off hers, but leaving the impression that he was flinging hers away. "There's just no winning with you, is there? I asked you to meet me here because it is private. I didn't think you'd want to be seen with me in any of the coffee shops closer to the courthouse. They're always crowded with people we both know."

She was free to stand up and walk out, but she remained in her chair and stared at him across the checked tablecloth. His exasperation was evident as his eyes bored into hers.

The waiter chose that tense moment to bring their drinks. He withdrew without speaking. She sipped her mineral water, wishing that she had heeded her instincts and never brought up the subject of their meeting place. Now, he was the injured party and she looked like a petulant brat. It seemed there was no common ground for them to meet on. She wanted to get this over with as quickly as possible.

"What did you want to see me about?"

He had wanted to avoid the issue as long as he could. When would he have another opportunity to be alone with her, to sit and look at her? He had put her on the defensive again and now he had to change tactics before she bolted without hearing him out. "Are you all right?"

She responded with a soft, surprised laugh. "Of course I'm all right. What do you mean?"

"I can't forget how ill you looked that night I came to your house. Are you fully recovered from your . . ."

"My miscarriage?" The bitterness behind the question was plain. "Yes. Physically, I'm recovered. Emotionally, I will take a long time to heal."

Why should she be delicate about it and spare his feelings? He had contributed to her poor emotional and physical condition, though she couldn't swear that he was the sole reason she had lost her baby.

In his mind, Hunter said a foul expletive. Would he ever stop feeling guilty? Rationally he knew that nothing he'd done had caused her to lose her baby. At least, not directly. But every time he thought about it, he became sick to his stomach. The topic should be left alone, but like a sore tooth, he kept going back to it, probing it just to see if any of the pain had diminished.

"Did your husband know about the baby?"

"No. I didn't find out I was pregnant until several weeks after Thomas . . . died."

She must have become pregnant during one of their last nights together. Jealousy pumped through his system like poison. It was irrational and downright stupid. But he couldn't stand the thought of her making love with another man, even her husband.

It occurred to Kari that this conversation was too personal to be having with a stranger. Or was he a stranger? Why did she always feel that he knew what she was thinking?

It must be the intent, penetrating way he sometimes looked at her. Like now. It made her uneasy. She pushed her unfinished drink aside. "Mr. McKee, I appreciate your concern over my health, but I can't believe you made this appointment to discuss just that."

Her sarcasm irritated him. How could she be so damn hostile when all he could think about was how much he wanted her? What if they were lovers meeting for a drink before going upstairs to a room, where they would make love for the rest of the evening?

Ah, that would be a different story. She wouldn't be frowning; she would be smiling the mellow smile of a woman who knows her lover is dying to have her. They would be sitting close, nuzzling, exchanging small, pecking kisses. Maybe, just maybe, her hand would be riding the top of his thigh. Maybe, just maybe, he'd accidentally-on-purpose graze her breast with the backs of his fingers. She'd act astonished at his boldness, playfully swat his hand away, but her eyes would be shining with heightening desire.

What was he trying to do? Drive himself insane? But, God, he wanted to be deep inside her. He wondered what she'd do if he pulled her into his arms and kissed that vexed tightness off her mouth, kissed it until her lips parted and worked over his hungrily.

Probably shoot him, he thought grimly and forced himself back to the business at hand.

"You're right," he said tautly. "I didn't invite you for coffee to discuss your health. I came to ask you to bury the hatchet."

She blinked. "What?"

"You know what I'm talking about."

"I'm afraid I don't," she said coolly.

"The hell you don't." He folded his arms on the table and leaned forward. "I know why you don't like me. I regret it, but I can accept it. Only this time you're going too far. You've become an obstruction to the wheels of justice."

"The wheels of justice!" she exclaimed. "Where'd you get that phrase? Perry Mason reruns?"

He was trying to sound stern and had ended up sounding trite and foolish. So he would appeal to her reason. "You claim that all your stories are unbiased."

"They are."

"Do you call a tearful interview with the mother of an accused killer unbiased?"

"I drew no conclusions."

"You didn't have to. The viewers did that on their own. But you failed to mention how that woman had stood by year after year and let her husband beat the kid until he became what he is. You didn't ask her why she failed to seek psychological help for him when he was brought in on an attempted rape charge. He was twelve at the time."

She knew he was right, but she couldn't admit it, even to herself. "I didn't know that."

"And you didn't make it your business to find out."

"I don't need you to tell me how to do my job!"

"Exactly my point. I don't act as your critic, so please desist in acting as mine." Their voices had risen to an angry pitch. They became aware of it simultaneously and both glanced worriedly toward the men at the bar. One winked and saluted Hunter with his highball glass.

Hunter looked back at Kari. The last thing he wanted to be doing was arguing with her. He wanted to be weaving his hands through that mass of blond hair and nibbling on the pearl in her earlobe.

"Your colleagues are going to be very upset if we close that courtroom to cameras," he said quietly.

"Meaning that's what you'll do if I don't depict you as a white knight?"

He sighed. So much for reasoning and friendly persuasion. "Meaning that that's what I'll do if you continue to make the accused out to be a victim, no matter how subtly you do it."

"Of course, you realize that television is a visual medium. Without visuals, I don't have a story."

His smile oozed charm. "Of course."

She looked away in exasperation. He was admitting that he would do all he could to render her useless. "You tried to have cameras barred once. The judge turned you down."

"I think he'll listen this time. If the press swings too far either way, the defense could set up a hue and cry for a mistrial. I don't think the judge wants to release a killer on a technicality."

She gathered up her purse. "I hardly want a killer running loose on the streets, Mr. McKee." She slid from her chair and stood up. He did the same.

"Then, you promise to be less of a distraction in the courtroom?"

"Do I distract you?"

She tilted her head back to look up at him. She had intended to sound flippant, not flirtatious. But the way his eyes lanced down into hers lent another connotation to her question. She would have given anything to recall it.

"Yes. You distract me."

More disturbing than his eyes was his compelling voice. It was low and husky, raspy and intimate. Though they weren't touching anywhere, she could feel that voice seeping through her clothes, touching her everywhere.

"I've got to get back to work," she said quickly, wondering why she was suddenly finding it hard to breathe. "I'm making you no promises, but thank you for the drink."

Hunter watched her go, wondering if he'd gotten his message across. She was damnably high strung.

Damnably desirable.

Sitting at the editing console, Kari did some serious soul-searching. Twice she viewed the unedited tape Mike had shot for her. It was unbiased. The focus of her story would depend on how she wrote her voice track. And it wouldn't be so much what she said, as how she said it.

Whether he had planned to or not, Hunter McKee had pushed the right button to make her stop and think about what she'd been doing. Her personal feelings for him shouldn't matter. They shouldn't dictate the slant of her stories.

In the long run, where would this lead? What would she gain? Perhaps the scorn of other journalists. She was well thought of by her professional peers. Was her vendetta against Hunter McKee worth risking her reputation as a good reporter?

But even more important, what was this vendetta doing to her as a person? She knew her father wouldn't have approved of her attitude toward McKee. Pinkie was disenchanted and made no secret of it. Was everyone else right and she wrong? Had she misjudged the man?

Looking at it objectively, not taking into account her personal feelings, she supposed that McKee was only doing what his job demanded of him. She still thought he was a scoundrel. She still didn't like the way he had handled the evidence against Thomas, nor the way he had bullied her in the courtroom. She especially didn't like the way he talked to her, looked at her, or made her feel when he looked at her.

But, and that was a crucial *but*, she was a news reporter, not an editorialist. Her professional reputation was as much at stake as his. What else could she do but report impartially?

She felt good about her story an hour later when she handed it to the producer completed and ready for airing. There was a lightheartedness to her step as she left the building for home. She had only one name for the feeling welling up inside her: relief. McKee would no doubt be glad to have her off his back, but she was just as glad to be rid of that compulsion to bring him down.

At his apartment, Hunter watched the evening news. He held his breath as Kari's report from the courthouse was introduced. When the story was finished, he let out a great long expulsion of air. She had been factual; her attitude toward him had been tempered considerably.

Thank God, he thought. They were over that hurdle. He wouldn't have to worry about her anymore.

The next morning when he entered the courtroom, his eyes immediately went on a busy search until they located her. Unlike previous days, she wasn't directing her photographer and causing a commotion among the spectators seated around her.

Today she was sitting quietly holding a notepad on her lap. She and the photographer were talking together. He must have said something amusing. She threw back that mane of hair and laughed softly.

Hunter's loins responded to the throaty sound of that laugh. When he passed her aisle, he glanced down the row of chairs and caught a glimpse of her leg in its smooth silk stocking. Her dress was green. The demure design only made it that much sexier. She was leaning back in her chair now, speaking over her shoulder to another reporter. In profile, her breast was clearly detailed.

He took his seat at the prosecution's table and consulted the clock on the back wall. He had a perfectly good watch strapped to his wrist, but the official court clock provided him with an excuse to turn around. His eyes found hers as though by prearranged meeting.

Her gaze was expectant, and he knew she was silently asking if he'd seen her story the night before. He dragged his eyes away from her face, nodded curtly, and turned to the front of the courtroom again.

Damn! he cursed to himself. He was faced with a challenging case to prove in court and his mind was centered on what throbbed with an aching hardness between his thighs.

This juvenile infatuation couldn't continue. Besides being physically uncomfortable and damned embarrassing, it was dangerous. As long as Kari Stewart had been hostile and vituperative, he had been safe from letting his emotions run free. But this docile Kari, this Kari who half smiled at him, was a threat he couldn't combat. With her looking at him like that, he would never be able to concentrate on the task before him, a task his whole career hinged on.

As soon as the judge entered the court, Hunter rose to his feet. "Your Honor," he said politely, "I request that the courtroom be cleared of all distractions, particularly those created by the video tape cameras."

Kari gasped in disbelief. "That *bastard!*" she said under her breath. She had fallen for his convincing insincerity. Once again he had proved just how cold-hearted and manipulative he was.

After viewing her story on one of the newsroom monitors, Pinkie pinched the bridge of his nose between his thumb and index finger. "You've really gone and done it this time, sweetheart."

After the debate that had followed McKee's request, the judge had ruled in his favor. Much to the annoyance of every television reporter, the video tape cameras had been evicted. The judge had consented to let sketch artists remain so the reports wouldn't be totally without visuals for their stories.

Kari's story strongly hinted that the banishment of cameras was an attempt on McKee's part to keep the public in the dark about his political machinations.

"It wasn't libelous."

"Just short of it." Pinkie pulled on his stained polyester sport coat. "I'm getting tired of it, Kari."

"Tired of what?"

"This childish game of yours."

"It isn't a game."

"Call it whatever you like. It's unprofessional and reeks of the shoddy kind of journalism I never could stomach."

Coming from Pinkie, her staunch friend and ally, that hurt. "I'm sorry you see it that way."

"So am I." He headed for the door. "I feel like hell. I feel so bad I may ask Bonnie to get drunk with me." He shuffled out.

Kari had never felt so alone in her life. She drove home wondering why she was feeling depressed instead of elated. She had bested McKee again, but since there was no one to celebrate the victory with her, there was no joy in it.

She unlocked her front door and stepped inside. In one fluid motion she flicked on the lights and tossed her purse onto a chair. Then she came to an abrupt halt.

Hunter McKee was sitting in an easy chair across the room. His moss-colored eyes glowed with satisfaction at having captured his prey so effortlessly.

His coat was lying across the back of her sofa. His vest was unbuttoned, as were the first two buttons of his dress shirt. The knot of his tie had been loosened and his cuffs were rolled to his elbows. His slouching posture indicated that he had been waiting for a long time. There was an unfinished drink in his hand. His hair was even more mussed than usual.

He eased out of the chair to a standing position, keeping his eyes riveted on hers. He downed the last of his drink and meticulously set the glass on the coffee table. Stepping around it deftly, he came toward her.

"How did you get in here?" She was breathless and suddenly frightened by the determined set of his jaw and the intimidating power of his body. He exuded a masculine anger that had been aroused and that wasn't going to be easily appeased.

"I majored in criminology."

"But the security system . . ."

"I disengaged it."

"Is it that easy to tamper with?"

"In fact, it's a very sophisticated system."

"But you managed to disarm it."

"Yes. It's working again by the way."

He was standing close to her now. Too close. She could feel his body heat, taste the whiskey-flavored breath that fanned her face and neck, smell the citrusy flavor of his cologne. Her heart began to race.

"What do you want, Mr. McKee?"

"That's a trifle formal, isn't it? Don't you think that as intimately as you've hated me, you could bring yourself to use my first name? Say it." He filtered the angry words through his teeth, and she jumped back slightly.

She'd never seen a man more furious. A vein ticked in his temple. He said he'd majored in criminology. Maybe he knew how to commit the perfect crime, the clueless murder.

But she wasn't really afraid he'd harm her physically. He threatened her with a kind of danger that was totally new to her.

"Say my name, Kari," he whispered as he moved a step closer.

"No."

Roughly he cupped her face between his hands and tilted it up. He ran his thumb along her lower lip. "Say it."

It was a softly spoken command, but his voice held a steely ring. Reinforcing it was the fierce gleam in his eyes and the tantalizing pressure of his thumb against her lip.

"Hunter," she whispered in fear.

"Again."

"Hunter," she repeated. His eyes watched her lips as they formed his name. He held her that way for a disconcerting length of time before his hands fell away and he stepped back.

Kari's head was spinning. She was disgusted with herself for surrendering to his superior strength of will, but at the same time she didn't want him to know that he had the slightest effect on her. "I've said your name. Is that all you wanted?"

"No. I wanted to paddle your butt." He put his hands on his hips. "That was a helluva story you aired tonight. Are you proud of yourself?"

"Very. Especially after the trick you played on me."

"Trick? What trick?"

The innocent act only made her madder. "You led me to believe that if I'd tone down my reports, you'd let the cameras stay in the courtroom."

"My request to have the court cleared of them had nothing to do with our conversation yesterday."

"Didn't it? Didn't you request that they be evicted because of me?"

"Yes, but not for the reason you think."

"What other reason could there possibly be?"

Because you make me horny! he wanted to shout. Instead he directed the blame for the whole mess back to her. "Let's have this out once and for all. For months you've been paying me back for finding your husband's hand in the till. It wasn't my fault I found it there."

"He was innocent."

"He was as guilty as hell, of a lot of things."

She pinched her eyes shut and drew a deep breath. "I know why you discredited him along with those others."

"He discredited himself."

"Because he disapproved of your appointment."

That unexpected piece of information brought him up sharp. He opened his mouth to say something, but no words came out. Finally he asked, "Who told you that?"

"Silas Barnes," she said triumphantly.

She had spoken with the former D.A. about him? "When?"

"I called him shortly after our first meeting. I couldn't believe your allegations against Thomas and I mistrusted your motives. You said yourself that you came here from St. Louis because you couldn't move up the ladder fast enough. I thought you were probably trying to make a big splash and were using Thomas as one of your springboards. I called Mr. Barnes to ask his opinion of you."

"And?"

"Oh, you're his fair-haired boy. He said if he'd had an army of young attorneys working for him, you would still have been his choice to take over when he retired. *But*—" she held up her hand when he attempted to interrupt—"he also said that Thomas hadn't approved of you. It was all off the record, of course. But Thomas had let it be known around city hall that he thought you were dangerously ambitious."

Hunter shook his head and ran a hand through his hair. "Well, if you think I was getting my revenge on Wynne for not liking me, you're wrong. I never knew that he disapproved of me."

She scoffed. "You don't expect me to believe that?"

"No, I don't," he said sharply. "You thought Thomas Wynne was a saint and you've put on blinders to the truth about him. When you were talking to Barnes did you also ask him about my allegations against Wynne?"

The haughty toss of her head was his answer. "Naturally he sided with you."

"God!" he shouted in frustration and slapped his thighs with his palms. "The truth is right there in front of you and still you refuse to acknowledge it. Your husband was the criminal, not me."

Rage shuddered through her. "Oh, I despise you. You're shrewd—"

"I'm smart."

"And manipulative."

"I take advantage of every situation."

"And ambitious."

"Ambition isn't a crime."

"You're a bloodthirsty prosecutor."

"And you're a vindictive bitch."

"I'm only doing my job!"

"So am I!"

He didn't even realize his hands were on her until he felt her body pressing against his. He looked down, and through the red fog of fury he saw his hands gripping her upper arms.

And suddenly he could feel her, all of her. Her breasts were heaving against his chest. Her belly was softly cushioning his hardness. Her thighs were straining against his.

Angry as she was, she had never looked more beautiful. Her eyes were wide and deeply green in the shadowy light of the room. She breathed through moist and slightly parted lips.

Without thinking beyond the moment, he bent his head and stamped his mouth over hers. His arms swept around her and he drew her closer until her small frame was imprinted on his.

He twisted his mouth over hers until her lips parted. His tongue investigated the row of perfect teeth and elicited a whimper of outrage from her. Still he went on kissing her hard and fervently, until her mouth was forced to open for breath. Then his tongue slipped inside.

It was imposition. It was violation. It was wonderful. And he kept up the rapid thrusts of his tongue until he felt her body weaken and become pliable against his.

At first Kari had been too stunned to move. Then when she began to struggle against him, she realized that she was no match for his strength. How dare he insult her this way? She hated him. But she began to hate herself more.

Because she began to like the kiss.

Could she accuse him of brutality when in fact his mouth gentled its onslaught? He still had her mouth fused to his, but his tongue was no longer hard and rough. It was velvety and sensuous. Its thrusts were no longer random and punishing, but practiced and persuasive. She felt her body's resistance to such sweet aggression giving way.

With no instruction from her, her arms had wound themselves around his waist. When he pressed his aroused sex against her middle, she realized that she was moist and aching with want and need for it. Her breasts were full and flushed. She had the maddest longing to feel his mouth against their tightened peaks.

He kissed her deeply once more, rubbing his tongue against hers and snuggling her middle against his hips. Then gradually he withdrew. His mouth lingered, dropping delicate kisses on her bruised lips, before he pulled away completely and took a backward step.

He stood perfectly still as he stared down at her. She wished she could vanish into thin air. She hadn't responded. She hadn't! she screamed to herself. Still, in case he thought she had, she was afraid to face him. Reluctantly she lifted her eyes to his face.

"What was my biggest fault, Kari? Discrediting Thomas? Contributing to your miscarriage? Wanting you? Or making you want me back?"

He picked up his suit coat. At the door he turned. "One of these days you'll admit the real reason you're angry with me."

He let himself out.

Hunter entered his dark apartment and walked straight to the telephone. He had held out for a long time. But tonight he had kissed, really kissed, Kari Stewart. That had changed his mind. He dialed the long-distance number and after three rings, she answered.

"Pam, it's me, Hunter. You've been right. I've been mule-headed. I'm going to give you your divorce."

Chapter Seven

HE HAD DECIDED TO SIT OUT ELECTION DAY AT HOME.

He knew there must be something wrong with him. He was a healthy, red-blooded American male. But he preferred solitude to a crowd. He preferred watching the evening television newscast to a party.

He sat in front of his TV set like a deviate at a dirty movie. He watched her, mesmerized. By now her speech patterns, facial expressions, and mannerisms were endearingly familiar. He would recognize the flowery scent of her hair anywhere. The texture of her complexion lingered on the pads of his fingers. He knew what her mouth tasted like. He wanted her.

And, by her own admission, she despised him.

What if they'd met under entirely different circumstances? What if he'd met her two years after Wynne's death? Or what if there'd been no Wynne at all? That would have been even better. They would have liked each other immediately. In fantasies anything was possible, wasn't it?

He would have invited her out to dinner a few times. They would have talked about their careers, current issues, movies and books. He would have told her his repertoire of jokes and she would have thought him extremely entertaining. They would have discovered that they had a remarkable number of things in common.

One night she would have invited him in for a nightcap. She would have been smiling invitingly. When he took her in his arms, she would have come willingly. Her lips would have parted obligingly beneath his. She would have been hungry for his kisses, craving his caresses.

"I think it's only fair to tell you that I was married."

"Was?" Her hair would sweep his hands as her head fell back. His mouth would skate down her throat.

"I'm divorced." Her breast would fill his palm and he would sigh her name as his thumb found her responsive nipple. "I've been alone a long time. Since I've met you . . . Well, I've never felt this way about any woman. I want you, Kari. I need your softness and sweetness in my life. Let me love you."

She would have taken his hand and led him into the bedroom and . . .

His telephone rang and he jumped. Snatching it up, he growled into the receiver. "McKee."

"Mr. District Attorney, you mean." Guy was shouting over the racket in the background. "You took it hands down. Of course you were a shoo-in, but the final results of the election have just been announced. You're officially the D.A. now."

"Thanks for calling."

"You've made a grand slam this week. First the conviction of that kid who wasted his old man. And now the election."

Hunter was ambivalent about sending a sixteen-year-old to death row, but this wasn't the time to squelch the enthusiasm of his junior assistant. "Thank everyone who helped."

"You're not coming to the victory party?"

"No."

"But, Jeez, McKee, we're all gathered in someone's apartment. I'm not sure who lives here, but there's booze galore and food and . . ." He dropped his voice to a conspiratorial whisper. "You know Marilyn in the tax assessor's office, the one with the set of knockers that would put your eyes out? She's been anxious to see you all night, if you know what I mean."

Hunter called to mind a leggy redhead with a penchant for tight sweaters. He felt a momentary flare of desire but didn't know if it was a remnant of his daydream about Kari or the thought of Marilyn of the tax assessor's office. "I don't know, Guy."

"You'll hate yourself in the morning if you pass up an offer like this. Take it from me, buddy, she's hot."

Hunter laughed. "In that case, how can I say no?" Maybe that was just what he needed, a rowdy tumble with an obliging sexpot. What better way to eradicate one woman from his mind than to absorb himself with another?

"What's the address?" Guy supplied it. "If Marilyn should need a ride home," Hunter said suggestively, "tell her to meet me outside in ten minutes."

"Gotcha!" He could hear Guy's grin through the telephone. "I guarantee she'll need a ride home."

Before his better judgment got to him, Hunter grabbed up his jacket, his car keys, and left his apartment. The substantially endowed Marilyn was waiting at the curb as promised. How easy it was to score these days. Where had girls like Marilyn been when he was in high school?

"Hi," she said, opening the passenger side door and sliding in.

"Hi."

She was wearing her trademark sweater and it was as tight as all the others in her wardrobe. If he were any judge of the female anatomy at all, she was wearing nothing beneath it. Her perfume was heavy and sweet and unfortunately reminded him of cheaply made, sleazy French films.

"It was so nice of you to offer me a ride home. The party was nice, but then the guest of honor didn't show up." She softened the reproach with a wink. "Things were getting a little wild. It was nice to get out of there."

Irritably he wondered if she knew any other adjective besides "nice." And just as irritably he wondered why they had to act out this charade. He hadn't thought he'd be expected to make small talk. Why couldn't she just say, "I'm glad you're taking me home to bed. I understand it's good therapy to work another woman out of your system."

Then he would feel at liberty to say, "That's right and I appreciate your candor, uh, Marilyn? Yes, Marilyn. You see what I'm after is a hard and fast roll in the hay. No emotion. No conversation. Just fun and games. You've come highly recommended."

But he didn't say any of that. Instead he smiled across the car at her and said, "You'll have to give me directions to your place."

She found them much easier to give when she was plastered against his right side, one of those legendary breasts tucked under his arm. Uninhibitedly she laid a hand on his thigh and began to rub it up and down.

He felt nothing but a mild annoyance. With each passing minute, his aggravation grew and unfairly it was directed toward her. He didn't particularly like the color of her hair, or her eyes. The notable body didn't seem so voluptuous and desirable now, but rather bawdy and blowsy, too much of a good thing.

A trimmer silhouette, a more compact figure, a slenderness with soft womanly curves. Riotous curly blond hair, green eyes. That was what appealed to him.

Kari Stewart appealed to him.

It was her hand he wanted to be flirting with the fly of his trousers. And only when he imagined it to be hers did he feel the first stirrings of arousal.

"Ummm," Marilyn said and squeezed him.

He pulled the car to the curb in front of her building. As he went around to open her door, he breathed in great quantities of air to clear his lungs of her perfume. He realized just how much he disliked it.

Subtlety was an art Marilyn had never mastered. But she was quite agile. Upon getting out of the car, she managed to brush the back of her hand against his crotch, shimmy her breasts against his chest, and find his ear with her lips. "My roomie is going to be away for the night," she promised seductively, before undulating up the sidewalk.

Suddenly he was furious with himself. What was the matter with him? Why didn't he want her? Why wasn't his body burning with lust?

Angrily, to prove that he wasn't hopelessly besotted with another woman, he reached for Marilyn, spun her around, and ground his mouth down on hers. After an instant of surprise, Marilyn responded.

Her mouth was slack and wet. Her hands seemed to crawl over him like furtive spiders. The embrace was thoroughly distasteful and repugnant. Trying not to show just how repulsed he was, he tore his mouth free of her sucking lips and broke away. He had the almost irresistible urge to wipe her sloppy kiss off his mouth.

"It's late and tomorrow is a workday," he said lamely.

Marilyn's face collapsed into a comic mask of stupefaction. "You're not coming in?" she whined. "I thought you wanted to, uh, you know, have a drink or something."

He forced himself to grin and ask with a mischievous lilt, "On the first date?"

"Oh, well." Apparently Marilyn wasn't acquainted with dating protocol. The idea seemed foreign to her. "Maybe you'll call me up sometime." She took a step toward him and laid a hand on his lapel. "Then it wouldn't be a first date, would it?"

He wasn't about to commit himself. He cuffed her gently under the chin. "Good night."

Let her read into it what she might. He had behaved like a jerk. It didn't matter if her morals didn't bear close scrutiny, he hated to treat any woman abusively. She was innocent. He was the heel.

He drove away feeling like a damned fool. If anyone found out about this, he'd be made a laughingstock. But he didn't think Marilyn would boast of her one failure to lure a man into bed.

And why hadn't he felt inclined to go to bed with her?

Because he knew it would have served no purpose. When he woke in the morning, he would feel only disgusted with himself. The longing would still be with him. Marilyn's body wouldn't ease his desire for another. His heart would be left empty.

Sex with Marilyn wasn't what he wanted. He wanted love with Kari.

"This is a great lunch, Kari. How'd you know it was my birthday?"

"I made it my business to know." She smiled at Mike Gonzales as he sliced into the thick steak he had ordered. Eating at one of Denver's finest restaurants was a real treat for him. His wife had just had a baby and on his photographer's salary, the household budget was tight. "How are Becky and the baby?"

"Doing fine, I guess," he said around a mouthful. "Becky's depressed. My mother told me that's to be expected." He laughed. "She's up to her eyebrows in diapers and bottles and heat rashes. I guess she's entitled to be a little cranky."

"I guess so," Kari said, listlessly stirring her crab salad. Reminders of babies always brought a pain that she didn't think would ever go away. Her own pregnancy would have been well advanced by now.

"Don't look now, but your nemesis just walked in."

Disregarding Mike's suggestion, she turned her head. Hunter McKee was being seated at a table across the room. He was with several dignitaries from city and county government.

He must have sensed her presence in the dining room, for his eyes sliced directly to hers. It was the first time they had seen each other in weeks. Both froze until Kari was made uncomfortably aware of how long they stared at each other. She glanced away just as he nodded a silent greeting and sat down to join the men with him.

She was shaken and admonished herself for letting the sight of him upset her. But why was she so upset? His good looks would be unsettling to any woman. He was dressed in a gray suit that fit his athletic body to perfection. His hair had been wind-tossed, and she knew that up close he would smell of expensive cologne and the outdoors.

But she had met many attractive men. Her heart usually didn't stumble over itself at the sight of a handsome man.

No, what disturbed her most was the way he looked at her. He didn't look at her as though she were his enemy, someone he had tangled with many times. There was no sneering, gloating look on his chiseled mouth.

He looked at her as though she was a woman he knew something about, a woman he had shared a secret with, a woman he had been intimate with.

And rightly so. Because there was no other word to describe the way he had kissed her that night at her house. It *had* been intimate. She detested him for forcing that kiss on her, but detested herself more for remembering it in such explicit detail. Since that night, there had been idle moments when she had dwelled on thoughts of that kiss.

Even now, as she lifted her wineglass, her hand was trembling. All the color had drained from her face, but her eyes glowed feverishly. She could still feel the hard pressure of his lips. His tongue had possessed her mouth in a thoroughly masculine way. The taut lines of his body seemed engraved on hers. Much as she wanted to forget, she couldn't. The memories wouldn't be banished.

"Gee, Kari," Mike said, noticing her distress. "If his being here is going to upset you that much, let's leave." Regretfully he glanced down at his half-eaten steak.

She shook her head and smiled at him with affected buoyancy. "Don't be silly. This is your birthday party. Would you like more wine?"

"I may not be able to get you in focus this afternoon," he warned, grinning as he raised his glass.

"That's all right." Unintentionally she spoke aloud her afterthought. "I haven't been in focus for a long time." She wasn't referring to Mike's camera work.

They finished their meal. Kari signed the check and they made their way toward the door. As they drew close to Hunter's table, he laid his napkin beside his plate and stood.

"Hello, Kari."

Behind his eyeglasses he was looking at her with that intensity that never failed to unnerve her. It automatically made her feel threatened. She reacted defensively. "Mr. District Attorney, I haven't seen you since the election. I suppose congratulations are in order."

"Thank you."

"Don't thank me. You earned it the hard way. But then, you don't have any qualms about murdering children, do you?"

Those within hearing distance lapsed into one of those awkward silences that occur when someone disgraces themselves in public. No one but Hunter knew about her miscarriage. Everyone assumed she was referring strictly to the recent trial that had ended with a sixteen-year-old being given a death sentence, a sentence she had editorially protested in her television news reports.

Even so, her stinging comment exceeded the bounds of every code of professional conduct. Had she been a man, Hunter would have been justified in slugging her. As it was, his eyes went as hard as flint, his body tensed, and his lips compressed.

Unperturbed by his anger, she gave him a terse nod, spoke a polite "Gentlemen" to the others, and moved toward the exit. Mike, flabbergasted and embarrassed, stumbled along behind her. He knew they would catch hell when Pinkie heard about the incident.

That was putting it mildly. Unfortunately the station manager heard of it first. One of Hunter's colleagues telephoned him that afternoon. He immediately sent word to the newsroom that he wanted to see Pinkie and Kari.

"Do you have any idea what this is about?" Pinkie asked her as he huffed down the carpeted hallway on the second floor, far removed from the gritty, noisy newsroom.

She had come away from the restaurant feeling worse than she had ever felt in her life. She didn't know herself anymore. The Kari Stewart she used to be could never have behaved that badly, never been that malicious and rude to anyone, no matter how bitter an enemy.

What was happening to her? Each day she felt little pieces of herself falling away. She didn't seem able to get them back. Soon there wouldn't be enough of her left to recognize. The thought frightened her.

Why hadn't she listened to Pinkie? He had been right. She had set out to destroy, and was destroying herself in the process.

"Yes, I think I know why he wants to see us," she said softly.

Pinkie stopped dead in his tracks and faced her. "Lay it on me. I'd rather hear it from you first."

He taught her a whole new vocabulary of obscenities when she finished with her account of the incident. "What the hell were you thinking about?" he shouted.

She shrank from his anger. "I wasn't thinking, I just—"

"Save the explanations. You're gonna need them," he snarled as he dragged her the rest of the way to the manager's office.

The secretary showed them in to the inner sanctum and discreetly closed the door behind them. Not only the station manager, but the sales manager, and the president of the company were there. No one was smiling.

"Please sit down," the station manager said. "I received a telephone call today from an old friend of mine. I could hardly believe what he told me. I hope, Ms. Stewart, that he was mistaken in what he heard you say to our district attorney today at lunch."

She wet her lips, threw an apologetic glance at Pinkie and replied, "He heard correctly."

Pinkie thought he was alone when he eased open the bottom drawer of his desk and reached for the secreted flask. He took a long pull on it and wiped his mouth with the back of his hand. When he looked up, Kari was standing in the doorway of the glass office. Everyone had cleared out after the ten o'clock news. The newsroom was quiet and shadowed behind her.

"Don't let them do this to me, Pinkie."

He hadn't seen her since they left the station manager's office. He had returned to the newsroom to find a fresh crisis on his hands. The producer of the early news show was ninety-seconds short of material. Should they run the story about the pregnant elephant at the zoo or the one about the blind typing teacher?

He had put out that brushfire and the myriad others that flame up during the production of a newscast. But Kari was constantly on his mind. He wondered where she had gone to lick her wounds. Now he could see that wherever she had been, she'd been crying.

He tilted the slender silver flask in her direction, but she shook her head. She dropped into the chair opposite his desk. He took another swig before capping the flask and returning it to its hiding place.

"You did it to yourself, Kari." He settled his bulk more comfortably in his chair. "I warned you, but you didn't listen."

"I'll apologize to him, publicly if I have to."

"You should do that anyway. But it's not going to change their minds. They're furious with you. And they should be. What you said to that man was inexcusable."

"All right. I did something wrong. I confess." She swallowed a sob. "But suspension for three months! Isn't that a bit severe? I thought maybe for a week. Two. But three months! I'll die, Pinkie. My job means everything to me. I've lost my husband, my baby. My work is all I have left."

She placed her hands flat on his desk and leaned forward in a pleading attitude. "Intercede for me, Pinkie. Tell them some of what I've gone through at the hands of that man."

"No."

She yanked her hands away from his desk as though it had suddenly burned her. "You won't help me?"

"Not this time, baby; I'm sorry."

"Why?"

Pinkie sighed and ran his hand down his face. "Because I think you need this time away. You're not the person you used to be, Kari. You haven't been for a long while."

She couldn't take his criticism, not on top of the chastising she had already received. "I'm doing my job!" she said heatedly. "The ratings are up."

"Not anymore. Remember my telling you that I was getting tired of your personal attacks on McKee? Well, I was only one jump ahead of our viewers. Our ratings are slipping and I can't help but think you're one of the reasons."

Her pride was hurt, but she knew Pinkie was right. Hunter had won the public's approval. The citizenry had officially endorsed him as their D.A. Her continual badgering of him would only antagonize her audience.

"I realize that I need to change the slant of my stories," she said quietly, twisting her hands in her lap.

"The city hall beat has already been assigned to someone else, Kari. That was one of the manager's orders."

Panic, cold and lethal, stabbed through her. "Then give me back my entertainment slot."

Pinkie was shaking his head. "Can't do it. Sally's locked into it."

"By sleeping with one of the salesmen!" Kari shouted.

"And he's liking it!" Pinkie roared back. "But that has nothing to do with it. Personally I can't stand her goody-two-shoes style, but the ratings say the audience feels otherwise. I don't know if they like her boobs or what, but the bottom line is, they like her. I warned you about this. Remember, I told you to think all this over carefully be-fore—"

"Stop lecturing me! You're not my father."

"No, but I thought I was your friend." His face went beet red and he forced himself to calm down. "Kari, if you'd been anybody else, I would have nailed your ass to a tree a long time ago. You've pulled one shenanigan after another with this McKee thing, but I've toler-ated it. If I weren't your friend, you'd be long gone by now."

"Meaning that you're not going to help me this time?"

"Meaning that I *am* going to help you. Really help you."

"By talking them out of suspending me?"

He sighed. "No. By making it stick. Use that time away to get your head together, to get things into perspective. McKee's become an obsession with you. It's unhealthy. You've blown his responsibility for your hardships way out of proportion."

"My God," she said, bolting from her chair. "Who are you all of a sudden? His campaign manager?"

"No," Pinkie said, trying desperately to hold on to his temper. "But the man's only doing his job. He had been all along. He's been like a burr under your saddle since he said things about Thomas you didn't want to hear."

"They were lies!" she yelled. "Would you have me mutely stand by and have him slander my husband?"

Pinkie looked at her sadly. His eyes dropped to his desktop for several moments before he looked up at her again and said quietly, "Are you sure they were lies, Kari?"

She recoiled as though he'd slapped her. "Of course they were. You . . . you don't think Thomas was a thief?"

"I don't know about that. I only know that he wasn't the god you thought he was. He was a man. He had faults. You just couldn't see them."

"You believe that he entertained whores when he was out of town? You believe all that?"

He knew it would hurt her, but it was time she saw things as they really were. "I knew about some of Thomas's flings. Everybody did."

She folded her arms across her stomach and bent forward as though in pain. "Please tell me you're lying, Pinkie." Tears rolled down her cheeks.

He shook his head. "I know nothing for fact. But when there's that much gossip, it's usually based on some degree of truth. You were vulnerable when you met Thomas so soon after your father's death. He was just what you needed at the time, strong, indulgent, protective. I was glad you had him. Damn glad."

She sank into the chair again. "The wife *is* always the last to know, isn't she? I feel like such a fool."

"Don't. Wynne adored you, too. His escapades had nothing to do with your life together. You were blissfully in love and probably would have been for years to come if he hadn't died that day. But he did."

He came around his desk and took her hand. "You've been blaming the wrong guy for Thomas's sins, Kari. McKee didn't have any choice but to bring them to light." He pondered his next words. "I don't think he enjoyed it any more than you did."

Her head rested on Pinkie's arm for just a moment, then she pulled away. Her tears had dried, but she looked thoroughly defeated.

"Maybe I do need some time away. I have a lot to think about, feelings that have to be sorted through." She stood and went to the door.

"What will you do?"

She gazed at him sightlessly for a moment before saying vaguely, "I don't know." Then she left, drifting through the empty newsroom, becoming one with the shadows.

The last person Bonnie expected to see when she pulled open her front door was Pinkie Lewis. "Do you have a drink?" he asked without one word of greeting or explanation.

With an irritated gesture, Bonnie jerked the tie belt on her robe tighter. "What happened? Did the bartenders go on strike?"

"Do you have a drink or don't you?"

She stood aside, giving him her silent and none too gracious permission to come in. "Whiskey?"

"Yes. Neat. A double."

One of the first things Bonnie had done when her last child left for college was refurnish her house. She had discarded all the pieces bearing the ravages of children. The new furniture was her reward for having survived the years of her sons' upbringing when treats to herself had been rare if not nonexistent.

Pinkie slung his coat over the back of a chair and sprawled on the couch. He pulled off his tie and tossed it on the corner cushions of the sofa. His shoes came off next. His rumpled presence spoiled the whole effect of her now-perfect house. She was surprised at how glad she was to see that disorder. Her house had been too tidy for too long.

She handed him the glass of whiskey and sat down beside him, resting her arm on the back of the sofa and curling her bare feet under her hips. "Do I owe this visit to unrequited passion finally given vent, or what?"

He shot her a sour look. "I don't feel like sparring with you tonight. I feel like hammered crap. Management suspended Kari for three months." He filled her in on the details. When he was done, she sat in meditative silence. His ruddy head came around. "Well, say something."

"It'll probably be the best thing that could have happened to her."

Somewhat mollified, he took another sip of the Scotch. "That's what I told her. I also thought it best to disillusion her about her late husband."

"You told her about his affairs?"

"I didn't go quite that far. I just raised the question in her mind that McKee might have told her the truth."

"How'd she take it?"

"How do you think? She thought the man was a saint."

"Then it's time she wised up. No man is a saint."

That won her another baleful look before he went on. "She's been irrational, blaming McKee for all this. She's been eaten up with him way too long. It's not natural."

"Or maybe very natural," Bonnie said cryptically.

"What does that mean?"

"I think there's more going on than appears on the surface."

He turned to her. "You know it really bugs the hell out of me to have to keep asking, 'What does that mean?' Why don't you just come out and say what's on your mind?"

"All right. Hate is sometimes as passionate an obsession as love. And vice versa. Often one can't be distinguished from the other."

His pale brows lowered over his eyes. "You think she acts like she hates him because she really loves him?" Pinkie showed the first trace of a smile. "I wouldn't mention that hypothesis to her if I were you."

"I don't intend to. I intend to let her discover it herself. And if Hunter McKee is as determined a man as I think he is, he'll help her discover it."

"You think he's got the hots for her?"

"Don't you?"

Pinkie uttered a noncommittal grunt as he finished his drink.

"Another?" Bonnie asked.

"No, thanks." He set his glass on the end table and stood. "I guess I'd better be going." Taking up his coat and tie, he ambled toward the door.

"Pinkie." He stopped and faced her. She was standing in front of the sofa. "Why did you come here tonight?"

He looked away, sullen and belligerent. "I felt like hell and needed a drink. Your place is on my way home. You're a good drinking buddy."

She smiled, but it wasn't the smile of a buddy, drinking or otherwise. It was the smile of a clever woman. "I'm good for a lot of things." She undid the tie at her waist and shrugged out of the robe, letting it fall to the sofa behind her.

The nightgown wasn't one she would have worn had she known the final step of Pinkie's seduction would take place tonight. But the baby pink color was flattering for a mature complexion already creamed free of makeup. The lace bodice cupped her generous breasts and gave her a slight advantage over gravity.

Pinkie's tongue felt thick in his mouth. He dragged his eyes away from the large dark nipples that teased him from behind the lace screen. "Now look, Bonnie. Don't go reading anything . . . into . . . uh . . ."

His voice dwindled to nothingness as she slipped the straps of her nightgown over her shoulders and let it slither down her body. She knew she wasn't ready for the *Playboy* centerfold, but she knew she wasn't a troll, either.

Pinkie's failure to comment vexed her. He could have said *something* instead of standing there with that stupid gaping-mouthed expression on his face. Putting her hands on her hips, she walked toward him naked. "Well, I'll bet you're no great shakes without your clothes on, either. But I'm willing to take a chance if you are."

She reached for the buttons of his shirt and within seconds they were undone. He wore an old-fashioned tank undershirt that made her smile, a smile she diplomatically hid as she eased his shirt off. His belt buckle didn't intimidate her in the least. She shoved his trousers down.

She leaned forward and kissed his lips as she slid her hand down the front of his shorts. Again she smiled. It had worked!

She turned on her heel and started for the bedroom saying over her shoulder, "What are you going to do, come to bed with me, or stand there with your pants around your ankles?"

"Mr. Lewis? Pinkie?"

"Yeah?" He was mad as hell. He couldn't find a photographer and there was some kook holed up in an apartment with a gun trained on three hostages not ten blocks away. He'd been trying to locate someone on the radio but so far had had no success.

Now, as he swung his head away from the radio panel, a cigarette ash fell to his shirtfront, burning a tiny hole in it before he could brush it away. He'd catch hell from Bonnie. She had ironed the shirt for him only that morning.

He almost forgot all his problems when he looked up to see Hunter McKee standing on the other side of his desk in the newsroom. "Hiya, McKee."

"Are you busy?"

The irony of that struck Pinkie as funny. He laughed as he ground out his cigarette. "Why don't you wait in my office?" He hitched his head in the direction of the cubicle as the speaker on the radio panel squawked and a scratchy voice said, "Pinkie, have you been trying to get us?"

"Hell, yes, I have," he yelled into the microphone as he grabbed it up.

Hunter jumped to his feet when Pinkie bustled into the office five minutes later, a batch of script sheets clutched in his beefy hand. "What can I do for you, McKee?" he said as he began thumbing through the scripts and slashing them with a red ink pen. "Wish somebody would teach reporters to write the English language."

"I guess I've caught you at a bad time."

"Naw, naw. Today's calm, believe it or not. What did you want to see me about?"

"I think you know."

Pinkie's hands stilled and he looked at Hunter from beneath his jutting brows. He studied the man across the desk from him. He looked like he hadn't been sleeping well. Even behind his eyeglasses, his eyes looked tired. The vertical lines running down either side of his mouth didn't look like laugh lines anymore but tracks of unhappiness.

"Yeah, I think I do," Pinkie said slowly. Then he yelled, "Not now!" to someone brave or stupid enough to come barging in without knocking.

"I missed seeing her reports on the news," Hunter said uneasily. "I went by her condo last week, but she wasn't home. It looked like she hadn't been for a long while. Earlier today I called here. I was told she didn't work here anymore."

"That's right, she doesn't. But that's temporary. I hope."

"Is she sick?"

"No. She was suspended for three months."

Pinkie could tell he was relieved that she wasn't ill, but distressed over the suspension. "Why was she suspended?" A level stare was his only answer. Hunter lunged to his feet. "Dammit, I told them that what she said didn't matter. She wrote me a note of apology. That was enough."

He turned his back on the desk and stared out over the bustling newsroom. He didn't even see it. When he spun back around, his jaw was as rigid as granite. "I want to see her. Where is she?"

"I don't know."

In a heartbeat Hunter covered the space that separated him from the desk. Placing his hands on the cluttered surface, he leaned over it. "I want to see her," he enunciated clearly. "Tell me where she is."

This guy has it bad, Pinkie thought. "I don't know where she is," he repeated calmly. "I tried to reach her the morning after the incident, but she'd already had her telephone disconnected. That afternoon a messenger sent me an envelope with the key to her condo and instructions on when to water her plants. That's all. She said she would be in touch."

"That was three weeks ago! And she hasn't been in touch?"

"No."

"Something could have happened to her."

"I don't think so. She went somewhere to be alone. To sort things out."

"What things?"

"Maybe you could tell me."

A spasm of emotion tugged at one corner of Hunter's lips, otherwise he gave nothing away. "If you hear from her, will you let me know?"

"Why?"

"I told you. I want to see her."

"Why?"

"None of your goddamn business," Hunter shouted.

Pinkie smiled as he came out of his chair and picked up the scripts. "I've got a news show to get on the air in exactly fifty-three minutes, Mr. McKee. I can't afford to spend any more of my valuable time on your personal problems." he stalked to the door of the office. "But keep in touch." He sailed through the door, cursing deadlines and shouting orders.

Chapter Eight

❧ ❦

BRECKENRIDGE WAS AS PICTURESQUE IN THE SUMMER AS IT WAS IN winter. Patches of unmelted snow showed up like white blossoms on the mountains. The majestic peaks still wore their sparkling caps. The season had little to do with the ski resort's charm. Its one main street was lined with shops and boutiques stocked with tempting merchandise year-round. The century-old buildings, many with gingerbread trim, looked just as quaint against a panorama of bright blue Colorado sky as they did with snow sifting around them.

Kari had been coming to Breckenridge to ski since she was in junior high school. But she'd never made the trip during the summer. She liked it this way, without hungry skiers queuing for valuable tables in restaurants, without the muddy slush, without the traffic jams at the one traffic light in town.

It was peaceful. That was what she needed.

She sat now on the deck at the back of the house and watched the sun sink behind the peaks. The snow at the summit glistened brightly, then took on a pink hue as the sun slipped behind the mountain.

She had been here for over two months. The year anniversary of Thomas's death had slipped by unnoticed by everyone but her. She hadn't been unusually sad that day. A year's time had blunted the serrated edges of the pain. What saddened her most was that he wasn't as clear in her memory as he once had been. No longer could she hear the sound of his voice in her imagination. Nor was his face as well defined in her dreams.

It was time to say good-bye.

How many had known about Thomas's "flings," as Pinkie had called them? How could she have been blind to his human frailties? She had tried to conjure up bitterness toward Thomas but couldn't.

He had loved her. No matter what else he had done, she knew that he had loved her. He had been exactly what she needed at the time in her life when he came along. And she supposed that she had been a boost to his middle-aged ego. They had been good for each other during the years they'd had together. How could she feel bad about that?

Her mind felt cleansed and at peace. Her body had recovered from the ordeal it had been put through during the last year. She was rested. In another week she would return to work.

But what if they didn't want her back? What if she had no job waiting for her? What if she had to start all over again for the third time in her life?

She stood up and stretched. "I'll cross that bridge when I get to it," she said aloud. Whatever the future held, she now felt ready to face it.

The refrigerator and pantry were grim reminders that she hadn't been to the market in several days. But she was suddenly ravenous and decided to dress and go out to dinner. Her reinstatement into society might be awkward. She needed to be around people.

She dressed in a denim skirt, a pair of low-heeled boots, a short-sleeved cotton sweater, and a suede jacket. The temperatures up in the mountains were considerably cooler at night.

It wasn't a long walk to the center of town, but by the time she was seated in a corner booth at one of the best restaurants, her stomach was growling rebelliously. She ordered a shamefully immodest dinner. It was while she was sipping a pre-dinner glass of wine that he walked in.

It was as if he had come looking for her and knew exactly where to find her. The moment he entered the room, his eyes lasered across the candlelit dimness to fix on her. The hostess greeted him and he responded, though his eyes remained on Kari. The hostess glanced over her shoulder, then smiled at him and nodded. He stepped around her and made his way through the tables toward the booth.

Kari set her wineglass down so he wouldn't see that her hand was trembling. She wanted to look away, but was held spellbound by his gaze. His face was expressionless, but he gave the impression that he knew exactly what he was going to do when he got there.

He didn't stop until he reached the edge of the booth. "If you don't let me join you, it's going to be mighty embarrassing. I told the hostess that you were expecting me."

And in that instant, Kari realized that she had been expecting him. Not specifically that night, but somehow she had known he would come.

"I wouldn't want you to be embarrassed, so you'd better sit down."

The light from the candle on the table was dancing in her hair, flickering in her eyes, and shining on her lips. He thought she'd never looked lovelier. Kari would never have guessed that his heart was beating just as fast and erratically as hers.

"You're sure you don't mind?"

She made no answer but slid over a bit and moved her purse and jacket aside to give him room to sit down. When he was settled, he folded his hands on the table and turned only his head toward her. They stared. Just stared. They didn't move, hardly breathed, but their eyes were busy.

"Sir, would you care to order?"

Hunter kept his eyes on Kari even while he responded to the waiter. "I'll have whatever the lady is having. And we'd like a bottle of wine. One that goes with . . ." He consulted Kari. "What are we eating?"

"Trout."

"One that goes with trout."

"Yes, sir. Thank you."

The waiter withdrew and they fell into that silent staring spell again.

"You look different," she remarked candidly.

"So do you."

"I've never seen you dressed in anything but a suit and tie." His slacks and shirt were casual. The collar of his poplin Windbreaker was flipped up and the sleeves were rolled back to the middle of his forearm. Even as she noted it, he took it off and laid it beside her jacket on the other side of the booth. The outfit was straight out of *GQ*, but it looked better on him than it did on the models in the magazine.

"Your nose is sunburned," he observed. Laughing lightly, she touched the tip of her nose self-consciously. "Have you been lying in the sun?"

"Some, not much. I get cold easily and it's usually too cool up here in the mountains for me to sunbathe. But I've been taking long walks."

They lapsed into another silence. He thought about how cute that sunburn looked on her nose. She wondered if the dark springy hair showing through the opening of his shirt covered all his chest.

"The wine, sir," the waiter said hesitantly after he'd stood unnoticed beside the table for long moments.

Hunter went through the tasting ritual. Kari was given another glass and it was filled with a golden wine that she could have sworn was already flowing through her veins. She sampled it and smiled appreciatively, but she hadn't really tasted it. She would taste nothing. The hunger that had compelled her to order a huge dinner had vanished.

They sipped at their wine and stared fixedly at the candle on the table as though it contained the answers to all the secrets of the universe.

"How did you know— Never mind. I know who told you I was here." Then, thinking she might have been too presumptuous, she said, "This wasn't an accidental meeting, was it?"

He shook his head. "This was no accident."

Her eyes returned to the candle. "You asked Pinkie where I was." There was little inquiry in her voice. It was a quietly spoken statement.

"Yes."

"I only called him last week. He was sworn to secrecy."

"I made a pest of myself and wore him down." He'd made it a daily habit to stop by the television station on his way home from the office to ask if Pinkie had heard from her. And just as habitually, Pinkie and Bonnie refrained from leaving until they had seen him. Finally last Wednesday Pinkie had had something to report.

"Breckenridge!" Hunter recalled exclaiming. He had expected Tahiti, or Tibet, not someplace as close as Breckenridge. He'd been a basket case for almost three months and she had been only seventy miles away.

"Please don't be angry that I tracked you down," he said.

She looked at him directly, staring straight into the gray-green depths of his eyes. "I'm not angry." Her lips barely moved and the words were whispered. "Not anymore."

He had been accused of many things, but being dense wasn't one of them. She didn't have to spell it out for him to get the message. He'd been forgiven.

A tightness inside his chest gave way and he began to breathe normally for the first time in a long while. He'd had a knot in his chest ever since the day he knew what destruction his actions were going to bring into her world, a world that had already fallen apart. He felt like laughing.

Instead he raised his glass. When she did the same, he clinked them together, toasting the truce they had tacitly made. They watched each other over the rims of their glasses as they drank.

It took every ounce of willpower he possessed not to lean over and kiss her wine-glossed lips. He longed to bury his fingers in the wealth of her hair. His mouth wanted to chart the satin smoothness of her throat and beyond, into the V of her sweater.

She was noticing what beautiful hands he had. They were tapered and lean and strong, with a sprinkling of dark hair on the knuckles. His wrist wasn't too thick. It was encircled by a gold watch. Suddenly she wanted to pick up his hand and study it in minute detail.

They ate each course of their meal unhurriedly. The restaurant wasn't crowded. The staff was attentive, but they were content to let their diners set a lingering pace.

The lettuce salads were cold and crisp. The baked potatoes were hot and fluffy and dripping with high-caloric garnishings. The trout was aromatic with herbs and grilled to perfection.

But Kari nearly choked on a succulent mouthful when Hunter asked, "How long have Pinkie and Bonnie been living together?"

The bite of food finally went down the right tube. She chased it with a swallow of wine and blotted her watering eyes with her napkin. "The Pinkie and Bonnie I know are living together?"

He shrugged. "I assume they are. They leave the parking lot of the television station together. The other day I heard her reminding him that 'they' were out of milk and should stop and get some on the way home. That sounds rather domestic, doesn't it?"

"Milk?" Kari squeaked. Flopping back against the padded booth, she laughed. "That low-down sneak! He didn't tell me when I talked to him. He didn't want to hear me say 'I told you so.' "

Hunter pushed his plate aside and relaxed with her against the back of the booth. "I take it their affair is a project you've been working on for some time."

"For almost two years. I knew they would be perfect for each other. She's crazy about him and desperately needs someone to fuss over. If anyone ever needed fussing over, it's Pinkie. He was just being pig-headed."

Hunter studied her as she smiled. "You like him very much, don't you?"

Her eyes came to rest on his. He was close. His hard thigh was only an inch from hers on the seat. She couldn't exactly feel it, but she knew it was there. "Very much. He's the friend everyone should have." She sipped at her wine. "Sometimes it's painful to have a friend like that."

"How so?"

"They tell you the truth when others would tell you what you want to hear." She sighed and closed her eyes. "You see, I counted on Pinkie to bail me out of the mess I got myself into. He made me take my punishment like a good little soldier."

"Kari." Her eyes drifted open. "I'm sorry I was the cause of your suspension. Please believe that I had nothing to do with it."

"I know." Her voice was as soft and quiet as the hand she laid reassuringly on his arm. She was as surprised as he that she had touched him voluntarily. She gazed down at her hand, but couldn't find a good reason to remove it from the hard strength of his forearm. "None of this was your fault, Hunter. I apologize for what I said that day in the restaurant."

"You apologized in your note."

"My stilted and formal note," she said and he shrugged slightly. "I was embarrassed by the scene I'd caused and didn't know what to write." Her eyes shone with tears and her voice was tremulous. "You should have punched me out."

"Kari, don't let it upset you again. It doesn't matter anymore." He covered her hand with his own.

"Dessert tonight?"

Kari was grateful to the waiter for intruding. Her head was buzzing, and it had nothing to do with the wine she had drunk. Things were moving too fast. They had to slow down. She was just coming to grips with Thomas's death, his infidelities, her career, her whole future.

Did she need another emotional upheaval now? She seized the opportunity to prolong the dinner, because she didn't know what would happen when it was over.

"Please. I'd like to see a dessert menu," she said quickly. "It must be the mountain air, but since I've been here, I've been eating like a horse." She tried to sound frivolous and gay, but didn't think Hunter fell for it. He was studying her closely with a half-formed smile on his lips, as though he knew her craving for dessert was a delaying tactic.

They perused the menu together. "New York cheesecake," Hunter commented.

"That sounds good," Kari said. "With strawberries, maybe?" The waiter nodded.

"What's the difference between New York cheesecake and plain cheesecake?" Hunter asked him.

"Seventy-five cents," he quipped.

They both laughed. "I buy only the best. One New York cheesecake with strawberries for the lady and I'll have apple pie. Two coffees."

"With cheese or vanilla ice cream?" the waiter asked, noting down their order on his pad.

Hunter turned to her. "Do you take cheese or vanilla ice cream in your coffee?"

"No," she said seriously.

"I meant on the apple pie," the waiter said with forbearance.

"Oh, on the *pie*! Vanilla ice cream."

The waiter went away shaking his head and they burst out laughing. Kari even went so far as to press her forehead against his shoulder as she giggled. She rather imagined she was tipsy, but it felt so good she didn't care. When she lifted her eyes to his, they melted together.

"The only other time I've seen you laugh was one day in court when your photographer said something to you. I like the sound of it," he said softly.

"I've never seen you laugh."

"This is a night for firsts, isn't it?"

His husky whisper found its way into her body. Once inside, it scattered to every erogenous spot and brought on a riot. Battling so many bonfires was futile, so she let them burn slowly and deliciously.

"It's a shame to waste that last bite, but if I eat it, I'm going to pop," she said a few minutes later.

"We can ask for a doggie bag. You could have it for breakfast."

"No, but thank you. Remember that fifteen pounds the television camera adds?"

"I remember everything you said that day."

She remembered it, too. She had walked into his office, curious but confident, having no inkling of the impact he was going to have on her life. And it wasn't over yet. She felt that the influence he had already had on her future was mild compared to what was coming.

Was she being naive? Were they truly on the brink of something exciting? Or was the wine making her feel and think recklessly and irresponsibly?

"Where are your glasses?" she asked suddenly.

"In the pocket of my jacket. I only need them to see." She laughed. "Actually," he explained, "I can see up to about four feet away without them."

"And you didn't think we'd be sitting farther apart than that?"

His voice lowered. "If you let me sit with you at all, I planned to sit as close as possible."

Nervously and shyly, her eyes flitted away from his. He cursed himself. *Go slow. Be her friend first.* "Shall we go?"

She murmured her consent and they moved out of the booth. Before he could help her, she settled her jacket around her shoulders. She also reached for the tab. He yanked it from her fingers.

"I intend to pay my part."

"My treat," he said succinctly, forestalling any further discussion. "What was that?" he asked when she mumbled something he didn't quite catch.

"I said you're bossy." He threw back his head and laughed.

Outside on the sidewalk he asked, "Do you feel like walking back or would you rather I drive you?"

So, he knew she had walked to the restaurant. She shouldn't be surprised. If he had been determined to come after her, he wouldn't have left finding her to chance.

"You don't have to do either."

He stuffed his hands into his jacket pockets and gazed at the dark silhouette of the mountains for a slow count of ten. "Surely we aren't going to start playing games with each other. Not after what we've come through already."

She'd almost bungled it again, first with the check, now with this. *Don't be so damned defensive.* "It's quite a walk," she said in a teasing manner, hoping to make a concession.

He smiled. "I think I can handle it." He took her arm as they crossed the street. Without even asking, he guided them up the hill in the direction of the house.

He matched his stride to hers. They walked in companionable silence. The night was still and quiet. Finally she asked what was uppermost in her mind. "Hunter, why did you come here?"

"I'm on vacation." This time his attempt at humor fell flat.

"You just happened to choose Breckenridge?"

"No, it wasn't a random choice." He stopped. They stood facing each other in the middle of the street. The street was deserted but it wouldn't have mattered. To them, they were the only people on earth at the moment.

"Pinkie told me you were here and I immediately notified my office that I was taking this week off. I came here with the sole purpose of seeing you. This afternoon as soon as I arrived, I located the house you're staying in. I drove past it several times and spotted you when you came out. I didn't plan to call you until tomorrow morning but couldn't wait. I followed you into the restaurant."

He took a step nearer and spoke more softly. "I know it's been a year since your husband's death. From what I've read that's the last hurdle. Now you should be ready to start again." He capped her shoulders with his palms. "I wanted to see you, talk with you, spend time with you."

"Why, Hunter?"

He probed the depths of her eyes. "You know why."

Her eyes met his steadily. She answered as honestly as she could. "There's always been *something* between us. I don't know what it is. At first I thought it was hatred, at least on my part. Now I'm not sure. Every time I've seen you it's been upsetting and unsettling. I've always been uncomfortable with you until—" She broke off and looked away.

"Until when?"

"Until tonight." Her head was bowed and she spoke into her collar. He tilted her chin up with his index finger until she was looking at him again.

"So, you don't think you'll mind having me around for a few days?"

"I don't know," she said with soft earnestness. "Don't expect too much. Don't expect anything. My feelings for you have always been ambivalent. They still are."

His grin was rueful. "I can't ask you to be more honest than that." He pressed her hands between both of his. "Tell me this. When you saw me walking toward you tonight, what was your initial reaction?"

She let her eyes fence with his for a moment while the knot of emotion in her throat tried to work itself out. "I was glad to see you."

She expected a reaction. She was disappointed. His face gave none of his thoughts away. She had expected him to smile, or maybe duck his head and kiss her cheek, or embrace her and kiss her passionately.

Instead he only said "You're shivering."

"I'm cold."

"Here." He lifted her jacket from her shoulders and helped her guide her arms into the sleeves.

"Thank you," she said politely and started to turn away.

"Wait." He pulled her back in front of him, bent his knees to put him on a more even level with her and reached for the two sides of her jacket. In the dark, it was difficult, but he managed to link the components together. As he slowly straightened his legs, he dragged the zipper up the front of her body. It was an intensely sexual motion.

Somehow he managed to draw close without actually moving. He just inclined toward her until there was barely room to navigate the zipper between their bodies without touching her. His hands passed her waist and hovered above her stomach. When it inched over her breasts, it left behind a heat that spilled over her skin like an ink stain.

She wondered what she would do if he dropped the zipper and slipped his hands inside her jacket to cover her breasts.

She knew what she would do. She would lean into his hands, for her breasts were aching with the need to be caressed.

His breath was hot on her face as he pulled the zipper all the way up to her chin and whispered, "There. That should feel better."

She didn't know if it did or not. Every nerve in her body felt like it had been singed. She had never felt so disoriented and confused in her life. She yearned for the feel of his body against hers. She wanted to see him naked, to run her hands over him.

"I'd better get you inside."

His quiet words were all that saved her from swaying against him and begging him to hold her. How foolhardy that would have been. Because if the workings of her mind were erotic, she could imagine what his were. She had barely confessed to enjoying his company, while he had made no bones about coming here specifically to see her and spend time alone with her. From the rigid set of his facial muscles, it was clear he was struggling to restrain his arousal.

Was she ready for intimacy with a man other than Thomas?

Tonight, tomorrow night, soon, in the distant future, ever? God, she didn't know. One minute she was burning, the next she was quaking with apprehension and fear of making another commitment. And sex for her would always be a commitment.

What if he tried to kiss her good night?

But she needn't have fretted about that tonight. At her door, Hunter outlined the shape of her chin with his thumb. "That was one of the most enjoyable dinners I've ever had. Thank you and sleep well."

Then he began walking back the way they'd come, toward the sleeping town.

The first thing she did the following morning was the first thing she'd been doing every morning during her stay. She rolled out of bed, went to the window with the eastern exposure, and reached for the drape cord.

She had slept later than usual. Sunlight struck her full in the face. She yawned and stretched and shook out her hair. It was only when her eyes came fully open that she saw Hunter leaning against the fire hydrant at the curb. He was watching her with evident delight.

A squealing sound escaped her as she reached for a robe and held it against her. It was a ridiculous attempt at modesty since he'd already seen her in her sleeping attire, a Denver Broncos T-shirt. It was the most comfortable thing she had to sleep in, being soft and faded from innumerable washings. It only reached the top of her thighs, a fact she was embarrassingly reminded of as Hunter waved jauntily and started jogging toward her door.

"Oh, my God," she groaned as she raced through the bedroom and caught a haphazard glimpse of herself in the mirror. She pulled on the robe just as his knock sounded.

"Good morning," he said as she opened the door.

"Good morning." She rested one bare foot on top of the other as the cool mountain air hit her toes. "How long have you been out there?"

"Long enough for the coffee to get cold and to give the neighbors something to talk about."

"There are no neighbors this time of year."

He smiled. "Good. Then you won't have any reservations about inviting me in."

She gave him an exasperated look and stepped aside. "Is that how you finagle a jury?" It was asked without malice.

"Practice makes perfect." He had carried a paper sack in with him and began unloading it on the dining table. "I have tepid coffee and moderately fresh donuts."

"Sounds wonderful," she said in a dubious tone. But she picked up one of the gooey donuts and bit into it. "Hey, these are good. I love this chocolate icing," she said, licking her fingers.

"I thought you would." He wadded up the now-empty sack and with a perfect arc, lobbed it into the trash can. When he turned around, he was mesmerized by the nimbleness of Kari's tongue as it flicked over the tips of her fingers. What he wished that tongue were doing to him was still illegal in some states.

He hadn't recovered yet from seeing her stretching in the sunlight. That ridiculous T-shirt was sexier than any negligee. Did she have any idea at all what a tantalizing picture she made when she arched her back and stretched with feline laziness? Not only could he see the silk and lace confection of her panties, but the cotton T-shirt had stretched over her breasts and made them a present for his eyes.

He loudly cleared his throat. "Should I heat this coffee up or do you want to make a fresh pot?"

"I'm out of coffee. You can heat that up in the microwave oven on the counter."

They demolished the donuts in record time. As they sipped the reheated coffee, Hunter surveyed the room. It had a tall cathedral ceiling, warm wood paneling, and a parquet floor dotted with braided rugs. The furniture was tasteful and expensive but not ostentatious. A stone fireplace took up one wall. From this central room, he could see into a dining alcove; the small kitchen and a hallway he presumed led into the bedroom, or bedrooms. It was small, but the vistas its wide windows afforded gave it a feeling of spaciousness.

"This is a nice house. Does it belong to you?"

"No. To friends of my father. It's their vacation home. They offered it to us anytime we wanted. I haven't abused the privilege, but I knew it wouldn't inconvenience them if I used it this summer." Perching on the arm of the sofa, she gazed out the wide picture window. "In the wintertime, you can sit here by the fire and watch the snow fall."

"Do you ski?"

"Yes, but I'm a better observer than participator."

Curious, he walked around the room, stopping to inspect this and that, thumbing through the magazines left on the coffee table. She marveled that he could be so composed. He had virtually barged in on a woman who hadn't even washed the sleep from her eyes or had her morning coffee. Yet he was making himself right at home. He'd offered no explanation for his untimely arrival.

But then she hadn't asked for one, had she?

Even though she was sitting here with nothing on but her nightclothes, her feet and legs bare, her hair straggling like an unruly mop and her eyes still puffy from a sound sleep, she didn't feel nearly as disconcerted as the situation warranted. Why not? she wondered.

Could it be because he seemed so at ease? Or could it be that her mind was so preoccupied with him, it didn't have room to think about anything else?

He looked lean and hard and infinitely male as he prowled the room. The down vest he'd worn against the chilly air of late summer had been tossed negligently over the back of a chair. His western-cut shirt tapered to fit his torso. His boots were scuffed and looked perfectly at home with his jeans, which were far from new. Their snug fit made his sex unquestionable. Frequently her eyes strayed toward his thighs.

He was wearing his glasses, she supposed, since he had driven over. She remembered seeing an unfamiliar car parked at her curb. She also remembered how the sunlight had painted streaks of fire through his windblown hair.

"What's this?" he asked, bending down over the card table where a jigsaw puzzle was spread out.

"I brought it with me," she said, moving off the arm of the couch to join him. "I knew I'd have to fill many idle hours up here. So I brought a stack of books I'd been wanting to read. This is another of my projects." She picked up a piece and after studying it a moment, locked it into place.

"Very good," he said, smiling down on her. "Do you do these all the time?"

"I never have before. But I've gotten in hours of practice."

The puzzle held a special symbolism for her. She hadn't started it as most people would, from the outside. She had started in the center and worked outward.

To her the center represented the nucleus of herself, the things she believed in, her mores and values, her thoughts and convictions, the things she held near and dear, the parts of her personality that had been nursed through childhood and that made Kari Stewart Kari Stewart.

That was what she had started with when she arrived. And gradually, daily, she had added pieces to the puzzle. She relived the frightening childhood experience of losing her mother, the life she'd had with her father, her college days, the beginnings of her career, the development of her friendship with Pinkie, her meeting Thomas. She recalled as many specific days of their life together as she could. She relived the horror of his death. She chronicled each time she'd seen Hunter McKee. The picture on the puzzle had begun to emerge from the myriad pieces.

It was almost complete now. "When it's finished, I'll feel that I know myself better." She hadn't intended to speak the thought aloud. Quickly she glanced up at Hunter. He would think she was a fool. But apparently he understood this self-therapy. He nodded his head. She hoped he wouldn't ask her to elaborate, and he didn't.

"You have chocolate on your mouth," he said softly.

She was enraptured by his eyes. The warm light from them seemed to shine over her whole being, inside and out. "Do I?"

"Uh-huh, right here."

His finger lifted the speck of chocolate glaze from the corner of her mouth. He let it melt against the tip of his tongue. She watched his mouth, intrigued and aroused by its flagrant sensuality. Her eyes remained fastened on his lips as he settled his hands on her shoulders and drew her against him.

"Kari?" Her eyes slowly climbed his face until they met his.

"Hmm?"

"The first time I kissed you, you were unconscious. The second time

I was so angry, I didn't know whether to kiss you or throttle you. I was blinded by rage and hardly aware of what was happening."

He moved his hands up to cup her cheeks between his palms. "Don't you think we owe it to ourselves to kiss when both of us know exactly what we're doing?"

Chapter Nine

SHE REMAINED PERFECTLY STILL. SHE DIDN'T EVEN BLINK. HE TOOK off his glasses and laid them on the card table. Her cheeks were again cradled between his palms. They were warm. His fingertips were gentle as they skimmed over her cheekbones. The pads of his thumbs alternately stroked her lips.

His eyes were still open when hers finally gave up the fight and fluttered closed. Then she felt his breath on her lips. It was moist and warm and coffee-flavored. His lips hovered over hers for what seemed like a small eternity before he actually touched them.

Lips closed, he rubbed her mouth with his, back and forth in a hypnotic rhythm. He made small nibbling motions, then lightly caught her lower lip between his teeth and laved it with his tongue.

Rockets exploded inside Kari's head. Before, she had thought such reactions to a kiss belonged only in the movies. This was all new to her. Either she had been kissed by inordinately unimaginative men, or they had felt bound by some code of ethics that didn't apply to Hunter.

Had she inspired men to give her protection rather than passion? Had she given the impression that there wasn't a carnal side to Kari Stewart? Or had that part of her nature just been born? For the first time, she was being kissed like a woman, and by a man who knew how. Hunter made kissing a frankly sexual mating ritual.

He laid his lips against hers and pressed, withdrew, pressed again. Each time their mouths met, his lips were parted more, until she felt the damp heat of his mouth. She responded to it. Her lips opened to take it in.

All of him moved at once with perfect timing and coordination. His head tilted to one side. His mouth settled over hers and with the sweetest suction, fused them together. He gave her his tongue. His hands slid from her cheeks, down her arms, and around her back until she was being held in the warmest, closest embrace imaginable.

Her bare toes stubbed against his boots as she instinctively moved closer. No longer docile, her body was restless to know his. Her arms lifted and folded around his neck. She heard a growl of approval rumble in his chest.

God, she had needed this!

She loved being held like this, loved feeling defenseless and feminine against such maleness. He had carried the cool outdoors in with him. It clung to his clothes and hair and skin. What a delicious contrast to her sleepy warmth! His scent was distinctly masculine. It reminded her of lemon peels and wood smoke and crunching autumn leaves.

He was hard. She gloried in that evidence of his desire by cushioning it with her softness. At every point along their complementing bodies, she was electrically aware of the differences between them. The rasp of his beard against her chin and around her mouth was exciting.

Her mouth was being made love to by a wicked tongue. With each rowdy thrust her entire body reacted. Tiny pockets of desire burst inside her and leaked their liquid fire into her veins.

Then the tempo changed. The strokes of his tongue became disciplined and controlled. She wanted to feel its knowledgeable caress all over, on her breasts, her stomach, her thighs. She wanted intercourse.

But when his hands untied the knot at her waist and the panels of the robe fell apart, she realized how far it was going and how soon she had lost control. She tensed. Her fingers dug into the back of his neck. Tearing her mouth free from his, she bowed her head against his chest.

"I only want to hold you against me, Kari." His unsteady breath fanned the top of her head. "I want to feel you against me, but it will go no further than that. I swear it."

Gradually her fingers relaxed. He tipped her head back with his finger beneath her chin. Her eyes were closed. Her mouth was red and kiss-swollen and dewy. A pulse as rapid as his own vibrated in the hollow of her slender throat.

He felt a rush of sexual desire so intense it was painful. But it was coupled with a tenderness he'd never experienced before.

His mouth touched hers briefly, experimentally. She didn't pull away, but her fingers stretched up into his hair and laced through it. He settled his lips more firmly over hers as he slipped his hands inside the robe on either side of her waist. As the kiss deepened and his tongue sank into the wonder of her mouth, he drew her against him.

His hands splayed wide over her back. The cotton knit T-shirt was soft beneath his hands. Her body heat came through it. He knew her skin would be silky to his touch, but he dared not lift the shirt and slide his hands under. God he wanted to.

Her breasts flattened against his chest and he moaned his pleasure. He could feel the hardness of her nipples even through their clothes. He wondered how the rough denim of his jeans felt against her bare thighs as he worked his knee between hers. He wished he could see their legs linked together. Just the thought of the way her hips were raised up against his sent his mind reeling.

He also wondered what she thought of that ridge behind the fly of his jeans. She had to feel it. It was nuzzling the beguiling triangle of her bikini panties. He couldn't get that image out of his mind either— the way she had stretched in the sunlight, back arched, arms raised, legs braced apart, head thrown back. Sensual abandonment personified.

He wanted to touch her, all of her. He wanted to smooth his hands over her skin while his tongue was lazily exploring her mouth. How would she react if he slipped his hands beneath—

No. If he touched any part of her bare skin, even her back, he'd want to caress it all. His hands wouldn't stop at the small of her back but would probably slide into her panties and squeeze that cute bottom. And if things should progress from there—Damn! Don't even think about her front—she would hate herself afterward.

She would condemn herself for consenting too soon. He would be called an opportunist for catching her lonely after nearly three months of solitude. He had arrived early in the morning when she was at her most vulnerable, only partially dressed. She would blame him for taking advantage of her again.

He could all but hear the accusations she would fling at him. And the hell of it was, she would be right. He *was* moving too fast. Maybe her response to him was only a result of her being without a man, any man, too long.

That thought was a slap to his pride, but it carried enough weight to make his hands move from the inside of the robe and settle affectionately, but passionlessly, on her shoulders. He forced his mouth away from the miracle of hers.

Her eyelashes lifted heavily and she looked at him through hazy green eyes. Hunter cursed himself for a damned fool for stopping so soon. Maybe she was ready. Maybe . . . No, not yet. He smiled and asked, "What's on the agenda for today?"

He was a bundle of contradictions. After the kiss they had just shared, while her senses were humming and her limbs were liquefying and her body was melting all over his, she would have expected a man of Hunter's virility to ask, "Where's the bedroom?" or "Do you mind if we forgo the bedroom?" and drag her to the floor.

His softly spoken inquiry was so different from what she had thought he would say that she blinked rapidly. When her vision cleared and she could feel the floor beneath her feet again, his words finally registered on her. "Agenda?" Her voice was reedy and weak. She tried again. "What did I plan to do today?"

He brushed back stray wisps of hair from her cheeks. "Yes. Whatever you were going to do, care for a companion?"

"I, uh, I need to buy groceries." She smiled wanly. "That doesn't sound very exciting, does it?"

His eyes took on a gleam that startled her. The wolfish grin sent a thrill of sensation feathering up her middle and back down again. "We can make anything exciting, Kari. Haven't you figured that out by now?"

He waited in the living room while she showered and dressed. When she came from the bedroom wearing jeans and a pullover, he whistled low and long.

Putting her hands on her hips, she asked flirtatiously, "Which turned you on? The jeans or the ponytail?"

"Both. Remember, lately I've never seen you any way but camera-ready."

"How soon you forget. You saw me fresh out of bed only an hour ago."

His eyes took on a smoky hue. "I'll never forget that."

She ducked into the kitchen to make a grocery list, but her fingers could barely control the pencil. During her shower, she had tried to tether her high-flying spirits, but they wouldn't be anchored down. She felt as lighthearted as a child in the springtime. No, amend that. She felt as if she were learning for the first time all it meant to be a woman. And what fun it was!

Suddenly a new emotion washed over her. It had been there, lurking on the edges of her mind, trying to get a foothold. Now she had no choice but to acknowledge it.

Guilt.

For the first time since Thomas's death, she was enjoying the company of a man, and having a helluva good time at it. She felt guilty about it. The pencil rolled from her listless fingers.

"It's perfectly natural, you know."

She jumped and spun around. Hunter was standing close but had moved so silently she hadn't heard his approach. "What?" she asked breathlessly.

"The guilt." He didn't touch her, but she thought that he wanted to. "It's natural to grieve when someone we love dies, Kari. But it's just as natural to eventually go on living, to enjoy life, to laugh again. Possibly love again."

She doubted that she would feel guilty if she weren't so attracted to Hunter. If he were older, chubby and bald, she doubted her conscience would be pricked at all. But he wasn't. He was young and handsome and virile. If he were someone she could establish a comfortable, affectionate friendship with, she probably wouldn't feel guilty at all. But she was thinking of him as a lover. And since the only man she had been intimate with was Thomas, she saw her passionate response to Hunter as unfaithfulness.

"I don't intend to replace anyone in your life, Kari. I intend to make a place there for myself."

"You said once that mind reading wasn't one of your strong points. You lied."

"That's the only time I've lied to you."

Both the subject and his ability to read her were disturbing. She turned back to her list. "Oreos or Nutter-Butters?"

"Why not both?"

"Remember that television camera and its cursed fifteen pounds? Oh, what the hell? Both." She scratched across the paper with the pencil. "If Pinkie sends me to a fat farm, the television station can foot the bill. What else?"

"Tomato sauce, oregano, onion, bell pepper—"

He was peering over her shoulder at the list as she wrote. She turned to face him in the small space he allowed her between the cabinet and his equally unyielding frame. "What's that for?"

"The spaghetti dinner I'm going to cook you one night."

"You can cook?"

"Spaghetti. Can you cook?"

"Spaghetti," she answered, laughing.

He shrugged. "So, we'll eat a lot of spaghetti or eat out. Or overdose on Oreos and Nutter-Butters."

They laughed together and finished their list. He insisted on taking his car. "I'm perfectly capable of driving on a mountain road," she said as he unlocked the door for her.

"And I'm a male chauvinist. Shut up and get in."

"Bossy."

He drove as capably as he did everything else. She liked to watch his hands on the padded leather steering wheel. Naughty mental images of those hands on her naked body flickered through her mind. The motor of the sleek sports car throbbed beneath her. She was throbbing all over.

"Penny for your thoughts," he said, catching her eyes on him.

"I was just thinking how much you and your car are alike."

He cocked an eyebrow in surprise. "Care to expound on that?"

She studied him, the lean symmetry of his body, the threat of a dangerous temper just beneath the surface, the power in every taut inch. "No. I don't think I do," she said saucily.

"Aw, come on."

"Nope."

"Then, I won't tell you how sensational you look. I won't tell you that until this morning I had a fairly good idea that your thighs would be just as perfect as your calves and ankles. Now I know for sure that they are.

"I won't comment that your tush is even better in jeans than it is in a skirt. Or that I love the way your breasts looked under that T-shirt and the feel of them against my chest. Or that I like the color of your hair in sunlight, which is almost as pretty as it is in candlelight. Forget my even mentioning that your face is exquisite and as easy to read as a first-grade primer.

"Nor will I tell you that your eyes are the most bewitching pair I've ever gazed into. As for your mouth, suffice it to say, it has played a major role in my fantasies for months. Is there anything else I shouldn't say?"

He swung the car into a parking lot and brought it to a jarring halt. He switched off the ignition and faced her. "Well?"

She swallowed. "No. I think that about covers all that you shouldn't say."

"One more thing." He took her hand and met her eyes with his. "I'm glad to be here with you like this." He smiled that heart-stopping smile that had convinced judges and swayed juries and seduced God knew how many women.

She joined their ranks and answered his smile with one equally as dazzling. "Me, too."

He winked. "Got your list? Let's go."

He had driven to Dillon. It was little more than a community of rental properties used by skiers during the season. The prices for life's necessities were outrageous but somewhat more reasonable than those in Breckenridge.

It was a new experience to stroll up and down the aisles of a grocery store with a man. Thomas's housekeeper had done all the shopping when Kari had lived with him. Before and after her marriage, no man had ever accompanied her on her whirlwind expeditions through the market where she picked up only the essentials and rushed out.

Hunter shopped impulsively. "Ever had any of this?"

"What is it?"

He studied the label on the can. It was printed in a foreign language. "I'm not sure." He tossed the can into their basket.

While she squeezed heads of lettuce, he peeled an orange and conscientiously put the peels in the nearest trash can. He fed Kari a wedge, then popped two in his mouth. "You do intend to pay for that, don't you?" she asked, trying to keep the juice from drooling out the sides of her mouth.

"Sure," he said in the middle of chewing his own bite. Then he bent close to her ear and whispered. "If they catch me."

She coughed. "I thought you were always on the side of law and order, locking away the bad guys."

"But I'm on vacation." He tweaked her nose.

"Why did you choose prosecution over defense? As sharp as you are, wouldn't you make more money as a defense lawyer?"

"Thanks for the compliment." He studied a bag of marshmallows, but returned them to the shelf. "And you're right. I guess it would be more profitable to go into business for myself rather than to continue being a public servant."

"So why?" she persisted. If she got to the bottom of this, she felt that many of her ambiguities concerning him would be resolved.

"I guess my parents taught me too well. It was ingrained in me from the cradle that there is a difference between right and wrong and that one must be held accountable for one's actions. I don't think I could defend someone I knew was guilty of committing a crime. Don't get me wrong. I respect defense attorneys and the work they do. They're necessary. The system can work. But that particular kind of law isn't for me."

"You're ambitious," she said quietly. The grocery cart beside her came to a halt. He waited until she looked at him before he spoke.

"Yes. I am. I don't deny it. But I don't consider it a fault, either."

"Even when it's blown out of proportion?"

"Do you think mine is?"

She glanced away. "I did. Now"—she lifted her eyes back to his—"now I'm not sure. Do you have political aspirations?"

His smile was mischievous and fleeting. "We'll see. Right now, I want to be a good district attorney."

"You are." She met his stare levelly. There was no guile in her eyes.

Again Hunter felt that rush of passion and tenderness sweep through him. She wasn't just a desirable woman, she was a person worth knowing. She was willing to admit her mistakes and to forgive. "Thank you," he said.

For a while their eyes held, then she took up pushing the cart. "Tell me about yourself."

He had grown up in Utah. His father had an insurance agency. Both parents were still alive. One of his sisters was married. The other was in school. "I'm the middle child. Very ornery and stubborn by nature."

"No comment."

He laughed. "I'd like you to meet my family."

"I'd like that, too."

"What about you?"

"What about me?"

"Your family, childhood, etc."

They had paid for their groceries and driven to a fast-food restaurant to have lunch. The hamburgers were thin, the french fries were greasy and limp, the shakes were foamy. But they didn't notice.

She told him about losing her mother when she was ten and going through adolescence with only her father to keep things on an even keel. "I loved him desperately. He tried so hard to be both parents for me. It couldn't have been easy for him."

"What did he do for a living?"

"He was a newspaper journalist. That's where I first got my love for a newsroom. I would meet him in the city room every day after school. It gave me a sense of superiority to be the first to read the news as it rolled off the presses. That thrill of being in on things as they happen has never left me."

"It must have been a real blow when you lost him, too."

"It was. I felt so alone, rootless, until I met Pinkie, then Thomas."

The name slipped out before she could recall it. Her eyes flew to Hunter's, but he only smiled at her. "Finished eating?" He escorted her to the car and drove back into the mountains toward Breckenridge.

They put the groceries away, then spent the rest of the afternoon on a driving excursion that took them everywhere in general and nowhere in particular. When he pulled up outside her house, she asked, "Where are you staying?"

He motioned with his chin toward the western side of town. "In some condos over by Peak 8. You know the Four O'clock Run?"

"Yes. Is the apartment yours?"

"No. I rented it for the week. It's not as fancy as your house. What are you doing for dinner tonight?"

"What are you doing?"

His grin was boyish and she thought his mother and sisters must have spoiled him terribly. "I was hoping you'd invite me over."

"You're invited," she said as she got out of the car. "But you have to do the dishes."

"Then, keep it simple," he called as he put the car in gear and sped away.

She heated up a can of chili and fixed nachos. Just before he arrived she put on a long, flounced printed skirt and a blue peasant blouse. It was the only impractical outfit she had packed, but tonight was the occasion for it. How long had it been since she had entertained a man? Such feminine frivolity felt good. She even plucked a silk flower from one of the arrangements in the house and stuck it behind her ear.

His slow lecherous smile of appreciation as she opened the door told her her efforts hadn't been wasted.

They ate, and after he dutifully stacked the dishes in the dishwasher, they worked on the jigsaw puzzle. She was miffed to find that he was better at it than she.

"Look, if you're going to sulk every time I fit a piece—"

"I'm not sulking!"

He reached across the table and ran his finger over her lower lip. "It looks like it to me."

His touch was like an electric shock. She clamped her teeth over her lip the moment his finger was withdrawn, as though she either wanted to capture the thrill of his touch or deflect it.

"How are you at mountain climbing?"

"Terrific," she boasted. "Why?"

"That's what I thought we'd do tomorrow if you're game."

He rose and pulled on his jacket. She felt a spasm of disappointment. After spending these weeks totally alone, the house seemed empty each time he left it. "I'm game. What time?"

"Sleep late. Say eleven o'clock?"

"Okay. I'll even pack a lunch."

"Great. Good night."

They were at the door. He opened it, turned back to hug her quickly, then left. Deflated, she closed the door.

She plucked the flower from her hair and threw it on the floor, hating herself for caring that he hadn't even kissed her good night.

"Are you all right?"

"Sure," she panted. "Are you?"

"I'm fine. Say when."

As though waiting for the slightest encouragement, she collapsed on the grass. "When," she gasped.

He dropped down beside her. For several minutes, they rested without speaking, their breath soughing laboriously through their lungs. At last Hunter lifted his head from its bowed position and looked over at her.

She was sprawled on the slope, her arms flung over her head. One knee was raised. He had thought she looked adorable when he picked her up that morning. She had on shorts, knee socks, and hiking boots, with a plaid shirt and an oatmeal-colored cardigan sweater. Her hair had been left loose.

About halfway up their climb, she had taken off the sweater and tied the sleeves around her waist. Now he could see the swell of her breasts beneath the cotton shirt. A cooling mountain breeze flirted over her and the nipples contracted. Inwardly he groaned.

She opened one eye and looked at him. "Are you still alive?"

"Barely," he confessed. "The air is thin at this altitude. How about a drink?"

She sat up as he fished in the picnic basket he'd been carrying. He popped the top off a can of soda and passed it to her. She took a long drink, then handed it back to him. He finished it in one swallow.

"When you say mountain climbing, that's what you mean," she said grudgingly, massaging her shins.

"Anything worth doing . . ." he said in a singsong voice as he rummaged through the basket. "What did you bring to eat?"

They were in the shelter of spruce trees but had kept one of the ski slopes in sight, knowing that they couldn't get lost if they followed it back down.

"Cheese, cold cuts, potato chips, candy bars."

He was finding the goodies as she enumerated them. He ate hungrily and she watched him. Her breath had almost stopped when she spotted him coming toward her front door that morning. He was dressed in shorts and hiking boots as she was. His calves and thighs were bunched with lean muscles and dusted with hair. He had on a blue chambray shirt. Now that he was hot from their hard climb and the sun, he had unbuttoned the shirt almost to his waist.

His chest was matted with an intriguing network of dark crinkly hair. Each time she looked at it, her insides seemed to thicken and a heavy pulse began to beat shamefully between her thighs. It was embarrassing. It was thrilling. And she had a hard time deciding whether to quell it or cater to it and keep on looking at him.

When sunlight caught on his hair, it burnished it with reddish highlights. His eyes, behind their thick screen of lashes, seemed a part of the woods around them, green with shadows of gray and flecks of brown.

When they were finished eating, she leaned her back against a tree and closed her eyes. She breathed deeply of the clean air. The languorous motion stretched her shirt over her breasts and brought Hunter's attention back to them.

"You don't wear a brassiere very often, do you?"

Her eyes snapped open and focused immediately on his. "What?"

He sat up slowly and inched across the ground on his bottom until he was close to her. Bracing his hand near her head on the tree, he leaned forward and came perilously close to bumping noses. "That day you fainted on the witness stand, you weren't wearing a brassiere. It surprised me."

"It surprised me to wake up and find—" She broke off suddenly.

"Find me kissing you?"

"Yes."

"And find yourself kissing me back?"

"I'm still not convinced I was."

"You were," he said softly, his eyes dropping significantly to her mouth. "Do you know why I unbuttoned your blouse?"

She made a soft moaning sound and turned her head. She pressed her forehead into the hollow of his elbow and squeezed her eyes shut. "You said it was to revive me."

"Partially."

"Then, you have lied to me on more than one occasion."

"Maybe that was a white lie," he confessed softly. His hand fiddled with the collar of her shirt. "I couldn't stop myself. I wanted to look at you, Kari." His hand closed around her neck and slid down the slender column. "I still want to." His voice was as tantalizing as the breeze that whispered through the dense branches overhead.

His fingers deftly unfastened the first button. "You're not wearing anything underneath today either."

"No."

"Or last night."

She rolled her forehead against his arm. "No."

"That's why I didn't kiss you last night. If I had touched you, I wouldn't have been able to stop. I would have had to touch your breasts. Kiss them. You know where it would have gone from there."

His fingers moved down to the next button. He toyed with it and when she made no move to halt him, he undid it. Then the next. The next.

Her flowery scent wafted up to him as he pushed aside the fabric so his hand could slip inside. His eyes closed in an agony of pleasure as his palm found her skin as warm and smooth and alive as he had imagined it.

He cupped the firm globe of her breast. It filled his hand. His fingers flexed in a gentle kneading motion. "Kari, Kari," he groaned. "You feel beautiful." His hand moved to her other breast and treated it to the same loving caress.

His thumb tenderly finessed her nipple. It beaded in response and he murmured endearments against her neck. When the peak grew pebble-hard, he rolled it between his finger and thumb, then fanned it lightly with his fingertips.

A small weeping sound brought his eyes open. He was alarmed to see a tear rolling down her cheek. His hand stilled instantly. "Kari? What's wrong? Am I hurting you?"

"No," she whispered, leaving her face buried in the crease of his elbow.

"Are you insulted? I swear—"

"No."

"Then, what is it? Why are you crying? Do you want me to stop?"

She raised her head. Her eyes were luminous with tears. "That's just it. I don't want you to stop. It feels wonderful." She shuddered. "And I don't know what to think about that."

He moved like summer lightning. Kneeling before her, he caught her head between his hands and pulled her mouth to within a breath of his. "Then, don't think about it. Don't think at all."

Chapter Ten

HIS MOUTH TOOK HERS HUNGRILY. THERE WAS NO PRELIMINARY PER-suasion to this kiss. It was rampant and wild from the beginning. Her lips didn't hesitate to obey the probing of his tongue. It slid deeply into the sweet channel of her mouth.

Kari's senses had been awakened by his fondling. Now they responded to his unbridled passion. Guilt, reservations, and ambiguities were banished. They surrendered to the all-consuming heat of his kiss. Her mind no longer ruled; she was being governed solely by her senses.

Hunter lowered them to the ground, his mouth never leaving hers. His arms went around her with such fierce possession, she doubted he would ever let her go. At the moment, she didn't care if he ever did.

He pressed her down into the thick carpet of grass, then, holding her tightly against him, rolled her on top of him. Her knee landed between his legs. His hard, lean thighs tightened around it and pressed it against his loins. She rubbed her knee against him.

"Oh, God, Kari," he hissed. "I've wanted you so long."

He turned them again until she was on her back and he was angled over half her body. The restraint he had imposed on himself for months was lifted. He had wanted her from the first time he saw her. Now he would have her.

He lowered his head for another deep kiss. Her mouth gave and took as freely as his. Working his hand between their bodies, he untied the sleeves of the sweater from around her waist. After he had pulled her shirt from her waistband, he spread it open. He relinquished her lips to raise his head and gaze down at her.

Dappled sunlight danced erotically across her breasts, highlighting and shadowing in playful patterns. She looked like a work of art, only better, because she was living and breathing, whispering his name, reaching for him.

His eyes devoured her greedily. But he had to touch her or die. He laid his hands on her breasts. He marveled at the texture of her skin, the softness of the curves, the delicacy of her nipples. "You're so beautiful." He gathered the fullness of one breast in his hand and pushed it up. Gently he stroked the coral tip with his thumb, drawing slow, repetitive circles over it. Its response was beautiful to watch. "Ah, look at you."

With his free hand, he yanked his shirt from his waistband and opened it. Gradually he lowered his bare chest over her, pressing her breast against him.

"Hunter," Kari groaned softly. "Oh, that feels good."

His chest hair felt crisp against her flushed nipples. She rubbed herself against the lush mat, reveling in a million sensations she had never known were available to her. She could feel the steely strength of his muscles beneath his warm, vibrant skin. Her hands closed around the back of his neck as he lifted himself over her, dipped his head, and kissed her breasts.

At first his touch was tentative. His lips sipped at her skin. His tongue tasted. But it wasn't nearly enough. He kissed her fervently, drawing more of her breast into his mouth and massaging the peak with his tongue. His head moved from side to side. Then down.

With ardent lips, he tracked the shallow groove that divided her stomach. His lips were hot; his tongue was bold; together they left a damp trail along her skin that made her writhe in an orgy of sensations. Unsnapping her shorts, he found her navel and kissed it wantonly. He inched down her body until his shoulders were propped between her thighs, his legs stretched out between hers.

Kari's blood was thundering through her veins. All her senses were alive and tingling with discovery. The heat of Hunter's body only made the ground beneath her seem cool in comparison. The smell of crushed summer grass filled her nose. The breeze blew over their bodies, lifting their hair, letting it fall. Sunlight flickered over her face, bathing it with warmth.

Sensation after sensation washed through her as Hunter's mouth continued its seduction of her navel. Her bare legs sawed restlessly against his. Mindlessly her hips began to lift and roll. His hand left her breast to venture down her abdomen where it pressed and rubbed in time to her movements.

"Kari? Sweetheart? Do you want me to?"

Her fingers grasped handfuls of his hair and she moaned incoherently. He pulled down the zipper of her shorts. Her bikini panties were a soft yellow. A butterfly, embroidered in silk thread, spread its wings over her mound.

Hunter lowered his parted lips to the butterfly and kissed it.

Kari cried out sharply as the world fell away and she was catapulted into a new realm. She was splintered with such arrows of pleasure that she sobbed. Small delicious spasms followed one after the other and continued to ripple through her long after the initial eruption.

"Oh, God," she groaned as she rolled to her stomach and buried her head in her folded arms. Her body was still trembling in the aftermath of a tempest, but her mind had returned to reason.

For a long while, she lay there, perfectly still, willing away that glorious lassitude and delightful heaviness. She didn't want to feel this good. She had made a fool of herself and didn't know how she would ever face this man again.

He laid a reassuring hand on her back and patted it. Long minutes passed. He didn't try to force conversation on her and for that she was grateful. At last he said, "I've got to go into the trees for a minute. I'll be right back."

She felt him rise and listened to his footsteps as he left her. She rolled over and spotted him disappearing into a thick copse. Despite what had happened moments ago, she smiled at his diplomacy. She could have stood a trip to the bathroom, too.

With fumbling fingers she restored her clothing and ran her hands through her tangled hair. She dabbed at her eyes with the back of her hand, knowing that her earlier tears had no doubt made a streaking mud of her eye makeup.

When she saw him coming from the cover of the trees, she busied herself picking up the refuse of their picnic and replacing it in the basket.

"We'd better start back down," she said quickly before he could say anything. She stood up and dusted off her seat. "It gets dark early up here." She retied the sleeves of her sweater around her waist and took two steps before Hunter grasped her wrist and turned her around to face him.

"We're not going anywhere until we talk this out. Since we met each other, we've had one big misunderstanding after another. I'm not going to let this develop into one."

She hadn't yet found the courage to meet his eyes, so she spoke to the third button of his shirt, which had been neatly rebuttoned and tucked into his shorts. "I don't know what happened. I—"

"You had an orgasm." It was quietly, emphatically, bluntly spoken. Her eyes flew to his. His expression was the gentlest she'd ever seen. "I fail to see the problem, Kari. Why are you acting like this?"

"Because that's never happened to me before."

His lips tried hard to hide a quick smile but failed. "Then, I think congratulations are in order."

"I mean, it has," she said in exasperation, "just not like that. Not so . . ."

She foundered for a way to describe her total lack of self-control. Would he understand that feeling of slipping toward a precipice and not knowing how to slow down, or of trying to stop an avalanche? Or by trying to explain would she make even a greater fool of herself? Because when it came right down to it, no description fit. "It came on so fast, without even . . . you know. You must think—"

"Will you let me do my own thinking, please?" He drew her closer. "I think that you're a passionate woman who, due to the sad circumstances of your life this past year, was starved for physical love."

"That's just it," she cried. "I can't stand being thought of as a sex-starved widow out for the first man who—"

"Listen to me." He shook her lightly. At the hard tone of his voice, she once again braved his gaze. "I thought it was beautiful. And I'm damn glad I was the one to bring it about. If any other man had even come close, I probably would have wanted to kill him, breaking one of the laws I hold dear. You were wonderful.

"All right? You got that? What else do I have to say to wipe that guilt-ridden expression off your face and take that closed, cautious wariness out of your eyes?"

It was at that moment she knew she loved him.

He could have reacted to what had happened with smug satisfaction, lording it over her that he could control her emotions and her body. But he hadn't. He had made her feel that it was her triumph, not his.

Her eyes glossed with tears, but she smiled as she said, "What else do you have to say? Say you'll cook your special spaghetti for me tonight."

The tight lines around his mouth relaxed and went from a frown to a lazy grin. "Come here."

He drew her against him. With his hand cupping her head, he pressed her face into his neck and bent his head over hers. His other arm was like a band of steel across her back as he hugged her tight. They remained locked in that embrace for several minutes, rocking slightly.

When he released her, he kissed her briskly on the tip of her nose. "You're right. It's already getting dusky. Let's go home."

He arrived early. She was sitting curled on the couch watching Sally Jenkins's entertainment segment on the news. She held the door for him as he came in carrying a grocery sack and two bottles of wine.

He searched for her mouth over the grocery sack and kissed her with a smacking noise. "Am I early or late?"

"Early. But thanks for interrupting. I was watching my number-one competitor gushing through her story."

"That Sally person?" he asked, making his way into the kitchen and depositing his burdens on the countertop.

"You know very well who I mean. Sally Jenkins. The new rage. The belle of Denver TV."

He popped his head around the corner. "Do you smell something rancid in here? Jealousy perhaps?"

"I'll admit I'm pea-green with it." She snapped off the TV and joined him in the kitchen. He laughed and handed her a glass of wine.

"You've got no reason to be jealous of her. She can't hold a candle to you. She's all boobs."

"I see you noticed."

"Who could miss them?"

"Yeah," Kari said. "One of the salesmen noticed them. Or at least that was the scoop when I left." She leaned against the countertop. Her finger traced the rim of her wineglass. "What if they don't give me my job back, Hunter?"

He saw the anxiety on her face, heard it in her voice. He straightened from his task of unloading pots and pans from the storage bin. Cradling her face between his hands, he said, "They will." His mouth met hers softly. "But if they don't, you'll do something else. And you'll be great at it."

"Thanks. I needed that." Then impulsively she set her wine on the counter and slid her arms around his waist. She laid her head on his chest. "I need you." She whispered but he heard her.

He pushed her away to look down into her face. "For what?" His implication was hazardous to a normal pulse rate. Hers skyrocketed.

She was still mortified over what had happened that afternoon and didn't want him to think she was that desperate. Cocking her head to one side she said, "To take care of my parking tickets. You can do me that little favor, can't you? You're the D.A."

He laughed. Grabbing her in a bear hug that lifted her off the ground, he growled in her ear. "Yeah, I can do that. But such favors are expensive." His hand shamelessly stroked her fanny. She had no doubt what price he intended to exact.

He put her to work on the salad while he set about mixing the ingredients of his spaghetti sauce. He worked with the concentration of a chemist. When the sauce was simmering, they carried their wine into the den and sat close together on the sofa. He lifted her bare feet into his lap.

"No shoes?"

"I think I rubbed a blister today."

His eyes took in the loose silk slacks she was wearing. They were the color of vanilla ice cream. Her matching silk sweater was loose as well, having wide sleeves and an oversize boat neck that was designed to slip beguilingly over one shoulder. "I like this outfit." His index finger trailed down her bare shoulder.

"Hmm, I wonder why?"

"Wear it on television and it'll boost your ratings."

"Yeah?"

He scowled. "On second thought, don't. I don't want thousands of men ogling you."

"Would you be jealous?"

"Damn right, I would." Unrepentantly he smiled. "Have you talked to Pinkie lately?"

She shook her head and dropped her eyes to the ruby wine in her glass. "I wanted to call and taunt him about his love life, but . . ." She let her statement dwindle away.

"But you didn't want him to taunt you about yours."

She brought her head up swiftly. "How do you do that?"

"What?"

"How do you know what I'm thinking? It makes me crazy when you do that."

"I'm sorry. But isn't that what you were thinking? He would be sure to ask if I'd found you and you'd have to tell him something. What would it be, Kari? What would you tell him about us?"

"I don't know."

He shoved her feet off his lap, stood and stalked into the kitchen. She sat for a moment, her face wrinkled in a grimace of frustration, then she bounded after him. He was stirring the sauce on the range.

"I told you not to expect anything."

His shoulders bunched angrily, but they relaxed a trifle before he turned around. "I don't."

For some reason she was suddenly spoiling for a fight. "Yes, you do. You expect me to sleep with you."

"Wrong!" he shouted. He was at the end of his rope, too. He'd been holding himself in check, doing everything by the book, going slow. But, dammit, his body could only take so much. And it had been in a state of emergency since he'd come to Breckenridge and joined her in the restaurant. "Yes, that's what I *want*. But I sure as hell don't know what to *expect*."

"Why do you say that?"

"Why? Because this has never been easy, or standard. Ever since I met you, you've thrown me one curve ball after another."

"So, why are you here?"

"Beats the hell out of me."

His anger only fired hers. "Supposing I did go to bed with you, then what?"

"I'd probably want to keep you there for a month."

The wooden spoon was dripping red sauce onto the floor. He tossed it down on the range and advanced toward her. "I've never waltzed around any woman the way I have you. And you know what? I'm tired of it. I've had to carefully measure everything I said so you wouldn't take it the wrong way."

He gripped her shoulders and pulled her toward him. Their chests came together hard. "Well, I don't give a damn how you take this. It's how I feel." He thrust his hips against hers for emphasis.

"I want you bad, Kari. I want you naked. As wild as you were in the grass this afternoon. Only the next time you experience that, I want to be buried deep inside you, feeling it happen around me, sharing it with you. There. Now is that crude enough and graphic enough for you? Have you got the picture? You have a real knack for choosing what you want to hear and closing your ears to everything else. I don't think you can mistake my meaning this time."

He released her so suddenly, she reeled. He had spotted a bottle of Scotch a few days ago in one of the cupboards. He took it out now, poured a generous portion into an orange juice glass, and threw it down his throat in one gulp.

She had a spontaneous desire to giggle. Thomas had never been one to lose his temper. Hunter's flare-up had been as strong a stimulant as one of his kisses. She wanted to spin him around, slap him as hard as she could, then kiss him with equal fervor.

"Hunter?"

"What?" he barked.

"Tell me when you're ready for me to set the table."

It took some effort on her part, but he came around. By the time they sat down to eat, his good humor had been restored. He joked as he opened the second bottle of wine and smiled when she praised his spaghetti. He was volatile but not moody. She liked that about him.

After the dinner dishes had been cleared away, they began working on the jigsaw puzzle again. This time Hunter sat back and let her muddle through it on her own. He watched her lips purse in concentration. He loved the way her hair fell over her face and the unthinking way she brushed it back.

They had moved the candles from the dining table to the card table after dinner. Now her bare shoulder glowed in the golden light they shed as she bent over the table. Her skin looked like warm satin and he wanted to take a bite out of that shoulder. He wanted to taste all of her.

The sweater she was wearing got his vote for the sexiest item in her wardrobe. She was wearing nothing underneath it. Every time she moved he could see the gentle sway of her breasts. She was sexy without trying to be. Her allure lay in her subtlety.

He thought about Marilyn and chuckled. How could he have ever thought to remedy his desire for Kari by taking another woman, any other woman, especially one as blatant as Marilyn? How stupid he'd been.

Kari looked up from the puzzle. "Did I miss something? What's funny?"

He laughed again. "I was just remembering a night I'd rather forget."

"Oh?"

"I had a lapse of common sense."

"That's it?"

"That's all you're going to get." She shook her head as though she doubted his sanity and returned her attention to the puzzle.

She held the three remaining pieces in her hand. Now that she was about to finish it, she was almost afraid to. Then she would have to face the picture she saw. Not the picture of the brightly colored balloons on the table, but the picture of herself that it symbolized.

Hunter McKee.

He had started out her enemy. Now she knew she loved him.

She locked in a piece. Two remained.

He wasn't all that easy to love. He was ambitious. He had a temper. But he also stood for justice, all-American wholesomeness, and old-fashioned values that she adhered to as well. He had been candid with her tonight. He wanted her in his bed. But she had already known that. In retrospect she realized she had known that for a long time. Maybe she had purposely goaded him so he would speak his feelings out loud.

But did he love her?

She thought he did. A man like him didn't have to wait over a year for a woman. Yet he had. After all she'd done to him, said about him, said to him, he had still come after her. And did it matter so much if he didn't love her? Thomas had professed his love frequently, yet he had deceived her. Did she need to hear the words, or were Hunter's actions sufficient to express his love?

She mashed the next to last piece in its place.

It had been difficult to love a god. That was the way she had loved Thomas. She could admit that now. He had been her knight in shining armor, just as Pinkie had said. In her eyes he had been perfect.

But it was intimidating to live with perfection. Hadn't she always been afraid that she would do something not to his liking? Had she ever felt truly free to express an opinion contrary to his? Hadn't she always strived to win his approval and felt that she fell short of the mark?

Would she ever have had the kind of physical and emotional release in front of him that she had had with Hunter that afternoon? Never. Thomas might have had prostitutes, but he would never expect that kind of passion from his wife. Instinctively she knew that. They simply hadn't had that kind of relationship.

Loving Hunter would involve no such constraint. She had loved Thomas, but now she loved again and it was different and wonderful. It was time to give her old love a special place in her memory but focus on the new.

She pressed the last piece into the puzzle and completed the picture.

Her fingers skimmed over it. She studied it for a long time, then she raised her eyes to the man who was silently watching her from across the table.

"All the pieces fit." Her voice was husky with emotion.

"Is it all right now for me to tell you that I love you? I have since the day you first walked into my office, Kari."

"I think I started to love you soon after that. That's why I was so angry with you."

"I know."

She looked at him in bewilderment. "You knew? Why didn't you tell me?"

"You weren't ready to hear it. Now you are. You love me and I love you."

Trancelike, but still knowing exactly what she was doing, she got out of her chair and went to him. He pulled her onto his lap and wrapped his arms around her.

Their mouths met in the sweetest, tenderest kiss, with just the tips of their tongues touching.

"Oh, sweet, so sweet," he murmured against her mouth. The kiss intensified. His tongue stroked and darted. He took delight in her mouth and gave as much in return.

His hand was warm on her breast as he fondled it through the silk sweater. The tip hardened beneath the gentle plucking of his fingers. Whispering endearments, he straightened and put space between them. He slid his hands beneath her sweater.

"I've wanted to do this all night." His hands coasted over her warm flesh.

"Don't let me stop you," she said raggedly as he cupped her breasts, lifted them, and teased the peaks with his fingertips and thumbs.

"Take off your sweater. I want to see my hands on you."

While his hands stayed where they were, she raised the sweater over her head and pulled it off.

"God," he sighed.

The sight of his large and tanned and hair-sprinkled hands against the smoothness of her flesh was purely erotic. She gasped softly when the pad of his finger finessed her nipple into a tight bud.

Then she saw his open lips close over it and felt the loving of his tongue. She watched his jaws flex as he sucked tenderly. His eyes were closed and his lashes left fan-shaped shadows on his high cheekbones. There were red glints in his hair. She ran her fingers through it as she held his head fast, hoping that the pleasure would never end.

It became almost unbearable. She ground her forehead against the top of his head and heard herself chanting words she had never thought she would say. Outrageous words. Sexual words. Words that made him leave her breast and recapture her mouth in a searing kiss.

He stood and swept her into his arms. He had never been in the bedroom, but he went to it unerringly and deposited her on the bed. He spread her hair out behind her head, combed his fingers down her breasts and stomach, then stood.

"If you have any reservations about looking at a naked man, you'd better turn your head," he warned with a smile as he began tearing off his clothes.

"I don't have any reservations about looking at you naked. In fact, I've fantasized about it." She flung her arms over her head and stretched in anticipation.

He groaned. Her position only made her back arch and her breasts strain toward him. "Are you doing that on purpose?" he asked as he grappled with his belt buckle.

A laugh rippled through her. "Yes."

"I thought so," he grated as he tugged at a suddenly inoperable zipper.

"It's your fault. You told me what to expect." Her voice dropped in volume to a sexy whisper. "I can't wait."

His oaths were heartfelt as he pulled down his pants and kicked them free. Then, hooking his thumbs in the waistband of his briefs, he peeled them off.

The sight of his aroused manhood brought an involuntary gasp to her lips and that in turn brought an abrupt halt to Hunter's rushed, frantic motions. He let himself down beside her gradually and took her hand between both of his.

"Don't be frightened of me, Kari. I couldn't bear that."

"I'm not frightened," she said breathlessly as he leaned over her. She touched his brows to smooth away the wrinkle of worry. "It's just that you're so beautiful." He didn't hear the words, but read them on her lips.

"Ah, my love."

Sighing, he pulled her into his arms. He buried his face in the wealth of her hair and breathed deeply of its perfume. He drew her closer, pressing her breasts against his chest, and arching her against his hips. His hands spread wide and smoothed down her back.

"Help me with my slacks."

She eased away from him and unbuttoned her slacks. With his help she dragged them down her legs. He laid them carefully at the foot of the bed, then turned back to her. This time her panties were pale ivory. He gave her time to protest when he curled his fingers into the elastic band. When she didn't, he lowered the panties past her hips, her thighs, her knees. He carefully slipped them over her feet and removed them.

He made a low, satisfied sound deep in his chest when his eyes took in her nakedness. His palms slid up her long silky thighs. One hand brushed over the soft tuft of dark-gold hair. Then his lips.

She sighed his name.

He lay down beside her and planted a warm, wet kiss on her responsive mouth as his hands celebrated her shape and the texture of her skin, each hollow and curve of her body.

He kissed her neck and ears. The base of her throat was outlined by his tongue. Fervent kisses were pressed into the plumpness of her breasts. Airy ones were dusted onto her nipples.

He parted her thighs and his caressing fingers found her dewy with desire. "Kari," he groaned and complimented her on her readiness. He knelt between her legs and draped her thighs over his. His hands slid beneath her and tilted her hips toward him.

"I know it's been a long time for you. Stop me if I hurt you."

"You won't." She raised her hands to his shoulders and clutched them as he guided himself into the smooth sheath of her body.

He was very thick and very hard. She was tight and small but yielding. He didn't take her all at once, but by slow precious inches. When he was fully buried inside her, he looked down into her face and smiled. His eyes said all that needed to be said.

His strokes were long and sure, extensive and exquisite. With each one, Kari was made ever more aware of what it was to be a woman being loved by a man. For the first time, she knew her true nature. This was what she had longed for. Now she had the answer to everything that had been unclear.

When the tumult came, he made certain she could feel all of him, then bathed her with his fire, even as she poured her love on him.

Chapter Eleven

SHE WAS GLAD HE WAS STILL SLEEPING. AFTER A NIGHT OF SUCH LOVing, she had wanted to wake up before he did so she could study him without his knowing it. Her smile as she gazed down at him was complacent. How handsome her lover was!

His tousled hair showed up darkly against the pillow and across his brow. His lashes were straight and black. She loved his eyebrows. They were thick and uneven, the eyebrows of a man with integrity and intelligence. Perhaps his nose was a trifle long, but it was slender and finely shaped.

Silently she scoffed at herself. She was thinking like a fool, but she was foolishly in love. Had anyone ever told her she would be lying naked in bed next to Hunter McKee, D.A., she would have thought that person insane.

Yet here she was, and she couldn't think of any place she'd rather be.

The lower half of his face was shadowed by morning whiskers. He might look very attractive with a beard, she thought. But then those grooves that were drawn down the sides of his mouth—during a particularly affectionate moment the night before, she had insisted they were dimples—would be covered up, as would that determined chin. And what a shame it would be to hide that sensuous upper lip behind a mustache. No, his face was too well chiseled to be covered with a beard and mustache.

Only the fear of waking him prevented her from touching his mouth. It was a pleasure-giving instrument with an uncanny sensitivity to her needs and desires. Even now her stomach experienced that delightful sinking feeling as she recalled the way his lips and tongue had introduced her body to carnal pleasure.

She was also tempted to touch his chest. When she had scooted from under his protective arm, he had rolled to his back and flung one arm over his head. The other arm looked like it had been caught in the act of reaching for her. His outstretched hand formed a loose fist on the sheet. She knew from experience that his chest hair could tickle her. The flat brown nipples nestled in that thick forest were as sensitive as hers. She had only discovered that last night under his patient tutelage.

His stomach was taut and corrugated with muscle. Over it, his body hair grew inward to form a sleek line that arrowed down past his navel before it furled around his sex. Her eyes scuttled in that direction now. She was almost relieved to see that the sheet reached his navel.

Recalling the pleasure he had given her, she closed her eyes and drew in a deep shuddering breath. But the pleasure hadn't been all hers. She couldn't help but feel proud of herself for the many times he had climaxed while holding her tight, whispering his adoration in her ear.

He was a fierce but tender lover, passionate but considerate, selfish but unselfish. Each time had been different, all of them exciting. If she made love to him every day for the rest of her life, it wouldn't become routine or boring.

Her eyes made one last sweeping inspection moving up his torso to find him watching her. She blushed at being caught. "How long have you been awake?"

"Long enough to get this." He kicked the sheet aside. She looked at him. Her blush deepened. He lifted her hand, kissed the palm, and laid it on his chest. He stroked the back of it. "I didn't mean to embarrass you. I'm sorry."

"After last night, I didn't think I could ever be embarrassed again."

His smile was wolfish, but his eyes were gentle. "So, why the maidenly blushes? Because it's daylight? Or because of my unabashed arousal?"

She ducked her head. "A little of both, I guess. It's ridiculous, I know, but I'm still shy with you."

He took a deep breath and laid his hand along her cheek. His thumb massaged her lower lip. "Don't be, Kari. I want you to know me as intimately as I know you." Then he quietly added, "You're allowed to touch, too, you know." He saw the panic flash in her eyes and laughed softly. "But for right now, I'll settle for a good-morning kiss."

He curled his fingers behind her neck and drew her down for a long kiss. Their mouths were as intimate as their bodies had been the night before. His tongue probed deeply and her lips moved warmly over his. When at last they pulled apart, he looked into her face and sighed. "Why don't you look like hell in the morning? Other women do."

She raised herself to a sitting position and put her hands on her hips. "I don't know whether to take that as a compliment or not. Just how many other women have you seen this early in the morning?"

Hunter was thinking how cute and pert her breasts looked and took a while before asking a question of his own. "Jealous?"

"No." She flung her legs over the side of the bed and shrugged into a robe.

"Where are you going?" he demanded.

"To make myself presentable," she said over her shoulder as she headed toward the bathroom. "I want to make sure I'm at least competitive with all those women you've awakened with."

Shortly she came out of the bathroom dressed in a long lightweight robe that zipped up the front. Her hair was wet from a shampooing. The scent of wildflowers followed her into the room.

Hunter, who had just come from the bed, caught her against him and kissed her breathless. With his hands kneading her derriere, he asked, "Do I at least get breakfast for my trouble?"

She bit his lip. "You are a chauvinist."

"Ouch!"

"Serves you right. That beard is scratchy."

"I'll forgive you if you'll lend me a razor."

"In the shower stall."

Nursing his lip, he went into the bathroom trailing the sheet he'd wrapped around him toga-style. Kari laughed, feeling happier than she ever remembered.

The bacon had been fried and she was on her way into the bedroom to ask how he liked his eggs, when she met him coming out.

His hair had been towel-dried, but the wet strands lay helter-skelter around his head. He smelled of hot water and soap and clean damp skin. He had pulled on only the jeans he had worn the evening before. His feet were bare. The towel he'd used on his hair was draped around his neck. The dark hair on his chest was still slightly wet and curlier than before.

She was immobilized by a wave of desire and came to a standstill in the middle of the living room. Her mouth fell open slightly and her vision blurred.

His broad grin became an expression of puzzlement. "What's the matter?" he asked.

"Nothing," she said on a soft puff of air. "I . . . you . . . I like the way you look right now, that's all."

"Get over here."

She flew into his embrace eagerly and tightly wrapped her arms around his neck. Any remnant of shyness fell away as she molded her body to his. Her lips met his hungrily. He tasted delicious and she couldn't get her fill.

"Kari," he moaned when she left his mouth to nibble on his neck. He felt the gentle rasping of her teeth on his skin and it set his body to raging. "Don't stop, baby. I like you this way. God, you're wonderful . . . Sweet . . ."

She ran her hands down his sides and over the rippling hardness of his ribs. Her palms smoothed over the sculpted curves of his chest. Her fingertips flirted with his nipples. When they hardened, she sponged them with her tongue.

His head bumped back against the wall and he grimaced with an ecstasy close to pain. But he remained passive. She had been a responsive lover, but throughout the night he had been the initiator. His masculinity wasn't at all threatened by this unexpected savage streak in her. He liked it.

Kari's hands slid down his stomach. Her fingers tweaked the hair whorled around his navel. She investigated the dent with a capricious fingertip. She unsnapped his jeans and lowered the zipper.

"Yes, Kari, yes."

Her hand slipped inside and encircled the hard, velvety warmth of his sex.

Hunter's breath hissed through clenched teeth. He cursed. He sighed her name. Her caress was all the sweeter for its innocence. Her fingertips explored him lightly, deftly, curiously, and stirred him to heights of passion he'd never experienced before. He wanted to be his hardest, his strongest, his most powerful, for her.

She dropped to her knees.

"Sweet heaven," he moaned. He knew he might very well die from the pleasure, but, God, what a blissful death it would be.

When he could bear no more, he knelt with her. In a frenzy, he unzipped her robe and tore it from her body. Together they fell to the floor and with one swift, sure thrust, he possessed her.

She cried out her joy, arching her body against him and receiving each pumping thrust greedily. The crisis was immediate and explosive. Afterward they lay panting against each other.

Still gloved inside her, he rubbed her ear with his nose. "Your timing is something else, madam."

Her fingers made languid passes through his hair. "What do you mean?"

His lips brushed a soft kiss over hers. "Why didn't you try that little experiment while we were still comfy in bed? You could have saved yourself from lying on the floor."

She grinned like a little girl caught doing something naughty. "Well, now I know where that old saying came from."

"What old saying?"

"The one about being between a rock and a hard place."

He chuckled between taking bites of her neck. "You're about to be again."

"Hmm? About to be what?" She sighed drowsily as he massaged her breast, then lowered his head and polished the tip with his tongue. When he pressed his hips forward, her eyes popped open.

He smiled down into her face. "*That's* what I mean." But he withdrew and stood to help her to her feet. "However, I'm going to be a gentleman and carry you to bed first."

They were still kissing when they reached the bed and he lowered her to the pillows. "I thought you wanted breakfast," she murmured, her lips moving on his chest.

"And I'm going to have it," he said, lowering himself over her. "Right now."

He was stretched out full-length between her legs. His cheek rested on her stomach. His arms were wound around her waist. Beneath him she lay in splendid exhaustion. She wore nothing but his eyeglasses perched on the tip of her nose. Her fingers idly strummed his shoulders and back.

"I've learned all there is to know."

"About what?" He blew softly on the white peach fuzz that dusted her belly. It could only be seen from this perspective."

"About foreplay."

He laughed and raised his head, propping his chin on her stomach. He rubbed it back and forth across her skin. "And what do you think?"

"That I'm too tired to ever move again," she said sleepily. "I'm beginning to think you meant it when you said that if you ever got me in bed, you would keep me here a month."

"I might."

Her stomach vibrated with a soft laugh. "Then you'll have to allow me food breaks."

"I gave you lunch."

She opened one eye and peered down her body at him. "Two stale Nutter-Butters and one cold slice of bacon hardly qualify as lunch."

He climbed up her body and dropped a kiss on her mouth. "What are you complaining about? I'm the one who should be weak from overexertion. Have you kept count of how many times I—"

"That's just it. You're already taking me for granted," she said with a delectable pout that he felt compelled to kiss away.

"So, what all this boils down to," he said when his lips were finally satisfied, "is that you think I should take you out for a bodacious dinner."

"An expensive one. Two entrées, double dessert."

"All right," he sighed. "But before I let you up, I want to see if I've missed anything."

He pulled his eyeglasses from her nose and put them on. When he glanced down her body, his jaw fell open and his eyes rounded as though in great surprise. He was staring at her breasts. "You've got two of them!?" he exclaimed.

Kari collapsed with laughter.

His tongue painted lazy circles up the insides of her thighs. "Hunter," she sighed his name, her breath disturbing the soft hair on his belly. "This is decadent and depraved."

"It certainly is." His lips were totally uninhibited.

"You admit it?" Her words came out in breathy gusts. Her fingers made deep impressions on the muscles of his back as they clenched reflexively.

"I'll admit to loving you."

"Oh, God." He kissed her with profound intimacy. "I'm going to die from your loving."

"No, you're not. You're about to be reborn."

His tongue was devilish and darting, sensuous and slow, unbridled and unashamed. Rolling her head from side to side over the furred warmth of his middle, she strangled out soft ecstatic cries as waves of pleasure surged through her.

But even that wasn't enough of a release. He repositioned them and lay above her. Her arms went around his neck in welcome. When he entered her, her body closed around him like the petals of some exotic flower.

"I'm shameless with you." He began to move within her. She covered the taut perfection of his buttocks with her hands and pressed him deeper.

"There should never be any shame between two people who love each other."

"It's not shameful to while away hours doing nothing but this?"

"What else are rainy afternoons during vacations good for?" He barely got the words out before their passions simultaneously erupted.

Later they watched the incessant downpour from the warmth of the bed. Heavy drops clung to the eaves like jewels from a chandelier. Silver rivulets coursed down the windows. She lay curled against him, her back to his front. Their legs were tangled beneath the covers. His arms were around her and his chin was hooked over her shoulder.

"Kari?"

"Hmm?"

"I'm truly sorry about the baby you lost."

She lay perfectly still. It surprised her that he would bring up such a touchy subject now. But she didn't need to look at him to verify his sincerity. His voice was full of it.

"I know you are. I am, too. Very sorry."

"You don't still blame me, do you?"

"No. Of course not. You were just a convenient scapegoat for my anguish."

His fingers thrummed her lower abdomen. "You'll have a baby some day. Maybe more than one."

She smiled, but her voice was sad. "Maybe."

His hand became still. "There was no permanent damage done, was there? I mean, there's nothing to keep you from having more children?"

She drew his hand back and pressed it flat against her. "No."

The sudden relaxing of his muscles gave away his relief, both that she could have another child and that they could discuss her miscarriage openly and without rancor. "You'll have a baby," he said firmly.

She laughed softly. "You sound certain of that. It takes two you know. Are you volunteering for the job?"

His lips found her ear beneath a clump of blond curls. "Always willing to oblige, ma'am."

And he was. Right then.

He pressed her back against him and entered her. His fingers trailed down her belly, sifted through the thick cluster of tawny curls, then moved between her thighs. He caressed her from without, even as he reached higher and higher within, stroking her toward oblivion with each sustained thrust of his manhood.

After they had climbed to the summit and glided back down, she lay panting in sweet exhaustion. Her body glistened with a sheen of perspiration and shuddered with delicious aftershocks. She rolled over to face him. He looked sexy in the most literal way, with his eyes drowsy, his mouth curved in a satisfied smile, and his hair clinging damply to his forehead.

She was awed by the emotions that inundated her. "Why did it take me so long to know that I loved you?"

"I'm just glad you know it now."

"Hunter, I love you."

"I love you, too."

She laid her cheek on his chest. He sank his hands into her hair and held her fast.

Pinkie looked down at the bowl set before him with undisguised distaste. "What the hell is that?"

"That," Bonnie said sharply, "is breakfast."

"Breakfast is a Bloody Mary."

"Breakfast is plain yogurt with granola cereal. I sprinkled some extra bran on the top."

"It looks like bird food. Or bird—"

"Pinkie!"

"Oh, hell." He picked up his spoon and took a mouthful. He knew she wouldn't let him have his first morning cigarette until he ate it. "It's disgusting. Give me some black coffee to wash it down with."

"What ever happened to 'please'?"

"Please," he grumbled.

She set the coffee within his reach and joined him at the table. "When are you going to marry me?"

He nearly showered her with hot coffee as he sputtered. "Marry? Who said anything about getting married?"

"I just did."

"Well, forget it."

"Why?"

"Because I don't want to get married."

"Give me one good reason why not."

"You snore."

"So do you."

"See? Do you want two snoring people in one bed? We'd never get any sleep."

"We haven't been *sleeping* much anyway. Which brings up another good argument. What if I got pregnant?"

The spoon stopped midway to his mouth. "Fat chance. You're too old."

"Thanks a lot."

"You're welcome."

"We're compatible," Bonnie went on doggedly.

"We fight all the time."

"Only because you're so mule-headed."

"And I suppose you're not?"

"We have a lot in common."

"Middle age for one."

Teasingly she laid her hand on the top of his thigh and squeezed it. "You've hardly acted middle-aged since we've been sleeping together. You wore me out last night, Pinkie Lewis."

A smile tugged at his mouth before he drew it into a frown. "You're trying to kill me." He eyed her suspiciously. "That's it. You want to marry me, kill me off quickly with one of those sexual marathons you put me through, and then collect my life insurance money."

She hooted with laughter. "Try another argument, Pinkie. What insurance company would have been dumb enough to insure *your* body?"

Before he could come up with a retort, the doorbell rang. "Who could that be?" Bonnie asked. The minute she was out of sight, Pinkie lit a cigarette and pulled the smoke into his starving lungs.

"Oh, my lord," Bonnie exclaimed. "It's so good to see you. Come in."

Pinkie assumed it was one of her sons. He dropped his cigarette in astonishment when Kari came sailing through the kitchen door and smothered him in an exuberant hug.

"Hi! I'm so glad to see you. Gosh. Three months. Can you believe it? What's that?" It all came out in a rush. The last question was asked as she stared into the bowl at Pinkie's place setting.

"She makes me eat junk like this all the time," he said, shooting Bonnie a poison look. "She's put me on a diet."

Kari laughed as she sat down in a chair across from them. Her eyes rested first on one, then the other. "I should be furious with you two for not telling me about your 'arrangement.' "

"We're getting married," Bonnie said happily.

"Like hell we are," Pinkie said.

"I think it's a terrific idea," Kari said. She didn't think Pinkie was half as opposed to it as he let on. Beneath his scowl, he looked like a happy elf.

Still, ornery as he was, he said, "I think the idea stinks. She's weird. You should see the kinky books she brings to bed with her."

"I'd love to," Kari laughed.

"Why you hypocrite!" Bonnie smacked him on his bald spot. "I haven't heard you complaining about those 'kinky' books before. You were ready to try it all."

Kari laughed even harder.

"She nags me all the time," Pinkie whined. " 'Eat this. You can't eat that. Remember your blood pressure. How many drinks does that make?' "

Kari ignored him and asked Bonnie, "What about his smoking?"

"Oh, she's rationed that, too," Pinkie answered before Bonnie had a chance. "I've had to cut down to five packs a day."

The women laughed. Bonnie bent down and kissed him soundly on the cheek. She left a proprietary arm across his shoulders as she said to Kari, "You're positively radiant."

"Am I?" she asked coyly. "It must have been the mountain air."

Pinkie was too shrewd to accept that blithe explanation. "Who told you I was, uh, staying with Bonnie?"

Kari challenged him back. "Who knew?"

Pinkie's face split into a broad grin. "He found you!"

She laughed, her happiness spilling over. "Yes, he found me." She wrapped her arms around her waist as though trying to contain the joy inside. "And he's wonderful and we're madly, deliriously, ridiculously, recklessly, hopelessly in love."

"Hot damn," Bonnie said, slapping the tabletop. "I knew it."

"*You* knew it?" Pinkie countered. "Remember, I'm the one who sent him up there after her."

"Well, whoever was responsible, the two of you or my guardian angel, I'm grateful. He's . . . oh, he's . . ."

"I think we get the point," Pinkie said dryly. He never wanted to be accused of being a softy, though his eyes were suspiciously damp. He was gripping Bonnie's hand beneath the table. To see Kari happy again meant the world to him. "I'm real happy for you, sweetheart. Where is this paragon of masculinity now?"

"He wanted to come over with me but had to go to his office. He said his desk would be piled high." She gazed down into the coffee Bonnie had poured for her, which so far had gone untasted. "Speaking of which, do I still have a desk? That's why I came here instead of waiting to catch you at work. I didn't want to make a fool of myself."

Pinkie sipped his coffee. Bonnie diplomatically excused herself to go finish dressing. "What makes you think you might not have a desk? Management didn't fire you. I'm still news director. Or I was as of last Friday evening when I left for the weekend. I still have the power to hire and fire."

"But I've seen Smiling Sally on the set every night. And last time we spoke you said the city hall beat had been given to someone else. Not that I want it back," she added quickly. "I think I'd find it harder than ever to be objective about our D.A." She flashed him a brilliant smile. Then her face became grave again. "Do I have a job, Pinkie?"

He sat back in the bentwood chair, which was too small for his barrel-shaped torso. "I've been giving an idea some thought. Let me bounce it off you."

"I'm listening." Though she didn't want to appear too eager, her heart had begun to pound. This would be the moment of truth. Would Pinkie trust her enough to give her another responsible position, a position worthy of her talent and experience? Or would she be given an assignment so insignificant that she'd be forced to resign?

He drew on his cigarette and squinted his eyes against the smoke. "Your strong point has always been the *human* way you approach a story. Whether you're giving a movie review or dissecting the D.A., you talk to the viewers as though you were chatting across the fence to your next-door neighbors. Your dialogue is natural and unaffected. No fancy stuff. They like that. It makes you a real person to them. I'm not talking about just credibility like a Cronkite or Brinkley has. You're where the viewers are at. You're *real*.

"So, what I was thinking of doing," he continued on a deep breath, "was to turn you loose, give you no specific beat, but let you do human interest stories. The real gut-grippers. For instance if there's a disaster, we report the disaster in the regular line up, but you do a human factor story that focuses on the people involved. Get my drift?"

She was already getting excited and it showed. "Yes, yes. I like it, Pinkie. I really do."

"All right, now listen up. Management is gonna be watching you with magnifying glasses. I don't have to tell you that you've got some fences to mend. Tread softly for the first few weeks."

"I will. I promise."

He saw her eager face, her shining eyes, and cursed. "I wish I could believe that. Hell, Kari, you've never treaded softly in your whole life."

* * *

The intercom buzzed.

"Damn!"

Hunter was up to his ears in paperwork and mail that needed his attention. All the details his secretary couldn't handle in his absence were waiting for him to attend to. He wanted to get finished with it so he wouldn't have to stay late. He planned to spend the evening with Kari.

"I asked not to be disturbed unless it was absolutely necessary," he said into the box.

"I'm sorry, but Mrs. McKee is here."

Hunter was momentarily taken aback. His first thought was that his mother had come to see him. But that was unlikely, as she rarely traveled from home without his father. If they were planning to visit, they would have called ahead of time. There was only one other Mrs. McKee it could be.

"Send her in." He stood up and buttoned his suit coat. He rounded the desk just as Pam came through the door.

She looked sensational. Her sable hair was still glossy and hung straight to her jaw, just curving inward toward her cheek at the last inch. Her body was as lithe and graceful as ever. She hadn't a trace of extra poundage. She was taller than Kari and attractive in a totally different way. While Kari exuded a feminine vulnerability, Pam was all cool sophistication. Even when Kari was playing her professional role, she seemed warm and approachable. Pam always maintained an aloof detachment.

Hunter grinned broadly as he went to her with both hands extended. "This is a surprise."

She laughed as she accepted his hands. "I thought it might be." Glancing at the paper-heaped desk, she said, "I know you're very busy."

He smiled ruefully and turned to offer her a chair. "You caught me on a bad day. I was out last week."

"Oh?" One dark brow arched eloquently, just the way he remembered.

"Vacation," he said succinctly, indicating the subject was closed to discussion. He sat on the corner of his desk.

She assessed him with dark, liquid eyes, eyes that promised more warmth than was there. "You look good, Hunter."

"So do you." He returned the compliment sincerely. Her suit was chic and fit her figure to perfection. As always, she was impeccably groomed. "You're as gorgeous as ever."

Her hair moved against her cheek as she laughed. "And you're as full of blarney as ever. But it's nice to hear." She cocked her head to one side. "I sensed an urgency when you said you were finally agreeing to a divorce. I'm curious. Was there a specific reason?"

His expression was guarded. "Yes."

"Hmm," she said coolly. "A woman?"

"Yes."

"Are you happy?"

"Very." There was no qualifying that. He'd never been happier in his life. "You?"

She shrugged. "My work is extremely satisfying."

That had been their problem. When he had met her, she was in her final year at medical school. He had been attracted to her intelligence, her courage, her ambition.

But that very ambition had finally been the undoing of their marriage. Like any man, he had wanted to be needed, just a little. He wasn't a chauvinist, much as he had teased Kari about it. His problem hadn't been that his wife enjoyed a successful career. His problem had been that her career came before anything else, even before her husband.

With each passing year, their life had become less a marriage and more a contest to see who could reach the top of his chosen field first. When he had been offered a chance for advancement in another city, she had refused to move with him and leave her position in a major hospital. He had seen that as a definite choice on her part between him and her career. It had been a bitter pill to swallow.

"You're stubborn, Hunter," she said now. "You held out for three years of separation before you called and said you'd grant me a divorce."

"You know I hate to fail at anything. I didn't want to fail at the most important commitment of my life. Which is what a marriage should be." He smiled lopsidedly. "I finally had to admit that we had. Or that I had. I'm willing to accept my losses and go from here."

"I never considered it a failure for either of us. We just outgrew each other."

She must be dating a shrink, he thought a bit unkindly. "I suppose." He agreed merely to avoid another argument on a tired subject. Besides, her opinion no longer mattered to him.

"I brought you this." She extracted a legal-size envelope from her purse. "Apparently the attorneys didn't have your latest address. They sent both copies to me."

"The final divorce papers?" he asked, not opening the envelope.

"Signed, sealed, and delivered. You can't ask for much more than that."

She stood and he joined her. Taking her arm, he escorted her to the door. "I'm glad to have seen you, Pam."

She gazed up at him. "Me, too, Hunter. We had some good times, didn't we?"

He recognized a plea for ego-salving. Now that she was no longer an element in his life, he could feel kindly toward her. And probably, if he thought about it very hard, he could remember a few good times before things had gone wrong.

"We had some very good times. I'm sorry we couldn't make each other happy." He wasn't about to say he was sorry it had come to this. He was now glad it had. Meeting Kari had made him glad. "Good luck to you, Pam."

"To you, too, Hunter. Good-bye." She rose up on her toes and kissed his cheek.

Kari virtually danced up the steps of the district attorney's building. She had stopped at a deli across the street and picked up two corned beef sandwiches, not even knowing if Hunter liked corned beef. But, busy as he must be, she knew he would welcome the distraction of seeing her. The few hours they'd spent apart already seemed like days. Besides, she couldn't wait to share the news about her job with him, and telephone calls were so unfulfilling.

The halls on the first floor were deserted and quiet. Most everyone was out to lunch. The outer office was empty. Hunter's secretary's desk was littered with memos and unanswered correspondence, but her typewriter was switched off.

Kari went straight to his door, knocked once, and then pushed it open.

Chapter Twelve

THE SCENE WAS STRAIGHT OUT OF A BAD FARCE: THE MAN CAUGHT IN the arms of another woman by his faithful lover.

The guilty culprits sprang apart. The scorned lover summed up the situation in one glance and wished the floor would open up and swallow her. Or that she could die on the spot. Or better yet, that the man would die a slow, painful death.

The other woman, as befitted the script, was strikingly beautiful. Her dark hair and almond-shaped eyes gave her the exotic look of a stereotypical temptress. And of the three of them, she seemed to be the only one with any poise remaining.

She stepped toward Kari. "From the guilty expression on Hunter's face, I suppose you're the reason for the rush on the divorce." She extended a slender hand. "Hello. I'm Pam McKee."

Kari ignored the offered hand. Instead her eyes flew to Hunter. "Your *wife*?"

"Until a few weeks ago."

Kari felt her whole body caving in and wondered if it were visible from the outside. She envied Pam McKee's composure.

The woman turned back to him and said, "Good-bye, Hunter."

"Good-bye."

"I'm sorry about this." She waved a hand toward Kari.

"I'll straighten it out."

Kari watched them share a sad smile, then Pam glided past her. They were silent until the tapping of her heels could no longer be heard, then Kari faced Hunter. "Don't count on it," she ground out.

"Count on what?"

"On straightening it out. Have a nice lunch." She flung the sack of sandwiches at him. He fumbled the catch but managed to keep the sack of corned beef from splattering open on the floor.

Turning, Kari made for the exit, but he was only two long strides behind her. He caught her arm and jerked her to a halt.

"You're not about to storm out of here, jumping to the wrong conclusions and thinking the worst."

She pulled on her arm, but he wouldn't release it. "Was this your way of paying me back?"

"Paying you back? What the hell are you talking about? Paying you back for what?"

"For all the negative news stories I did on you?"

He cursed elaborately. "I don't play petty games of revenge like you do."

"No? Didn't you decide it would be a great joke to trick me into sleeping with a married man?"

"I wasn't married!" he shouted.

The words echoed down the empty corridors. He pulled her into his inner office and slammed the door. "I wasn't married," he repeated in a more reasonable voice. "Now are you going to go off half-cocked, or are you going to behave like an adult and let me explain?"

She finally succeeded in tugging her arm free. Because she knew she couldn't get past him if he didn't want her to, she went to the window and sightlessly stared out at the noon traffic. She pressed her forehead on the cool panes of glass. A headache was coming on and it was going to be a dilly. How could things have gone from so good to so bad in so short a time?

"Pam and I haven't lived together for three years," Hunter began.

"You said she'd been your wife until a few weeks ago."

"We've been legally separated. The marriage was over, but I stubbornly refused to admit it."

"Why? Did you still love her?"

"No, Kari," he said with a long-suffering sigh. "I hated to admit defeat."

She glanced at him over her shoulder. "*That* I can believe. Go on."

"The fact that I was still married didn't become important until that night I went to your house and kissed you. I knew then that I wanted you and that it was serious. I came home, called Pam immediately, and told her I would finally consent to a divorce. She didn't even ask the reason, because she had wanted the marriage ended years ago. I told her to make it as expeditious as possible."

Her soft laugh was derisive. "Fool that I am, I thought you had patiently waited for me to get over Thomas before making your move. Actually you'd only been holding out until your divorce became final, protecting yourself in case of any 'difficulty.' "

He spun her around, his hands gripping her shoulders. "I *was* waiting for you to get over Thomas. You had to come to terms with yourself before you came to me."

"Then, why didn't you tell me about Pam?"

He sighed heavily. Good question. Unfortunately he didn't have a good answer. He had made an error in judgment and it was going to cost him.

"We had enough to deal with, Kari. It wasn't important. Listen to me," he said firmly when she began to squirm away from him. "I never would have taken you to bed if my divorce hadn't been final, at least not without telling you first. It became final the week before I heard you were in Breckenridge. Pam wasn't an issue between us. She'd had no place in my life for years. Any mention of my marriage would have only further complicated the situation. It was as simple as that."

He trapped her face between his hands, drew it up close to his and forced her to meet his eyes. "I'm sorry. I should have told you. But that's all I have to be sorry for. I don't love Pam. I haven't for many years."

"Why was she here today?"

"She had sensed my urgency about the divorce and came to deliver the papers. They had mistakenly been mailed to her."

"Are you sure she's over you?"

"Absolutely. She was giving me a good-bye kiss on the cheek, which I neither asked for nor returned. That's all you saw when you walked in. I'm not even sentimental over our breakup. It happened so long ago. You're the woman I love, Kari. *You.*"

His voice had taken on a desperate edge and his hands pressed harder against her cheeks. "Why are we arguing about this? Don't you know by now how much I love you?"

Then his mouth came down on hers possessively. He wanted to impress his sincerity on her. He moved his head to one side, slanting his mouth over hers and parting her lips for the ardent penetration of his tongue.

Her craving for him hadn't abated. She melted against him, aligning her curves to his hard frame as his arms closed around her. She moaned against his lips. He was already full and hard and she wanted him. But, dragging her mouth free, she pressed her forehead to the middle of his chest. "Hunter, no, no."

He lifted his mouth from hers, his breath uneven. His hands rubbed her back. "Thanks for stopping me," he whispered into her hair. "My career can't stand a scandal right now and that's what we'd have on our hands if my secretary came back from lunch and found us, uh, inappropriately engaged."

She could feel his smile against her temple. He hadn't completely understood her. "When I said 'no,' I meant no to more than just that, Hunter."

She slipped out of his arms and went to stand at the corner of his desk. Her finger traced the wood grain in its polished surface.

"What else did you mean no to, Kari?" There was a slight hint of irritation in his voice. That brought her around to face him squarely.

"I meant that we can't go on this way."

He didn't even pretend to misunderstand. He jumped right into what he sensed was going to be a debate. "Why not?"

"It's happening too fast."

"Not for me."

"Then, for me." She drew a deep breath that made the cloth across her breasts flutter.

He wished he hadn't noticed. "What's bothering you?"

"Up there in Breckenridge, it was easy to lose our heads. We were alone. We had no one to account to but ourselves. Down here, you have your life, I have mine."

"Why can't they be one and the same life?"

"You know why! You have a high public profile. So do I."

"I must be dense. What's your point?"

"I don't want to sneak around and have a secret affair."

"I hadn't counted on sneaking anywhere or keeping our love affair a secret."

"You'd flaunt it?"

"I'd shout it from the rooftops."

"Then, you don't know me at all. I won't live with you, Hunter. And I can't believe you would even consider it."

"I didn't. I want to marry you."

That effectively silenced the next point she was going to make. Her jaw hung slack as she stared at him speechlessly. "Marry me? We barely know each other."

His eyebrows went up. "Taking last week into consideration, don't you think that statement is ludicrously inaccurate?"

"I'm not talking about sexually." Her tone was sharper than she had intended.

He responded in kind. "Neither was I!"

Now wasn't the time to lose his temper. He drew a few deep breaths and spoke calmly. "I know what kind of woman you are. You couldn't possibly have been so free in bed if you didn't love me first."

She spread her hands wide. "I do love you, but don't you see, Hunter? I was on an emotional high. You wooed me. I admit it. It was romantic and wonderful and just what I needed. But we can't base a relationship solely on sexual attraction."

"Goddammit!" His temper won over good intentions. He raked impatient fingers through his hair. "Yes, I'm sexually attracted to you. I was from the first day you walked into this office. I could barely keep my eyes off your legs and your breasts. But even then, it was more than that. I started loving you. I loved you for a year without *any* sex."

"But I didn't," she cried softly. "What if I am just a sex and affection-starved widow who responded to the first man who came along?"

His eyes narrowed as they ran up and down her body. "You're trying to tell me that you would have done everything we did with just any man?" Her face turned scarlet and that was his answer. "Try again, Kari. I ain't buying it."

She avoided the hot, knowing look in his eyes. "No, I'm not saying that. It's just that you've had a year to adjust to the idea that you love me. I've only had a few days to get used to it. I need time."

He put his hands on his hips. "Do you know what all this is?" He didn't wait for an answer. "This is all just so much crap. You're punishing me for not telling you about Pam."

"That's not true."

"Isn't it?"

"No! I'm tired of petty games, too." She rubbed her forehead, which had begun to throb. "Hunter, I need time, time to assimilate all this. Pinkie's given me a new project to work on. That's what I was coming to tell you."

"Oh, I see." He had a sensitive spot where work was concerned. Career conflicts had destroyed his first marriage. "When you were down and out, not so sure about your job, you could love me. Now that everything is looking up, you don't need me anymore."

She recoiled as though he'd slapped her. Tears came to her eyes. "I guess that's how it looks to you, but that's not the way it is. I do love you. And I do need you."

He was beside her within a heartbeat, holding her close. "Kari, why are you so damn stubborn? Why can't you take anything at face value? This is crazy. We love each other. Why examine the whys and wherefores? Say you'll marry me."

"I can't just now. Please understand and be patient." She lifted her head to look up at him. Her fingers yielded to the impulse to brush back wayward strands of hair lying across his forehead.

"Pinkie said something this morning that hit the nail on the head. He said I never tread lightly, and I don't. I loved my father with all my heart. When he was gone, I soon fell blindly in love with Thomas. I depended on him far too much for my own happiness. His death devastated me. I suffered more than grief. A piece of me had died, too."

He wiped a tear from her cheek with his thumb, but he didn't interrupt her.

"You know how I throw myself into things, exactly the way I dedicated myself to hating you. I gave it all my energy. Now I love you, Hunter. But this is one time I must tread softly. When I saw you holding another woman, I thought I'd die."

"You know the reason for that."

"Yes, but it proves my point. I'm falling into that same pattern. I'm depending on you and your love too much and too quickly. If anything should go wrong, I couldn't bear the disappointment."

"My darling, nothing's going to go wrong."

The gentle earnestness in his eyes almost dissuaded her. But she remained resolute. "Then, a respite won't hurt us."

"A respite?"

"From being lovers." Her throat closed around the words, but she squeezed them out.

"You mean start as friends who date occasionally?"

"Something like that," she said softly.

His arms fell to his sides and he moved away from her, going to the window and staring out as she had done minutes before. When he turned back to her, his expression was bleak.

"No, Kari. In my own way I'm stubborn, too. I can't be your pal. I don't need another buddy. I need a fulfilling relationship with a woman. A lover and wife. If I see you at all, I'll pester you until you're in my bed again. You'd come to dread seeing me and . . ." He lifted his arms in a helpless gesture. "It would be a helluva lot of pressure on both of us. I don't want that, do you?"

She rubbed the tears off her cheeks. "It's all or nothing, then?"

His shoulders heaved with his sigh. "Yeah. I guess that's what I'm saying. I love you."

"I know that."

"But I've come to you for the last time. The next time, if there is one, you'll have to come to me."

"I know that, too."

At the door she glanced at him over her shoulder. She called herself a fool and wanted to run back to him, wrap her arms around him, and beg him to hold her for the rest of her life. But she couldn't entrust her life into his care. She had to learn to stand alone before she leaned on anyone else.

She left the office and walked down the deserted hall.

She was already lonely.

The news staff of WBTV welcomed her back, as did the viewing audience. After her first week on the air, letters came pouring in. The viewers were glad to see her again. She was flattered. Usually a television audience's memory was short, their allegiance fickle.

Pinkie's comments on her first three stories were reserved, but she knew he was pleased. She produced a story on a family of aerial artists who, despite the fact that several of them had died from falls, continued to perform in the circus. While Pinkie was watching it, his cigarette burned down without his even knowing it. If she could hold his jaded attention, she could surely capture the viewers'.

Her nights were spent quietly at home. She lost count of the number of times she reached for the telephone to call Hunter. If she called and he came over, she knew what would happen. They would go to bed. And they would be right back where they had started. He would want her commitment to marriage and she would be unwilling to give it.

Or what if she called him and he wasn't at home? She would go crazy wondering where he was and whom he was with. So it was better not to call at all.

She yearned for him. She missed his keen sense of humor, his intelligent observations. She even missed his temper. If she allowed herself to think about it, her body ached for the feel of his against her. Before loving Hunter, she had been ignorant of the array of sensual experiences one could enjoy. She had never had the small of her back kissed before, or the backs of her knees, or the soles of her feet. She blushed to think of all the erotic pleasures he had acquainted her with, but she burned to experience them all again.

She was making strides forward. Each day she felt stronger and more sure of herself as an individual. But she hadn't reached the level of confidence she aspired to. When she did, Hunter McKee would find her on his heels.

"Is this Kari Stewart?"

"Yes."

"I need to—"

"I'm sorry, you'll have to talk louder. I can barely hear you."

Was this a breather? It wasn't unusual for her to get an obscene phone call. When she first started doing on-air work, the calls terrified her. Now she took them more or less in stride. She had received an untold number of illicit propositions and twenty-three proposals of marriage. This caller had the gruff, breathy voice of the perverted type.

"I can't talk any louder," he said. "I have a story for you. Are you interested or not?"

She was accustomed to this, too. Wackos called to report everything from Russian invaders in the Laundromat to spaceships in the school-yards.

"I'm always interested in a story," she said mechanically. A harried assistant producer rushed into her cubicle and thrust a script at her. "Cut it fifteen seconds," he mouthed. She nodded and gave him the okay sign. "I'm very busy right now," she said into the telephone. "Why don't you give me your name and number? I'll have our assignments editor call you tomorrow."

"No, I can't do that. It can't wait." There was no denying the fear in the voice. Kari's red pen abruptly ceased its slashing track across the script. "I wanna talk to you or nobody."

"About what? Tell me." She forced herself to sound calm, though her heart had accelerated. Maybe this wasn't a nut.

"You know those babies that are being stolen from the hospital?"

Over a period of fifteen months, three newborns had mysteriously disappeared from one hospital nursery. It was assumed they had been kidnaped, though since there had been no ransom notes, the FBI hadn't been called in. The case was still baffling police, who hadn't been able to find a trace of evidence. "Yes, what about it?" She reached for a pad and pencil and waited, poised to take down any forthcoming information.

"A friend of mine might know something about it."

Not a friend. Him. Or her. She wasn't sure which. It sounded as though her caller was speaking through a handkerchief placed over the mouthpiece. "Why are *you* calling me? I'd like to talk to your friend."

"I . . . he can't talk to you himself. He's afraid he'll get in trouble."

Adrenaline was pumping through her now. This could be the biggest story of her career. "Would he talk to me if he was assured his identity would be kept a secret?"

"Can you do that?"

"Certainly. Could we set up a meeting? A secret meeting."

"He doesn't want to be on TV. That would be as good as getting himself killed. Maybe I'd better go. I've changed my mind."

"No, wait! Please," she said anxiously. "If you . . . I mean your friend . . . if he knows something about those babies, shouldn't he tell? Just have him meet me. It won't do any harm to talk. No one would know."

There was a weighty silence on the line, while he pondered his dilemma. "There wouldn't be no cameras, no tape recorders, or nothing?"

"No. I swear it."

"All right," he agreed cautiously. "Meet him in the hospital employee parking garage. You know where that is?"

"I'll find it." She didn't ask which hospital. She already knew. "What time?"

"Nine o'clock. Second level. Row B. Fourth car from the north end. If you're not alone, he won't stop."

"Tell him I'll see him at nine o'clock."

Her caller hung up. For several seconds she sat there staring down at the script in front of her. Suddenly it seemed mundane. She had a *real* story on her hands now.

Leaping from her chair, she ran to tell Pinkie, then thought better of it. He might not let her go. Maybe he would pass the caller off as a kook or send one of the "hard news" reporters in her stead. That would blow everything, because the informer had said he would talk only to her.

Pinkie certainly wouldn't want her going to meet an unidentified caller alone. She decided to keep it to herself until she had something. It might pan out to be nothing.

Still, she didn't know how she could stand the suspense until nine o'clock.

By nine fifteen, she was pacing impatiently. By nine thirty, she was deriding herself for being a gullible idiot. She had wasted her evening on a wild-goose chase when she could have been at home thinking about the new bedspread she was tempted to buy, or redoing her shelf paper in the kitchen cabinets, or fantasizing about Hunter, or anything more constructive than spending the time in a deserted parking garage that was giving her the creeps.

She turned around with the intention of going back to her car and almost bumped into the young man who stepped from behind a concrete pillar. Kari gasped and flattened her hand over her chest. Her heart jumped into her throat. She had the fleeting notion that all this might have been set up by a weirdo with an obsession for her.

"Hi."

"Hello," she said breathlessly. This was the guy. His voice had been disguised over the telephone, but she recognized it.

"I've been watching to make sure you were by yourself."

She tried a smile, but her lips were rubbery with fright. She had been very stupid. No one on earth knew where she was. No one would notice she was missing until tomorrow morning when she didn't report for work. But it wouldn't do to let him know she was afraid.

"What did you have to tell me?" she asked with an air of impatient authority.

He wet his lips and ran his palms down the side of his pants leg. She relaxed somewhat. He was more nervous than she. He sidestepped her and opened the door of a Volkswagen bug. "Can we talk in here? If anyone sees us . . ."

Knowing she could be making another dumb move, she slid into the front seat on the passenger side. He closed the door, went around, and sat behind the wheel. He gripped it with tense fingers and gnawed the insides of his jaw. "Thanks for coming."

"Thanks for calling me." Neither pretended there had ever been a "friend."

"I had to talk to somebody. I didn't know who to tell. I didn't want the cops after me, ya know?"

That was when she began to trust him. He wouldn't quite look her in the eye, which told her he was almost as nervous about meeting a "celebrity" as he was about the information he had to give. He was young, early twenties, she guessed. His hair was blond and fuzzy, a trifle long, but clean. His complexion was clear but showed scars of adolescent acne. He had on gray slacks, a plain white shirt, and Adidas.

"What's your name?" she asked in a confidence-inspiring tone.

"Grady. Grady Burton. You're not going to use it in the story, are you?"

"I don't have a story yet. But if you don't want to be identified, you won't be. You have my word."

His shoulders relaxed appreciably and his hands released the steering wheel. "I think you're all right, Ms. Stewart."

"Call me Kari. Now tell me what you know."

"I'm not sure it's anything."

"It may not be, but tell me anyway."

"I work as an orderly, sometimes on the maternity floor. There's this doctor, see, a snooty, rich sonofabitch. Drives a Porsche and thinks he's God-almighty and expects everybody to treat him like it. Anyway, him and this nurse; well, at first I thought they were just screwing around." His face blushed crimson. "I mean—"

"I know what you mean."

"They were always meeting in secret and closing themselves up in vacant rooms and all, ya know? There was talk, but there always is about who's, uh, you know, who's doing it with who. Then that kid vanishes."

He hitched a knee up in his seat to better face her. "I'd heard that doctor say something strange to that nurse a few days before it happened but didn't think nothing of it. So, then when the kid drops out, I thought it must be my imagination and why should I risk my job? I kept my mouth shut. Then another kid." He whistled and made a sliding motion with his hand. "Disappears clean as a whistle. I couldn't help but put two and two together. When that last kid went the way of the other two, it began to eat at my gut, ya know?"

She smiled at him. "You've done the right thing, Grady. Why don't you tell me everything you've overheard and seen. In chronological order, if you can. Be as specific as your memory will let you. Do you mind if I take notes?"

"No. But I ain't gonna give you no names."

"Fair enough."

He talked for half an hour and the longer he talked the more excited she became. He knew more than he'd given himself credit for. "Are you gonna put it on the news?" he asked when he had finished.

"I don't know. I have to check with my producer, but this has to get out, Grady. Whoever these people are, they've committed several crimes. It's got to be stopped."

"That's the way I figured it."

"Can I call you?"

He frowned. "Naw," he said with uncertainty. "But I swear if I see or hear anything else, I'll get in touch with you."

"Please do. Is there someone who can confirm what you've told me?"

"Confirm?"

"I really should have two sources."

"Yeah, well, there is someone else. Only she's afraid to talk to you."

"Who is she?"

"All I'll say is that she's a nurse and has much more clout around that place than I do."

"And she's overheard things, too?"

"Let's say she's just as suspicious."

"If I asked her questions, would she at least answer yes or no?"

"I think so. Anyway, she said I could give you a phone number, but no name." He took a piece of paper from his pocket and gave it to Kari.

"You both realize that if we do air this story, the hospital is going to become a hornet's nest."

"Yeah."

She patted his hand. "Good luck, Grady, and thanks." She paused as she stepped from the car to ask him one last question. "Of all the reporters in town, why did you call me?"

He grinned. "I knew I could trust you. There's this guy here in the hospital. He said you covered his ass one time when he gave you a patient's room number."

She smiled. "I'll cover yours, too. I promise."

Pinkie let a long, slow expletive filter through his teeth. He was at an editing machine watching the finished product on the monitor. "I should paddle your fanny for going into a parking garage to meet that guy. Don't ever do anything that stupid again. Who was he?"

"I call him Deep Throat."

"Very funny. For god's sake, he could have been a rapist setting you up."

"I thought of that," she said honestly. "But he wasn't and this is dynamite and are you going to air it?"

"Why do you always do this to me? Why am I always getting my rear chafed for sitting on the fence trying to decide if I'm going to air one of your stories or not?"

He must really like it. He was working himself into a lather over it. Kari smiled placidly. "I'm good, that's why."

"I thought we were out of the woods with you. My stomach was beginning to settle down. Now this. Why don't you call McKee, have a great roll in the sack with him, and come back tomorrow with a nice little story about a retired maiden school teacher?"

Kari crossed her arms over her chest. "Stop being abusive. Are you going to air it or not?"

"On the word of one flunky?"

"How do you know he's a flunky?" she challenged. "He might be the chief of staff." Pinkie frowned at her threateningly. "All right, I'll admit he's not very high on the pecking order, but his story was confirmed by an R.N."

"Who?"

"She refused to give me her name but assured me that she has seniority."

He cursed beneath his breath and studied the wall for a moment. "All right. I'm going to air it. You've got us covered on libel with enough allegedly's and supposedly's. You know the police will be on you like frogs on a June bug, don't you?"

"Everything I know is in the story."

"What they see is what they get?"

"Exactly."

"They ain't gonna like it. They ain't gonna believe it, either."

"What's up?" Bonnie popped her head around the door.

"I'm getting drunk tonight and I don't want any argument from you," Pinkie said, poking his finger close to her nose.

She only smiled, kissed him full on the mouth, and said, "I love you, too."

Before he left with her, he glanced at the monitor again and made a regretful sound. "I have a premonition that I'm going to hate like hell approving this, but it's too damn good to put a lid on."

Kari sat curled in her easy chair, her eyes glued to the television screen as she watched her story air on the six o'clock news. Visually it wasn't much. The only thing she could get on tape was an exterior shot of the hospital. She had edited in file tape of the stories done when each child disappeared.

It was what she had to say that would have the impact: It had been reported to her by two reliable sources that the kidnapings, for lack of a better word, had possibly been committed by members of the hospital staff.

It was a terrific story.

She was almost too excited to eat, but she cooked herself an omelet.

She had just slid it onto a plate when her doorbell rang. Before opening the door, she checked the peephole.

Hunter! Her heart thudded at the sight of him. It had been three weeks, the longest twenty-one days in her life. Quickly she unlatched the door and swung it open. Her joy was premature.

He was livid.

Chapter Thirteen

WITHOUT SAYING A WORD, HE BRUSHED PAST HER AND CAME INSIDE. She closed the door and turned to face him. Behind his glasses, his eyes were dark with anger. The brows over them were glowering. His body was drawn taut with rage. His fists balled and relaxed reflexively at his sides. He looked like he'd had a very trying day.

"Do you have any idea what you've done this time?"

"Hello, Hunter. How nice to see you, too."

She smiled up at him provocatively. After taking off the dress she had worn to work, she had put on an oversize sweatshirt. It rode low over the oldest, most ragged pair of jeans she owned. The sleeves were pushed up past her elbows. Her feet were bare. Her hair had been wound into a loose knot that was slipping from its precarious perch on the top of her head.

Her composure was an effective retaliation against his fury. It snapped him to attention like nothing else could have. He saw past his anger and looked at the woman. She looked adorable. Desire engulfed him, desire that was as rampant and consuming as a wildfire.

Reaching across the space that separated them, he grabbed a handful of her sweatshirt and hauled her against him. His other hand wrapped around that slipping mass of hair and lifted her face close to his.

"I want you so bad it's killing me."

His lips were rapacious. They moved over hers hungrily. His tongue reclaimed her mouth for its own.

Kari didn't even pretend to resist. She didn't care that he was obviously furious with her. Whatever reason had brought him to her, she was glad for it. Her head fell back and her mouth surrendered itself to him. She tunneled her fingers through his hair.

Assured of his conquest, he slowed down, gentled. He released the wad of cloth in his hand and with the other lifted the sweatshirt until her breasts were bare against his shirt. He sighed her name when his hand covered the warm fullness. His thumb coaxed her nipple to a hard peak.

". . . feel so good . . ." he mumbled incoherently.

"Oh, Hunter, yes." She pressed the sides of his face between her palms as their mouths fused.

He covered as much of her fanny as he could with one widespread hand and lifted her tight against him. She came up on bare toes to fit herself to his hardness. His tongue repeatedly dipped into the hot sweetness of her mouth. The kiss was unashamedly evocative and she moaned.

Then abruptly he released her and stepped away. He turned his back to her.

Kari stared at him mutely, feeling rejected and humiliated by the willingness she had demonstrated. She pulled down her sweatshirt and raised a trembling hand to her lips. They felt bruised and swollen. To her further dismay, tears filled her eyes.

He must have heard her tremulous sob because he turned back to her instantly. The tension in his face collapsed. "Oh, baby, don't. I can't go on kissing you like that." With infinite tenderness, he touched her lips with the back of his index finger. Then he dropped his hand to his side. "Because I want to make love to you." His voice lowered to a husky whisper. "And I can't do that, either." He took off his glasses and rubbed his eyes. When he reopened them, he looked at her wearily.

"Kari, do you have any idea what you've done with this hospital story of yours?"

She opened her mouth to speak, but closed it without making a sound. She hadn't expected him to be upset about that and was unprepared to answer his question. "I'm sure it opened a can of worms over there."

He laughed shortly as his gaze hit the ceiling before bouncing back to her. "A bit more than that. You've destroyed months of undercover work."

She gazed at him blankly. When she read the frustration on his face, she sank onto the edge of the sofa. Clasping her hands together, she began to shake all over. "You had undercover detectives working in the hospital?"

He nodded. "And now, with this story you aired tonight, you've destroyed the progress they were making. No one will be talking anymore. They'll be walking on eggshells over there for fear of reprisal. Those officers are as good as useless to me. And they were making good headway. Now it's all shot to hell."

"I'm sorry," she said with genuine regret. "I had no way of knowing."

"Then you should have cleared the story with me first," he shouted.

She shot off the couch, immediately defensive at his heavy-handed tone. "I never clear a story with anyone but Pinkie."

"He hardly had the authority to approve this one."

"In that newsroom, *he* is the authority, not you, Mr. District Attorney." When his face went dark with fury, she retreated. "I'm sorry. That was unnecessary." She sat back down on the arm of the sofa and looked up at him. "A story like that can't be suppressed, Hunter. It was a dynamic news story."

"Good for ratings, I suppose."

"Yes!" To hell with appealing to his reason. If he was going to play hardball, so would she.

"And your ratings are more important than months of police work?"

"No, of course not. But how was I to know you had men planted over there? I had no way of knowing that I was sabotaging a whole network of investigation."

"Did you think I laughed off the disappearance of three babies, told the parents that I was very sorry, but I couldn't find their kids, better luck next time? Do you think when I'm not actually in court I'm sitting over there twiddling my thumbs?"

Her chin went up at his condescending tone. "You don't have to justify your job to me any more than I have to justify mine to you."

He cursed beneath his breath. "Dammit, Kari, this isn't a contest between you and me. It's bigger than that. Do you realize what we're talking about? We're talking about three missing babies, six desperate parents, and an army of frustrated investigators."

All the fight went out of her then. He was right. This had nothing to do with them and she was behaving childishly. "I said I'm sorry,

Hunter, and I am. Of course I realize the gravity of the situation. To think that someone, *anyone*, could steal an infant from a hospital nursery. . . ." She shuddered. "I sympathize with those parents. That's why I wanted to get that story on the news. Did you ever stop to think that instead of impeding the investigation, my story might help it?"

Hunter's anger had abated, too. He looked tired as he shook his head. "Not this time. We have a strong suspect. We've been keeping tabs on him for months. He's come into large, unaccounted-for sums of money. But that's not enough to arrest him. We need evidence, facts, dates. Now he'll burrow under, cover his tracks, and we may never get him."

He took a step closer and drilled into her eyes with his. "Can you help me, Kari?"

"Not any more than I have. Everything I know was in the story."

"Did your source mention the name of the doctor? The nurse?"

She was shaking her head emphatically. "No. I swear it."

"Who was your source?"

She stared up at him for a long moment. Her eyes were sad and apologetic. "Please don't ask me that, Hunter. You know I can't tell you."

"This isn't a game, Kari. You've got to tell me. Your informant might be the culprit. He might be suffering a guilty conscience, wanting to confess but afraid to."

"No, he isn't the one. And I use 'he' as an impersonal pronoun, not to specify gender."

"You took the word of one individual and—"

"Two. I have two sources. I met one face-to-face. The other confirmed over the telephone what the first told me. They're both frightened."

"We'll protect them until we have enough evidence to arrest the suspects. Their names won't be divulged. I promise."

"*I* promised, Hunter, before you did. I can't reveal my source."

"Even if it means going to jail?" he asked quietly.

She could feel the blood draining from her face. "Jail?"

Hunter began to pace. "When I came over here tonight, I was mad as hell at you. I saw months of hard work going down the drain. But I'm a pussycat compared to the chief detective assigned to this case. He's a hard-nosed cop, Kari. I pleaded with him on your behalf. I begged him to let me talk to you first. I promised to deliver you and the names of your sources to him first thing in the morning."

"You shouldn't have promised that. I can't give them to him."

"And me?"

"I can't give them to you, either."

He caught her to him, pressing her face against his throat. "Kari, for once in your life, don't be stubborn. Relent this time. Give me a phone number, an address, something to go on, anything."

She clung to him, her eyes squeezed shut. Her lips were touching the skin of his throat. "And if I don't?"

With the pads of his fingers, he rubbed her scalp. "They'll put you in jail for obstruction of justice."

She raised her head. Her eyes were glassy with tears of apprehension. "You'd let them send me to jail?"

His eyes roved over her face, taking in the loveliness and the fear. His heart twisted with pain, but he replied, "I'd have no choice."

Her eyes closed, forcing the tears between the lids. They rolled down her cheeks. "No, I guess you wouldn't," she said softly.

He drew her closer to him and bent over her protectively. She felt so small in his arms. Barefoot as she was, the top of her head came only to the base of his neck. He was overwhelmed with a need to protect her, but she was making it impossible. He spoke into her hair. "I told them there was no need to send a car for you in the morning, that you'd come in on your own."

"Thank you."

"Nine o'clock tomorrow. For convenience sake, let's meet in my office."

"Nine o'clock," she repeated. Her hands slid around his waist. The muscles beneath the stretched cotton of his shirt were familiar. The palms of her hands glided over his back. He felt so strong. She wished he could imbue her with strength and courage.

"Change your mind. Please," he whispered desperately. "How in the hell do you think I could lock you in a jail cell?"

"How do you think I could betray my professional code of ethics?"

He muttered a curse of frustration, as he pulled back. Then he lowered his head and stamped his mouth over hers. He kissed her long and deep, but the passion was stimulated by anxiety, not desire. When they broke apart, they stared into each other's eyes for a long minute.

He left as he had come, without a word.

She was at Hunter's office by eight forty-five, not wanting to take a chance on being late and having them send the police after her. Being put under arrest and hustled off to jail didn't bear thinking about.

Hunter's secretary greeted her and solemnly led her into the inner

office. The moment she stepped through the door, Hunter jumped
from his chair and came around his desk to take her arm. Did she look
as faint as she felt? she wondered.

The other man in the office was less eager to put her at ease and
much less courteous. He came to his feet slowly, a triumphant smirk
on his thick lips. He both frightened and repelled her.

He was short and brawny. The lower part of his jaw was shadowed
blue with a heavy beard. He had oiled black hair with flakes of dan-
druff in it. He looked like he would eat meatball sandwiches with
garlic for lunch and make crude comments about women.

She had heard of Lieutenant Harris. He was reputed to be a valuable law enforcement officer, a cunning detective, with the tenacity of
a bulldog and a mind as shrewd and analytical as his piercing black
eyes intimated.

"Lieutenant Harris, Ms. Stewart," Hunter said without fanfare.

"Ms. Stewart," he drawled.

"Lieutenant Harris," she murmured.

Hunter led her to a chair and she sat down, just before her knees
buckled. She hoped she wasn't giving away her nervousness, but
Hunter's worried look told her she might be. He didn't look as though
he'd gotten any more sleep than she had.

Harris leaned back in his chair and crossed one ankle over the
opposite knee. "You're in a real jam, Ms. Stewart."

"So Mr. McKee told me." She congratulated herself on answering
in a voice that was surprisingly cool.

"But you can get out of it," Harris went on. "Who did you talk to
over at the hospital?"

"I can't tell you."

He lowered his foot to the floor and leaned forward. "You'd deliberately withhold evidence pertinent to a police investigation?"

"I have no evidence."

"Let us be the judge of that. Tell us what you know."

"I did. In my story. Look at it again if you need reminding. I can
even provide you with a copy of the script."

"Then, you won't cooperate?"

"I'm trying. I just offered—"

"I heard what you offered," he snapped. "I want the name of your
source."

"I'm sorry. I can't tell you that."

"Then, you'll go to jail, lady."

"I suppose I will," she said defiantly. She despised being called "lady." She glared at him. He glared right back. She was the first to lower her eyes.

"You ever been in jail, Ms. Stewart? Of course you haven't, a nice girl like you. Well, let's see if I can paint you a picture. First—"

"That's enough, Harris," Hunter said firmly. "I'll take it from here."

"But—"

"I said I'll take it from here," he shouted. The detective made his aggravation known by taking his time leaving the room. When the door closed behind him, Hunter took the chair the detective had just vacated directly in front of Kari. "You're not going to tell us, are you?"

"No."

"Kari, think of the parents of those babies."

"I have," she said in anguish.

"Have you? Have you really? Can you imagine going to the hospital to deliver a baby and having it snatched from you, having it disappear without a trace, never knowing what happened to the child you had created with someone you love?"

"Stop, please."

"You lost a child—"

"Stop!"

"—but you never saw it. Imagine holding your baby once or twice, feeding it from your breast—"

"Hunter, no."

"Imagine going home to the nursery you'd spent hours decorating, preparing, rearranging, anticipating the baby who would sleep in the crib. And then coming home without it."

She came out of her chair and began to prowl the office aimlessly, as though looking for an escape from an invisible cage. "You're being cruel. I know what those parents are suffering. But I can't compromise myself."

"What happened to those babies, Kari? Maybe they were sold on the black market to childless couples who will love them. Or maybe they're being used in bizarre medical experiments. Or maybe they're being reared to be used in child pornography. Or maybe they were sold to perverted old men who—"

"Oh, stop, please," she cried, placing her hands over her ears. "Why are you doing this?"

"Because, dammit, I don't want to put the woman I love in jail and will use any tactic necessary to keep from doing it." He gripped her shoulders hard. "Don't make me do this, Kari," he pleaded.

"I have to, my darling." She touched the lines on either side of his mouth, trying to erase the fatigue and stress there. "My heart tears in two every time I think of those families, Hunter. You know me well enough to realize that."

She eased out of his arms but kept her eyes level with his. "But if I revealed a source, my career would be over. I'd lose my standing with other reporters. My credibility wouldn't be worth a dime. No one would ever trust me again. I gave my word. I can't break it."

His head dropped forward as though a band at his neck had been severed. For several seconds, he stared at the floor. Then, drawing a deep sigh, he crossed to the door and opened it.

"Harris," he called out harshly. The detective was slouched in a chair. He got to his feet and lumbered toward them. "She's ready to go now," Hunter said briskly, as though if he didn't speak the words quickly, he might never say them.

Kari stepped through the door. Harris snapped his fingers and two uniformed policemen rushed in to flank her. She looked at Harris with open contempt before being led into the corridor and through the door to the outside where a police car was parked at the curb.

Harris smacked his lips. "Well, that's that. A couple of hours on ice and she'll come around. I'd lay odds on it." He yawned. "Still, she's a saucy little piece, isn't she?"

Hunter went into his office and slammed the door behind him to keep from yielding to an overpowering urge to bury his fist in Harris's beer belly.

By the time she had been put through the red tape of incarceration, word had gotten out. News of her arrest had spread through the journalistic community. The corridors of the jail were thronged with reporters and photographers as she was led toward the cell block.

Questions were hurled at her. Flashbulbs exploded in her face. The sun-bright lights accompanying video cameras blinded her. She was reminded of the days just after Thomas had been implicated in the city hall scam. But this time, the mood wasn't hostile.

"Kari!" a familiar voice shouted.

She whipped her head around and spotted Mike Gonzales. His camera was mounted on his shoulder, but he wasn't looking through the eyepiece. His face was animated with excitement.

"Mike, what's going on?" She tried to make herself heard over the clamor. A policewoman was firmly urging her to move along. Kari craned her neck around to keep the photographer in sight.

"You're a heroine. Every journalist in town is behind you one hundred percent. Pinkie's raising hell. McKee's name won't be worth two cents after this."

"But—"

"Please move along, Ms. Stewart," the policewoman said and pushed her through the crowd.

Disoriented by the events of the morning and confused by what Mike had told her, she didn't realize until several minutes later that she was being led down the narrow hallway of a cell block.

"I called my husband when I found out you were going to be here," the matron said. "I can't believe I'm seeing you in person."

Kari's skin was crawling with goose bumps. She ran her hands up and down her arms. "I wish the circumstances were different." She gave the woman a weak smile.

The matron shook her head in disgust. "This really tears it. I can't believe they're locking you up in here while criminals go free."

"I don't hold it against you." What was she doing? Comforting her jailers? She felt a laugh bubbling up in her throat. *Am I becoming hysterical?* she wondered. She forced the laugh down. "There's no one else here," she commented. They passed cell after cell. All were empty.

"Not on this aisle, no. Word came down from the D.A.'s office to put you here."

"I see." But she really didn't.

The matron held the door of the last cell open for her. "You've got a window," she said in the friendly fashion of a bellhop saying, "You've got a room with a view." "If you need anything," the matron went on, "you just call for me."

"Thank you," she said, before realizing how ridiculous it sounded. Was she trying to win Miss Congeniality of the cell block?

The matron swung the heavy door closed. Kari jumped at the clanking sound of steel on steel. The bolt sliding home was the most nerve-racking sound she'd ever heard. It seemed to go straight through her. How did one keep from going mad?

"Could you give me your autograph before you leave?" the matron asked through the bars.

"Yes, of course." Her teeth were chattering.

"And make it out to Gus. That'll tickle him to death."

"All right."

"I'll be at the desk. You remember to call out if you need anything."

Her rubber-soled footsteps died away and Kari was left alone with a stool, a cot, a basin, and a commode. The cell was clean. It looked new. It was stark. And cold.

Shivering, she lay on the cot and pulled the blanket over her. What would her father have thought of this? And Thomas? He would have been horrified.

Rolling to her side, she drew her knees up to her chest and began to cry.

"You know how I feel about that girl." Pinkie was morosely twirling his glass of Scotch over the plastic tablecloth. Bonnie was frying hamburger steaks at the range.

"She's a woman, Pinkie. Not a girl. She's taking a stand on something she believes. It was her decision. There's nothing you could do even if she would let you, and she wouldn't."

"I know, I know," he said irritably before swilling down the liquor. "Why does she have to be so damned obstinate?"

"She feels strongly about this."

"Hell, I feel strongly about it, too. The first thing I did this morning was notify the station's attorney. Management was backing her all the way. The lawyer could have gotten her out on bail within hours, but no." He thumped the glass on the table for emphasis. "Stubborn brat that she is, she uses her one phone call to tell me not to do anything until tomorrow."

"Did she give you a reason?"

"She said as long as she was going to do this, she was going to make it amount to something. She didn't want to go through the motions and then buy her way out. I think she wanted her sources to see that she was willing to suffer in order to protect them."

"That's admirable."

"Admirable, hell!" he shouted. "She has to spend a night in jail! And what does McKee think about it? Huh? How could he do this to her?"

"It's his job." Bonnie resignedly turned off the burner beneath the skillet. Pinkie wouldn't be in the mood to eat for a long time. "I would imagine that McKee's feeling much worse about this than you are."

She came to stand beside his chair. With a hand on either side of his face, she guided his head to her breast and pillowed it there.

"No one feels worse than I do," he mumbled. "Even whiskey's not making me feel any better." He shoved the glass away and turned his face into Bonnie's maternal warmth. His arms went around her waist.

She smoothed her hand over his head. "Don't worry about Kari. She'll be fine. McKee won't let anything happen to her. He loves her."

"You think so?"

"I know so."

Pinkie moved his head against her breasts. "I'm glad you're with me tonight, Bonnie. I need you."

Above him, Bonnie's eyes closed and she compressed her lips tightly against a glad cry. She wondered if he could feel her heart expanding with love and joy. "If you married me, you could have me every night. And every day. I'd be yours all the time." She positioned the crown of her breast against his mouth and rubbed it back and forth over his lips. "I'm good for you, Pinkie."

Through her clothes he could feel her nipple pouting with pleasure from the moist caress of his mouth. "And I'm good for you."

She tilted his head up until he was looking at her. "You're *very* good for me."

He pulled her onto his lap. "Well, since we're so damn good for each other, why don't you make an honest man of me?"

He stopped her laugh with a kiss.

The ringing sound echoed through the long dim chamber, and Kari sprang to a sitting position. Her muscles were sore from being held tense for so long. She was still cold and had lain in one position beneath the blanket for hours trying to ward off the horror of the place.

But it was the sound of heels striking the concrete floor that sent a new thrill of fear coursing through her. With a steady cadence, they came closer to her cell.

The visitor cast a long shadow on the floor. She stared at it with increasing panic. It stopped directly in front of her cell. The jingle of keys could barely be heard over the pounding of her heart. Her visitor turned his head back toward the warden's desk and the light fell on his face.

"Hunter!" she exclaimed breathlessly.

Chapter Fourteen

HE STEPPED INTO THE CELL. IN ONE SWIFT MOVEMENT, SHE VAULTED off the cot and launched herself into his arms. His embrace was encompassing. He held her tight against him, repeating her name like a religious chant and nuzzling the side of her neck.

"Are you all right?"

"Hold me, just hold me," she whispered frantically.

"For as long as you want."

They clung to each other. Neither spoke. Nor did they move. She pressed as near him as she could without actually becoming a part of him. His body was strong and warm. It was her security in this living nightmare. The minutes passed silently.

Within his embrace the darkness began to lift and the feeling of entrapment receded. She could breathe again without the sensation of impending suffocation.

At last, she eased herself away from him. "What are you doing here?"

"Officially I'm questioning a prisoner. Unofficially I'm rendering aid and comfort. And love." He kissed her mouth softly. "Have you eaten?"

"Sergeant Hopkins brought my dinner a while ago. I didn't want it."

"I'll go get you something." He started to leave, but she clutched at his arm and snuggled against him again.

"No, don't leave me. Please don't. Hold me."

He maneuvered his way to the cot and lowered her onto it. He sat on the edge and gazed down into her shadowed face. Purposely he had requested that Sergeant Hopkins not turn on the lights. He had access to jail cells for the purpose of questioning suspects. But that wasn't his reason for being in this particular cell at this particular time of night. He was going beyond the limits of his office and, at the risk of appearing downright furtive, would rather be exceeding the limits in the dark.

"Has it been too bad?" he asked gently.

She reached for his hand and held it to her cheek. "Yes. I never thought it would be this bad. Perhaps at first I envisioned it being rather quixotic to spend a night in jail. Perhaps I wanted the attention, the glory. But the reality of it is a debasing thing.

"I've been terribly afraid. It's unreasonable, I know. But I have been. I was scared that by some quirk of fate or some terrible accident I might never get out."

She sounded on the verge of hysteria. He'd never seen her so shaken. "Shhh, shhh." He smoothed back her hair with a comforting hand. "I'd never let that happen."

"But you might not have been able to help," she argued irrationally. "I've been so cold."

Before he weighed the consequences, he lay down beside her and pulled the blanket over both of them. Making the noises of a small wounded animal, she cuddled against him. Her arms went around his neck like a frightened child's and she buried her face in his neck.

"I love you, I love you. I'm so afraid. Hold me."

Her misery knifed through him and he felt it just as keenly. "Oh, God, I love you, too." He folded his arms around her and held her tight.

But she wanted to get still closer. Her lips found his. He sealed her to him with a fervent kiss. His tongue speared deep into the wet silk of her mouth.

After long minutes, he lifted his mouth from hers. "God almighty, this is insane." He covered her throat with quick random kisses. "I could strangle you for getting the two of us into this predicament."

She laid her cheek against his chest. "I deserve to be strangled. I had to make my stand on a reporter's right to protect his source, but I've learned I'm not martyr material. I came face-to-face with the fact that I'm basically a coward. How do convicts stand imprisonment day after day, year after year?"

"Few are as sensitive as you, love."

"I'm going to do a piece on convicts. I'm going to study their—"

He groaned. "Let's get you out first before you start thinking about your cellmates and how you can call the public's awareness to their plight." He tilted her chin up to peer into her face. "Why didn't you let the TV station's attorney bail you out?"

"What would have been the point of all this if I had? The real issue here is the First Amendment. I know you think I'm just a trouble-maker, stubborn, and—"

"I respect what you've done." Her eyes widened in surprise and he chuckled. "That's me the man talking, not the D.A. Me the D.A. is still upset with you. But I love you, Kari Stewart, and all you stand for." He pressed her head back onto his chest. "Why else would I risk my career by coming in here and holding you like this? They could throw the book at me."

"Sexual abuse of female prisoners?"

"Something like that."

She kissed his chin. "I promise not to squeal on you." They kissed and it was so satisfying that long moments passed before the severity of their situation took preeminence again. "You may have the book thrown at you for a different reason," she said quietly, recalling the chaos her arrest had caused in the corridors of the police department.

"Your cohorts have already seen to that. I was made out an ogre in the headlines today. And I think you bumped Joan of Arc off the roster of leading lady crusaders. You've got a staunch army behind you. They declared me their common enemy and came at me from all sides."

"I'm sorry, Hunter. Truly I am. I didn't want this to look like a personal attack on you."

"Well, that's a switch."

She laughed. "What will you do to get back in the public's good graces?"

"Find out what happened to those babies and return them to their families. I've got a gut instinct they aren't dead."

"I hope not," she said softly.

They fell quiet and she listened lovingly to the thudding of his heart beneath her ear. Only minutes ago, this small cell had seemed threatening. Now, with him lying beside her, his arms around her, the chilly gloom had been dispelled. She felt safe and warm and at peace.

"They took my watch. What time is it?"

"Late."

"You planned this rendezvous, didn't you? That's why I'm in a cell block with no other prisoners."

"Yes, I planned it. I couldn't let you spend the night in jail alone."

"How did you explain your visit to Sergeant Hopkins?"

If the grin he smiled down on her was anything like the one he had smiled at the matron, Kari's question was answered. "She has a romantic nature. I merely appealed to it."

"Doesn't that constitute a bribe?"

"Bribing the emotions, maybe."

"And you never did pay for that orange you pilfered in the grocery store." She pretended to consider him carefully. "I think that with just a little encouragement, you could become quite corrupt."

"I'm already there. I'm lying in a jail cell with a female inmate and wishing with all my heart that I could have carnal knowledge of her."

Giggling, she pressed closer to him. "Is that what you're wishing?"

"Cut it out, Kari, or we're both going to be in more trouble than we're already in. Are you warm enough?"

"Hmm, yes," she sighed. "Stay right there. Don't move. There's something to be said for narrow beds."

"I can feel your breasts against my chest."

"Can you?"

"Yes. Have I ever told you what beautiful breasts you have?"

"Yes."

"Next time we make love, I'm going to give them special attention."

"I'll look forward to that."

The arm around her waist tightened and drew her closer. His lips wandered through her hair. "I've missed you. I've missed making love to you, reaching for you in the middle of the night and finding you there, waking up in the morning with you lying beside me. Remember that afternoon in Breckenridge?"

"I remember them all. You'll have to be more specific."

"When it rained."

"Hmm, yes."

"Do you?" His lips slid down the length of her nose before they planted a sweet kiss on her partially opened mouth. "Which part did you like best?"

"All of it. I like it when we slowly explore each other with our hands and lips. I love the feel of your skin and the hair on your chest and abdomen. My mouth waters when I think about the way you taste. And I love to feel you inside me. You fill me so completely."

His breathing was harsh and rapid in her ear. "You're tight and warm," he whispered, making the words wonderfully forbidden. "Always perfect for me, perfect." Then his mouth found hers in the darkness and made love to it with his tongue. When at last they fell apart, he tucked her head under his chin. "Go to sleep," he said roughly.

"You'll stay with me?"

"I'll stay with you."

"I love you."

"I love you."

Their hearts pulsed together. Kari slept.

When she awakened at first light, he was gone. But the cot was still warm where he had lain with her through the dark night.

WBTV's attorney looked like David Niven. He had the same debonair mannerisms and dressed in a dapper fashion, even down to the fresh carnation on his lapel. When he appeared before her cell later that morning, he smiled charmingly. "Good morning, Ms. Stewart." Kari had the distinct impression that if he had had a hat, he would have doffed it while executing a quick bow. "You're being released."

She felt considerably better about the jail cell than she had the previous night before Hunter's appearance. Still she couldn't get out of it fast enough when Sergeant Hopkins unlocked the door. "Thank you," she said breathlessly. The attorney took her arm and led her down the corridor. At Sergeant Hopkins's desk, Kari paused.

"Do you still want my autograph?"

The policewoman beamed. "I wasn't going to bother you about it. Thanks for remembering."

Kari signed her autograph to Gus on the top sheet of a tablet. When she handed it to the woman she asked, "Aren't your shifts rather long?"

"I worked a double one. Mr. McKee asked me to so I could look after you."

With a soft private smile Kari nodded and left the cell block with the lawyer. Downstairs they collected her possessions. She checked the contents of the manila envelope against the inventory that had been made the day before, signed the release, and gathered her things to leave. It was then that the booming voice halted her.

"Wait a minute!"

Kari turned to stare into the intimidating scowl of Lieutenant Harris. "I wanna see you." He pointed a blunt finger at her. The nail had been bitten to a nub.

Fear clutched at her throat again. Did she have to go back to jail? Where was Hunter?

"Ms. Stewart has been released on bail," the attorney said crisply.

"This is between me and her," Harris said belligerently, dismissing the attorney with a wave of his hand. His beetle eyes remained on Kari. "You coming or not?"

It was a dare. And as Pinkie and Hunter knew well, she never backed down from a dare. "Of course." Much to the lawyer's consternation she followed Harris. He had no choice but to trot along behind.

They went up one flight of stairs, turned right into a hallway, and then turned left into a small room. As Harris opened the door and led the way inside, he said, "Friends of yours, I think."

She had never seen the woman with the iron-colored hair and kind brown eyes. But she would recognize the fuzzy blond mop and acne-scarred cheeks of her companion anywhere.

"Hi," Grady Burton said. "Guess I'm on your blacklist, huh?"

In spite of her weariness, Kari laughed. "Let's just say I'm awfully glad to see you."

"This is, uh, Mrs. Plummer," Grady said. "After we heard about you going to jail on account of us, we got together last night and, uh, decided to come in on our own."

"That's very conscientious of you," Kari said. She smiled at both of them. "You're doing the right thing. I never would have given you away, but I think the police need to hear whatever you have to tell them."

"So do we," Mrs. Plummer said.

"Since they came in, that lets you off the hook," Harris said. "I'm dropping the charges against you." He expected her to grovel with a tearful thank you. Kari merely nodded in acknowledgment. Harris frowned. He could scare almost anybody, but this dame was as cool as a cucumber. Again he wagged that unmanicured finger an inch from her nose. "You stay out of my hair from now on."

She glanced up at the flakes on his scalp. "I'll do my best." Her sarcasm was wasted on him. And she had been wrong. He didn't eat garlic for lunch. He ate it for breakfast.

Without another delay, the lawyer hustled her outside. Bright sunlight chased away the chill of the jail. Closing her eyes, she drew deep breaths of fresh air. When she opened her eyes, a horde of reporters were swarming up the steps, microphones and cameras aimed at her.

"Be careful of what you say," the attorney cautioned. "Every word will be quoted."

She had come to terms with her night in jail, but would she be able to explain her feelings about it? Where was Hunter? Why hadn't he come with the attorney to release her? Why hadn't he been with Lieutenant Harris? She didn't have time to sort out all the perplexities before a reporter asked the first question. Setting aside her misgivings, she faced her peers confidently.

"How was jail, Ms. Stewart?"

"I wouldn't recommend it." She smiled shakily.

"Were you mistreated?"

"Not at all. I was made as comfortable as possible."

"Were you questioned by Lieutenant Harris?"

Careful, she warned herself. Someone might have seen Hunter going into the cell block last night. If she failed to mention it, suspicions might be aroused. "I spoke with Mr. McKee last night," she said evasively.

"What about?"

"About naming my sources. I wouldn't."

"We understand two hospital employees came forward this morning and are willing to tell their story to the police."

"Yes, and I'm glad, for many reasons. I didn't relish another night in jail." Everyone laughed. "But I'm especially hopeful that what they tell the police may lead to finding the missing children."

"If you had it to do over again, would you keep your sources a secret?"

"Absolutely." She addressed them with conviction. "This is one of the most ambiguous issues of our time. I believe in freedom of the press. I believe in the privacy of the individual and in the sanctity of that privacy. I also believe in justice being carried out. I certainly don't condone the crime of kidnaping babies from a hospital nursery.

"Had I personally known any factual evidence I would have given it to the district attorney without hesitation. But at the same time, I would go to jail again to protect the identities of my sources, who until this morning wished to remain anonymous."

"Did Mr. McKee use this issue to pay you back for the attacks you had made on him?"

"Did I ever attack Mr. McKee?" she asked innocently. Her audience laughed again.

"At one time your stories were rather slanted," a reporter observed. "You all but accused the D.A. of using his present office to advance his political career by fair means or foul."

She was very tired. She knew she looked a wreck. She had dressed for jail, not a press conference. Her twenty-four-hour makeup felt like caked and peeling paint on her face. Her clothes were wrinkled.

But that particular question sharpened her wits. She had come to a meaningful conclusion sometime during the night, but it had remained fragmented and incomplete. Now it came into sharp focus. "At one time, my attitude regarding Mr. McKee was biased."

"Because of his allegations against your late husband?"

"Yes."

The attorney stepped between her and the cameras. "These questions have no bearing on the current situation. Ms. Stewart has no further comments."

"Yes, I do," Kari countered. A hush fell over the jostling crowd. Even the noise of passing traffic didn't seem to affect the sudden quiet.

A few months ago she would have grasped this chance to lambaste Hunter McKee. Now she was going to take the opportunity to defend him.

Rather than telling them how he maligned the reputations of dead men, how he victimized their widows, how he used controversial trials as stepping-stones to further his own career, she was going to take his side. She had the power to ruin him by revealing that he had sneaked into her cell in the middle of the night.

Oh, what a sweet secret that was to keep!

How could she have ever thought he was a manipulative opportunist? The man she loved was a man of integrity, who didn't need to play political games to win the public's confidence. To uphold a principle he firmly believed in, he had sent the woman he loved to jail. But he had also risked personal ruination by spending the night with her in her cell.

The eager reporters staring up at her would hang onto every word she spoke. She would be quoted and recorded and photographed. A year ago she would have used every means of ammunition available to destroy Hunter McKee. Yet now all she could think of was how much she loved him.

"It's true," she began quietly, "that at one time I did hold a personal grudge against District Attorney McKee. But that's just what it was—a personal grudge. In a most unprofessional way, I used my access to the media to slander him."

Emotion welled up inside her and she desperately hoped she wouldn't cry. "Unlike me, he separated his personal feelings from his professional duty in this case. He is a man of integrity. He refused to compromise that integrity, no matter what it cost him personally. He felt strongly about my withholding information. He acted upon it in the only way he could."

She could tell they were disappointed. What she had said came straight from her heart. She had organized the thoughts in her own mind, reconciled them, acknowledged them, before speaking them aloud. But they hadn't been the tantalizing kind of statements that made good news copy.

"Now if you'll excuse us," the attorney intervened once again, "Ms. Stewart has suffered a terrible ordeal." Taking her elbow in a surprisingly strong hand, he escorted her toward his car.

Newswise, it was a record day. The late evening television newscasts carried numerous stories about the doctor and nurse who had been operating a blackmarket baby ring from one of the city's major hospitals. The three children who had been kidnapped and sold had been located. Their tearful parents had been interviewed at length. The doctor was seen hiding his face as he was led handcuffed from a police car into the jail.

Kari felt resentful that she hadn't been a part of all the excitement, but Pinkie had refused to let her work that day. When the attorney dropped her off at the TV station, Pinkie had blown a fuse. He wouldn't even let her check the mail on her desk.

"Go home. Rest. Bonnie and I will come by after work. Now get out of here; I'm busy. Has somebody gone out to talk to the Hus . . . Hoos . . . hell, whatever their names are? Is someone on the way there now? Come on, let's haul some ass around here!"

When they arrived at Kari's condo, Pinkie nursed the two drinks Bonnie allowed him while she converted a sack of groceries into a home-cooked meal. They left as soon as the dishes were done.

The empty evening yawned in front of Kari. She had taken a long nap that afternoon, so she wasn't sleepy. Her mind wouldn't stay on a book; there was nothing to watch on television; there was no one to talk to. There was nothing to do but fill the hours with worry.

Why hadn't Hunter called? She knew he must have been busy all day, but surely he could have taken five minutes to call and ask about her health or her mental state or *something*. Why hadn't she heard from him?

She was still agonizing over it when her doorbell rang close to midnight. She ran to the door. When she saw him through the peephole, she sighed her relief and pulled open the door.

"May I come in?"

She stepped aside.

"May I have a drink?"

Without waiting for her consent, he went straight to the portable bar and poured himself a stiff Scotch. He drank it down in one stinging swallow.

He looked haggard. When he'd come in, he'd been holding his coat and vest over his shoulder by a crooked index finger. They had been dropped on the sofa as he passed it. His shirt was wrinkled and limp. His tie had been loosened. There was a shadow of beard on his chin. His cheeks looked gaunt and there were bruises of fatigue around his eyes. For once his glasses didn't make him appear distinguished but looked heavy as they sat on the bridge of his nose. If anything had combed his hair recently, it had been impatient fingers.

To her loving eyes, he had never looked better.

He brought his gaze to where she was still standing in the middle of the floor. A trace of a smile lifted one corner of his mouth. Her blouse was paint-splattered. There was a hole in the knee of her jeans. Her hair was an unruly mass of blond curls. She looked frumpy and comfortable and sexy as hell.

"No ill effects from last night?"

"A crick in my neck."

He answered her smile, remembering the way he'd held her head against his chest. "Nothing else?"

"No." Her eyes darted around the room restlessly. For some unnamed reason, she was incredibly nervous. "Did you see the early news?"

"Yes."

"Oh," she said in a small voice. "Did you see the story about me?"

"Yes."

"You heard what I said about you?"

"Yes."

His cool indifference finally ignited the fuse of her temper. She bent one knee slightly, making her stance arrogant. She dug her fists into her waist and demanded, "Well, dammit, what did you think about it? Say something!"

He came to her slowly. For endless moments, he stared down at her. Then his hand whipped out, caught her behind the neck, and hauled her face up to his descending mouth.

He kissed her with searing passion. Her lips gave way to the mastery of his and her mouth had no choice but to submit to the plunder of his tongue.

Hesitantly she raised her hands to his shoulders. Then when the tip of his tongue stroked that sensitive spot just behind her upper teeth, she sank her fingers into the endearing dishevelment of his hair.

His arms went around her and held her close for several seconds. "You're some woman, did you know that?" His hands went on a bold search that left her clinging to him weakly.

"I love you."

"I know. You practically announced it to the whole world. God, when I saw that news story, I—" His mouth took hers possessively.

When at last he released her, she gasped, "I could kill you, Hunter McKee. Where have you been all day? Why didn't you call me? I've been frantic with worry."

Between the kisses he was dropping on her face and throat he explained. "All hell broke loose this morning when Burton and Mrs. Plummer walked into my office. I turned them over to—"

"Oh, yes, there," she sighed, twisting her body against his to accommodate his questing hands. Her teeth tugged lightly on his earlobe.

"—over to Harris. I knew you'd be released within a matter of minutes. I honestly didn't have time to seek you out and celebrate your liberation."

"I forgive you," she whispered into the mat of hair on his chest as she tore the buttons of his shirt free. His tie was already lying on the floor at their feet, a victim of her eager hands. He reached for his glasses. "No, leave them on."

"On?"

"So you don't miss anything," she teased. "What happened then?"

"I went to the hospital myself and confronted the nurse involved. She . . . God, Kari, how long has it been since we made love? I can't—"

"Tell me about the nurse."

"The nurse? Oh, yeah, the nurse. She broke down and started talking. I sent her back with the police to get her confession and went after the doctor." Her blouse was dropped to the floor. His hands covered her breasts. "It's been a busy day."

With a slow twirling motion, his tongue delved its way back into her mouth. Her body molded itself against his and dual sighs of desire issued from them.

"Go on . . . ah, Hunter." Her nipples hardened against his persuasive fingertips. "Tell me everything."

"Then I rounded up the parents of the missing children and informed them that law enforcement agencies were picking up their babies in the cities the nurse had named. They'll all be reunited tomorrow."

"You're a hero." She pulled the tail of his shirt from his pants.

"End of story." His mouth moved hotly over her breasts. "I want you. No more chitchat."

"One more item. Pinkie and Bonnie are getting married." Her fingers tangled in the hair circling his navel.

"Bully for them." He unzipped her jeans and scratched her tummy just above the bikini line.

"He's mad at you for letting me go to jail." Nimble fingers worked at his belt buckle, then his zipper.

"I'm not too keen on him, either."

"Why is that?" She purred against his throat. His talented fingers knew just where to touch, just where to stroke, just what to do, to make her melt.

"He can't keep you out of trouble. Oh, my God," he hissed. Her fingers were talented, too. In a voice none too steady, he continued. "From now on I want him to assign you only the most uncontroversial stories."

"Oh?" Her one-syllable question came out as a soft sigh. He slid his hands into her panties and, with her jeans, eased them down her legs. She stepped out of them. "Why?"

"We're getting married. After that, I can't be sending you to jail or anywhere else away from me." His hands cupped her derriere and lifted her up, settling her against his lap. She took his hardness inside her and folded her legs around his thighs. "Not even for one night."

He rolled his hips forward and she began to groan with pleasure, but not before getting in the last word.

"Bossy."